POSSESSION

POSSESSION

RENE GUTTERIDGE

TYNDALE HOUSE PUBLISHERS, INC.
CAROL STREAM, ILLINOIS

Visit Tyndale's exciting Web site at www.tyndale.com.

Visit Rene Gutteridge's Web site at www.renegutteridge.com.

TYNDALE and Tyndale's quill logo are registered trademarks of Tyndale House
Publishers, Inc.

Possession

Designed by Mark Anthony Lane II

Edited by Sarah Mason

Published in association with the Books & Such Literary Agency, 52 Mission Circle,
Suite 122, PMB 170, Santa Rosa, CA 95409-5370, www.booksandsuch.biz.

This novel is a work of fiction. Names, characters, places, and incidents either are the
product of the author's imagination or are used fictitiously. Any resemblance to actual
events, locales, organizations, or persons living or dead is entirely coincidental and
beyond the intent of either the author or the publisher.

Library of Congress Cataloging-in-Publication Data

Gutteridge, Rene.
   Possession / Rene Gutteridge.
     p. cm.
   ISBN 978-1-4143-2434-0 (sc)
   1. Ex-police officers—Fiction. 2. Marital conflict—Fiction. 3. California—Fiction.
4. Domestic fiction. I. Title.
   PS3557.U887P67 2010
   813'.54—dc22
                                                      2010036323

Printed in the United States of America

16   15   14   13   12   11   10
7   6   5   4   3   2   1

For Sean, John, and Cate
my three gifts from God

Prologue

"Can you please state your full name?"

"Lindy Graegan."

"Your real name is Linda. Is that correct?"

"Yes."

"Your middle name?"

"Michaela."

"Mrs. Graegan, do you know why you're here?"

"Yes."

"You've waived your right to an attorney. Is that correct?"

"Yes."

"And for the record, your husband is Vance Mitchell Graegan, correct?"

"Yes."

"For your information, you are being tape-recorded."

"Fine."

"Mrs. Graegan, do you understand that you are being questioned in the death of—"

"I understand. I have nothing to hide. Just ask me the questions, okay? Can we just get on with it? Can I get a drink of water or something? Coffee?"

"We can get you a drink of water."

"Thank you."

"Let's start from the beginning."

"I'm tired."

"I understand. But we need to piece together exactly what happened."

"You can't possibly understand it all. You can't possibly know what this has done to my family."

"If we could just start from the beginning."

"Well, I fell in love with a cop. And that was my first mistake."

1

LIKE THE SUFFOCATING, squeezing atmosphere of D.C., the small, tattered banquet room at the Montgomery County Fraternal Order of Police closed in, one friendly handshake at a time. Smoke and lively conversation drifted from the bar that was attached to the back of the building. Laughter spilled forward, reaching Vance and Captain Barra just as Vance was about to thank the captain for his kind words.

"We're going to miss you around here, Graegan," Barra said, slapping him on the shoulder and causing his seltzer to slosh.

"Thanks." Vance shook the liquid off his hand.

"Come on, let's go see if Detective Short is wearing her favorite red blouse." Barra winked and wandered toward the commotion of the bar, holding his Solo cup high in the air like something from the linoleum might jump up and grab it.

Finally Vance found himself alone. He hightailed it to the back exit, where he indulged in his only vice: fresh air. The sounds of the city swarmed like angry bees, but he didn't care. They sounded like old friends.

"Hey." Andy Drakkard hung out the door. "What are you doing, man? We were just about to give a big toast when we realized you weren't even in the building!"

Vance laughed. "Sorry, man. Just needed some air."

"I know what you mean." Drakkard joined him, leaning against the cold concrete wall. The dim light of the setting sun colored the sky in a way that reminded Vance of campfires and cold nights.

"So you and Lindy gonna be okay?"

Vance nodded. Offered the reassuring smile that came free with every handshake he gave out tonight. "This is going to make us okay."

"A deli? I'm having a hard time wrapping my mind around it. You serving up cold cuts? Not seeing it. I mean, yeah, Lindy makes the best Monte Carlo I have ever eaten in my life, but still . . ."

"Lindy's the genius behind it. I'll just be crunching numbers."

"Sounds like more excitement than you can handle."

"Funny." Vance sipped his drink. "I think I've seen enough excitement in my lifetime."

Drakkard blinked slowly. "Yeah, I know, man. We all have. But you gotta push through it all."

"I'm not running," Vance said. "I would've done that a long time ago."

"You were never the same, though. Maybe none of us are." He pulled a pack of cigarettes from his pocket. "Short's in there with that famous red blouse."

Vance smiled. "What am I going to do without you guys?"

"Serve up salami."

"Yeah."

"Seriously, your wife makes outstanding sandwiches. Never had better." Drakkard puffed on his cigarette, killing the fresh air that was there just moments ago. He flicked the ash into the metal bucket beside them and opened the door. "You coming?"

"In a sec."

"This is your party, man. You can't be scooting out early."

"No way."

"Don't make me come hunt you down again."

Drakkard shut the door, and Vance breathed in the dense air. He closed his eyes. He was tired and just wanted to leave. What was the use in all this celebration? Twenty years on the force. Five years short of retirement. Leaving the only world he knew.

Cheers.

Familiar images flickered through his mind. A bench by a bus stop. Blood dripping onto the concrete.

The sound of a rifle, distant. Cold. Vanishing into the night like a ghost. It never let him rest.

And that's why, somehow, the deli made sense. At least it used to. Until the reality of it was one road trip away.

He pushed out the despairing thoughts and focused on Lindy. He smiled at the thought of when he first fell in love with her. They were at lunch on a Saturday afternoon, and he was complaining about having to be on hold with the phone company. She told him she always pushed 2 for Spanish.

"You don't speak Spanish, do you?" he asked.

She smiled wryly. "No. But they speak English. There's never a wait because fewer calls come in, and when you apologize for hitting the wrong number, they offer to help you anyway."

She then went on to deconstruct the sandwich she was eating, offering an explanation of why the quality of salami matters.

It seemed like two lifetimes ago.

The disappearing sun left only cold air, chilling him quickly. He stepped back inside to say his final good-byes.

* * *

The zipper sound. Again.

Lindy sighed and put down the packing tape. Three more boxes to go. The house always seemed so small, but now it looked expansive. It reminded her of when they bought it. She'd walked in and known it was to be their home.

"Conner . . ."

"Mom, I'm uncomfortable. This floor is hard. I want my bed."

Lindy walked to the living room, where the tent was pitched right in the middle of the floor. Conner's black hair emerged, followed by the sweetest face she knew. The flashlight in his hand tilted toward him, highlighting the apprehension in his eyes.

He crawled out and sat on the carpet, picking at the edge of his Star Wars pajama top. "I know this is supposed to be an adventure, but it doesn't seem like very much fun."

"You'll get to see new parts of America. Some people go their whole lives and don't get to see as much as you'll see on our drive." She tickled his tummy, and he cringed with laughter. "Plus, hotel rooms! You love hotel rooms."

He smiled, his deep dimples emerging, just like his father's. Where the black hair came from was anyone's guess. But his piercing eyes, speckled green with a dark ring of hazel encircling each pupil, had charmed many women in his life. Luckily, at eight he could hardly comprehend what those eyes were capable of.

Pulling him into a hug, she let him rest against her body for a little while. He looked up at her. "I might cry, Mom."

"When?"

"When the truck takes all our stuff."

"I know. But we can't move all our stuff by ourselves. And

they're professionals. They know how to get it there safely."
She stroked his hair. "It's okay. This is a new start for us, and
I know it's scary, but you're going to love California. It's very
warm and sunny. And we can go to the beach and play in
the sand." She stood and pulled him to his feet. "Now, you
have to get some sleep or you're going to miss our whole trip
tomorrow because you'll be sacked out in the backseat."

"Backseat? Can't I ride in the front? I'm eight."

"I know how old you are, and no, you cannot." She guided
him back to the opening of the tent. "I'll be in there a little
later on to sleep with you. I've got a few more things to get
packed before we leave tomorrow."

"I really like this house. I was born here."

"It holds . . . a lot of memories." She sprouted a smile as
her words trailed off. "We'll never forget it, right?"

"Right." He folded his arms. "Well, I'm going to pray,
Mom. I'm going to pray hard that we don't move."

Lindy groaned. "Conner, please. Not this again. Not right
now."

Hurt flashed across his eyes, and she hated that she couldn't
be more patient with him, but she had little tolerance for his
infatuation with prayer. It all started two years ago, when he
was six and couldn't find the Sunday morning cartoons. He
somehow landed on a religious program and hadn't been the
same since, insisting on praying and talking about God. And
every once in a while, she'd catch him watching a televangelist again. It got so bad that at one point they took him to a
specialist, afraid a vaccination might've gone haywire in his

system. The doctor assured them he was fine and that in due time it would go away. But it hadn't.

Conner dropped to his knees and started praying, one hand shooting up like a disco move. Lindy rolled her eyes and was about to tell him to quit it when the phone rang.

She caught it on the third ring.

"Hello?"

Silence.

"Hello? Vance?" Lindy listened carefully but heard nothing. She hung up the phone.

"Mom? When is Dad going to be home?"

Lindy leaned against the counter, her arms resting on its cold surface. That was always the question these days—and one that she could hardly ever answer.

* * *

Vance flipped on the switch, and his side of the office buzzed to life under flickering fluorescents. On the other side of the room a woman ran a vacuum back and forth, moving around like it might be the only dance partner she'd ever known.

His desk stood out among the office clutter, nearly naked now. Two boxes sat next to it, and a few unopened cards lay on top, probably from people who couldn't make it to the FOP.

The hum of the vacuum moved closer. Vance decided there was no reason to linger. He should just take his stuff and go. Except he couldn't get himself to leave the chair.

Then his phone rang. He stared at it for a moment,

wondering who would be trying to call him at his desk at this hour. His former desk. Maybe it was a wrong number.

Maybe not.

"Graegan." He dropped the *Detective*, since that wasn't true anymore.

"I thought I'd reach you there."

Vance paused. "Erin?"

"Surprised?"

"We haven't spoken in . . . a while." Vance swiveled his chair away from the vacuum's noise. "How'd you know I'd be here?"

"Just a lucky guess. If I were leaving the force after twenty years to move across the country and start a deli, I'd probably sleep on my desk. Maybe chain myself there."

His grip tightened around the receiver. "I, um . . ."

"What can I say? News travels fast—and far. All the way to Chicago."

"So you're still in Chicago?"

"I thought you might keep better tabs on me than that." A soft noise clicked in the background, maybe a pencil tapping. "Yeah. I'm in Chicago."

"How's everything going?"

"I don't know if I can sum up three years with that question. But overall, things are going fine. Chicago's different, but I like working here. I mean, I'll never go inside like you did, because I want the streets and have always wanted the streets."

"You know it was more complicated for me than that."

"I know."

There was an edge to her voice, and Vance regretted it. But it wasn't unusual.

"Look," she suddenly said, "I just wanted to offer my congratulations to you. I know this is a big step for you and Lindy. I think it's a good thing. I hear California is very sunny."

"I can hear it in your voice. You think I'm making a big mistake."

"I can't sit here and judge you, Vance. I've made my own mistakes, and I'm not about to judge how people deal with what life hands them. Life handed us a lot. I nearly drank myself to death. You're starting a deli. We all do our thing."

Vance leaned back in his chair. It was good to hear her voice. Comforting in a strange way. Maybe it connected him to a life that was more normal, years and years ago. "It's hard to believe we're leaving here. We don't even have a place in California yet. Conner and Lindy are going out a couple of days early to try to find us a place to live."

"Sounds like an interesting adventure. One that should come with a stiff drink." She paused. "And yes, I'm sober. I realize that I can't make drinking jokes around you because you're like an A.A. sponsor I can't shake."

"And that's a good thing."

"So," she continued after an awkward pause, "there is another reason I'm calling, besides to offer you the best of luck with your sandwiches."

Vance laughed. "I can tell the sandwiches are bothering you."

"I was wondering if you might want to swing by Chicago on your way? It's been a long time. I'd love to catch up."

Vance leaned back in his chair, eyeing the cleaning lady, who had now worked her way to the other side of the room.

"Hello?"

"Sorry. I'm here. I, um . . ."

"Okay, listen, Vance, I know we had unusual circumstances before. But that was a long time ago. And I just think it would be nice to put all that behind us. Just sort of move on. Why not, right?"

Vance closed his eyes, trying to keep memories—the kind that had caused him to change a lot of things in his life—from racing into his mind. "I know. It seems like another lifetime, doesn't it?"

"Yeah."

The faraway drone of the vacuum filled the momentary silence.

"Look, maybe this was a mistake. Maybe there's a reason we haven't talked in three years." Her tone had soured.

"Erin, don't go there. We don't need to go back to that place. We've moved on from all that."

"I thought we had."

"We have. And it's good to hear from you. I'd love to swing by and see you."

Even as Erin gave him directions and her cell phone number, Vance wondered if he'd done the right thing. He hung up the phone, staring at plans to detour to Chicago. How was he going to explain this to Lindy?

"You must be a popular man." The cleaning lady leaned against her cart, her thick South African accent smiling through her words.

"Am I?"

"Yes, my friend. That phone has been ringing every fifteen minutes for the last two hours."

2

Lindy's body ached. Even reaching for her purse was a task. She'd definitely be popping some ibuprofen once they got on the road. And stopping for a forty-eight-ounce coffee.

Through the window, she watched Vance watching the movers maneuver their dining room table.

"The leg!" she suddenly shouted. But Vance couldn't hear her. She ran out the front door.

"The leg, Vance!" Lindy pushed through the stacks of boxes on the lawn. She glared at Vance, who looked clueless, then hurried toward the guy in the hat, kind of burly and seemingly void of personality. "Sir, please. My husband was supposed to tell you that you can't hold on to that leg. It's unstable. We've had it repaired twice." She caught her breath as she looked between the two men holding the table. "It was my grandmother's, and it means so much to me. Please, please be careful with it."

"Sure, ma'am," the guy whose shirt read *Joe* said. His skin looked pasty and rough, like instant mashed potatoes.

"And, Joe, I also wanted to mention the couches. They're real leather, so please make sure they're not leaning against something sharp, okay?"

A hand patted her shoulder. "Sweetie, they're professionals. Everything's going to be fine."

Lindy shrugged Vance's hand off and walked to the car, where Conner sat on the hood playing with binoculars. "You have everything you need? Do you have your Etch A Sketch and your DS? We're going to be taking off soon. Have you gone to the bathroom?"

Conner hopped off and went into the house. Lindy tried to run through her mind what she might be forgetting, while keeping an eye on the movers as the coffee table now wobbled between them.

"Hey."

Lindy sighed and turned. "What?"

"Why are you in such a bad mood? Conner is nervous about leaving. You've got to make this all right for him."

Lindy crossed her arms, staring hard at her husband. "No kidding. In fact, I spent the whole evening making things all right for him. And you decide to come back home at—what was it—2 a.m.?"

"I had a few things to get from my office, Lindy. And I had to stay at the party. It's kind of what you do when a party is thrown for you." His eyes looked tired and heavy, dark circles sinking into the skin under his lower lids. "And you could've come, you know. I didn't ask you to stay home and finish up."

"Well, someone had to. The movers were coming today." She turned her glare to the movers. They were picking up the headboard. They seemed so careless. Once she found a place in California, she had fun times to look forward to, finding all the scratches and nicks on her furniture.

"Lindy."

"What?"

Vance squared his shoulders up to her. "Look at me."

Lindy begrudgingly obliged.

"This is our new start. I know it's kind of crazy right now, but you're getting ready to live your dream. You're opening your own deli, sweetheart. We're moving all the way across the country. Together. As a family."

She stared at the dying grass under her feet. It was what her soul felt like sometimes. "I know."

"So let's celebrate this. Everything is going to be fine." He nodded toward the movers. "I talked to Joe earlier. Not the brightest guy around, but he's been doing this for twenty years."

A sound caused them both to look toward the large moving van, bright yellow like a rectangled smiley face. Joe had knocked the bed railing against the side of the truck. He gave an apologetic wave.

Vance was brushing her hair off her neck, but she couldn't stand it. She stepped away and turned toward him. "What are you not telling me?"

"What are you talking about?"

"I can see it in your eyes. I saw it this morning. I still see it. We're starting over, but we're right back to where we were."

"No, we're not. This is real."

"Then tell me what's going on."

Vance turned his face toward the wind, his hair blowing up and out, his eyes blinking against it. Except maybe it wasn't the wind. She knew it wasn't. This morning his eyes held the same heaviness they did seven years ago, when he shut down and stopped talking about his day, his life, himself.

Finally he looked at her. "All right. I know honesty is important."

Lindy felt her heart skip. So she was right. There was something. But *what*? She searched her husband's eyes, hopeful that he might start sharing something from that awful time. He'd gone to counseling but wouldn't talk about the events with her. She'd lost her husband. He went inside himself and never came back.

But this new beginning for them . . . it seemed like he had crawled out.

"What's going on?" she asked, her voice softer.

"Erin called."

"Erin? This is about Erin?"

Vance's expression started to harden, and Lindy regretted

her tone. She swallowed back all the other words that wanted to escape.

"She heard we were moving. She wanted me to drop by Chicago to see her on my way to California."

Lindy forced her expression to freeze. He was talking, and that was a good thing. But the last name she wanted to hear was Erin's.

"What did you say?"

"I told her I would." He faced the wind again, closing his eyes against it. "It's been three years since we talked. She's doing fine in Chicago. Seems to have everything together."

Lindy took a few steps back, turned, pretending to be interested in the two movers and the lamps they were loading. It would take a few moments for her to grasp this and process it.

Conner came bounding out of the house but got distracted by two huge, empty boxes and disappeared inside one.

Memories crawled over her thoughts. . . . Conner was a one-year-old, and she was about to go crazy, captive in her own house for the eighth straight day. She found an old box, and Conner loved it. It had saved her sanity.

Her hair tickled her face, annoying her as she scraped it off her cheeks. What was she supposed to do? It was an impossible situation. She didn't want Erin back in their lives, but at the same time, Vance had told her the truth . . . opened up about something difficult. Even as they stood there, she could sense him drawing back into himself.

She turned and touched his arm. "Okay."

"Okay? You're okay with it?"

"I'm okay because you told me." She stepped forward and took his hands, looking him in the eye. It had been getting easier and easier to do. "You're just going to say hi, right? Just catch up."

"Yes, exactly," he said, a relieved smile emerging.

"And maybe this will help you put everything behind you."

"It will. I promise."

Lindy pushed out a smile and checked her watch as Conner, still inside the box, scooted across the grass. "We better get going if we want to make the hotel by dark."

"You've got everything you need? Conner's got his Etch A Sketch?"

"Yeah. We'll be fine. Just keep your cell phone nearby, okay?"

Vance pulled her into a hug. "Deli, here we come."

"I bet the guys were giving you a hard time about it last night, weren't they?"

Vance smiled. "You have no idea." He grunted as Conner jumped out of the box and onto him, piggyback style. "Buddy, it's time for you and Mom to get going."

Conner sighed and slid off his back. "Why can't you come too?"

"I'll be right behind you. You guys are going to find us an awesome place to live."

"It can't be small," Conner said, his face wound up with seriousness. "I have to have a room that can fit all my toys. *All* of them."

Vance laughed. "I know. Top priority. I promise. You have all the toys you want in the car?"

"He's got enough toys to keep him busy all the way to Japan."

Vance wrapped them both in his arms, and Lindy leaned her head against his chest. As frustrating as the last few years had been, they were starting to come out of it. It felt good to be in his arms.

Conner climbed into the backseat and hung out the window. "Bye, Dad! I'll be praying for you!"

Vance looked at Lindy.

She shrugged. "He's on this kick again. I'm trying not to make a big deal about it. Maybe it'll just go away."

Vance opened the car door for her, and Conner scrambled into the front seat. Lindy pitched a thumb for him to move into the back.

"Dad," Conner said, "talk some sense into her."

"Backseat, buddy. It's the safest." He closed the door but leaned in when Lindy rolled down the window. "Drive safe. Call me every time you stop, okay?"

Lindy nodded. Vance kissed her, then stepped away and gave a short wave as she slowly pulled out of the drive.

Tears stung her eyes, and she swiped at them quickly, keeping her voice light. "You okay back there, buddy?"

"I guess."

Lindy stared at the house and all her belongings shrinking in the rearview mirror as she drove away. A new beginning awaited her, but she knew that new beginnings didn't always mean happiness. Especially if this deli thing didn't work out. The deli thing really, really needed to work out.

As Conner settled quietly into the backseat, she started making up sandwiches in her head. Nothing relieved stress like building an imaginary, out-of-this-world sandwich that might actually make it on the menu someday.

*   *   *

Lindy's black Camry disappeared around the corner of the neighborhood, Conner waving from the backseat. Vance felt relieved to be able to decompress a little. He'd tried to keep up an excited spirit around Lindy. He knew how much this meant to her and how much hope she'd put into their new beginning. She'd spent years working as a caterer—and making good money at it—but her dream was her own restaurant. Deli, to be precise. And she had this amazing talent for sandwiches. That was the first thing she'd made him when they were dating. Double-decker fried bologna sandwich with melted blue cheese and olives. He thought it was the grossest thing he'd ever seen but tried it to be polite.

After the first bite, he knew he'd found the woman of his dreams.

So much of her unhappiness stemmed from him, and it was a guilt that weighed him down constantly. But he knew she couldn't fathom what he bore. He'd wanted to tell her. Tell someone. But he never did. He never would.

Vance stood and watched the movers as they loaded the final boxes. He stepped to a nearby tree and leaned against it.

He liked shadows and sturdy objects. After all these years, he still hated standing in open spaces. He still hated gas stations or walks in the park.

He'd seen car wrecks and burn victims and small children drowned in his years on the force, but the days of the snipers . . . it had felt like it would never end.

More memories. They'd vanish for a little while but come back. More often these days. He figured it was just stress.

He stared at his house, trying to shake the image of the slate gray parking lot and the fifty-five-year-old man slumped on top of its concrete, his hair lifting in the wind.

Suddenly Joe, the mover, was in front of him, holding a clipboard. "All right, Mr. Graegan. Looks like we have everything loaded in. You've read the contract?"

Vance blinked. Contract?

"I gave it to your wife to read and sign."

"Um . . . I'm sorry. I don't know what we did with that. My wife might still have it."

"That's no problem. I can get another copy. Hold on."

Vance followed Joe to the truck, where the man dug around between the seats for a moment and emerged with a fistful of documents. He clipped them to his board and handed it over. "There's one copy there for us and one for you to hang on to. Make sure you fill out the last page that gives us all your contact information. We're scheduled to arrive in California in four days, and the way the missus explained it, you don't have a place yet, other than knowing what city you're landing in."

"My wife is headed there now to find us a residence."

"All right. We'll be in contact when we arrive in California, and then we can make arrangements to get it over to your new place."

Vance flipped through the twenty-page contract. He checked the rates and the arrival date, everything he was sure Lindy would check. "You're insured, correct?"

"Yep. That's on page 9. Everything's covered. But haven't needed to use the insurance one time in my career." He grinned, revealing two teeth, gray like petrified wood, clinging to purple, swollen gums. He checked his watch and said to the other guy, "We'll be cutting it close for the next stop. Get on the phone and tell them we may need a couple of extra hours."

Vance came to the back page of the movers' copy and put his cell phone number and Lindy's. He signed at the bottom and handed it over.

Joe smiled again and offered a hand. "We'll take good care of your things, sir. Have a safe trip to California. Driving or flying?"

"Driving," Vance said. "Not looking forward to it. You guys are probably used to it."

"I've been a trucker since I was twenty-three. Seen every part of these states." He signaled for his partner to clear the ramp and close the back door of the truck. "If you have any questions, just call the number on the bottom there. Especially if there's going to be a delay. There is a fee for holding it over the time agreed upon in the contract."

"Understood."

Joe climbed into the rig and started her up. The engine roared to life like a dragon waking from a deep sleep. Exhaust clouded the driveway and choked out the clean, suburban air. The truck slowly rolled forward, its air brakes negotiating the steep driveway of their home. Vance watched it rumble down Pheasant Street, monstrous next to the mailboxes and tricycles lining the sidewalk.

He'd never actually parted with every one of his belongings all at once. It was strange to know that they were traveling apart from him. But he didn't have time to dwell on it. There were several things left to take care of before he started toward California. Electricity and gas had to be cut off. Bank accounts needed to be closed. He felt in his pocket for the list Lindy had made him. He scanned it, trying to decide what to tackle first.

Inside, the bedroom that had once been a source of many fights now looked barren, as if no soul had ever dwelled between its walls. And it smelled different. It used to be sweet, like a Popsicle. Now it smelled of wood, like the stick after the Popsicle is gone.

His suitcase lay in the middle of the floor. It had tipped over at some point. He knelt down and opened it. From underneath the clothes and the toiletries, he retrieved a large yellow folder wrapped in rubber bands.

With the bright daylight flooding in from every direction, he sat down on the carpet and undid the rubber bands. The folder, ripped almost in half from the weight of its contents, spilled open like it had entrails.

Vance spread the articles apart, fingering each one. Some were from magazines, others from newspapers and reports he'd printed off the Internet. The vibrant colors in the pictures were now starting to fade, and though it seemed like yesterday to him, the evidence proved otherwise.

There was something strangely comforting about revisiting the articles over and over. He never understood why. Lindy didn't know they existed. Nobody did. They'd been hidden for years.

The last article he'd put in was from the day that John Muhammad was executed. It should've closed the chapter for him. He expected it to. But it didn't.

He walked to the living room, carrying the armful of papers. The dark pit of the fireplace called his name.

Outside, neighborhood sounds seemed clearer, maybe because all the drapes were gone. Their neighbor's dog, Woodstock, was barking furiously at something. Probably the squirrel that liked to terrorize all the neighborhood pets.

Vance flipped a switch, and the fire appeared instantaneously. One by one, he fed the fiery mouth each article. He'd kept the obituaries of every victim of the snipers and all the articles on the recovery of those who managed to live through being randomly shot. He'd even kept all the stories about Chief Moose, his book deal, and subsequent humiliation over the sniper case.

It seemed impossible, but in less than five minutes, a lifetime's worth of nightmares was burning to ashes. He had to find a way to put this all behind him. To find healing and peace. His wife and son depended on it.

Surely, from three thousand miles away, the sounds of that rifle could not be heard.

The fire crackled, consumed, and devoured.

This part of his life was over. He wouldn't look back. He would put away his deepest regrets.

He was going to become a different person. He wasn't sure if he could return to the life he knew before the snipers, but he was certain that he could live without their long shadows cast across his path.

One last stop in Chicago and then a brand-new life.

3

VANCE'S LEGS ACHED and his back begged for a good stretch, but he was stuck going five miles an hour on the 94 express-way. He'd pushed himself longer than he should've, but he was anxious to get to California. Lindy and Conner would arrive sometime today and start house hunting. He hated missing that.

His car crept slowly toward the towering Chicago skyline until he finally reached Lake Shore Drive, where the day instantly seemed brighter. The sun sparkled against the blue waters of the lake, and the traffic became decongested at the very place he wanted to drive slowly.

The road, embraced between clear sparkling water and

shiny silver skyscrapers, wound lazily northward. Taxis still honked. But on Lake Shore, nobody seemed to seethe. He found his way to Navy Pier, where Erin wanted to meet. He'd been hoping to see her station, but she was on her days off and didn't want to go in. He could appreciate that.

It took him thirty minutes to park and find the restaurant. A familiar tension coiled through his body, and he tried to shake it. This was the closing of a chapter, and he should expect good things.

It had been years since he'd seen her, and three years since they'd even talked. It felt strange not to have talked to her for that long, but he expected, like good friends do, that they would pick up where they left off. If they could get past the shadow of awkwardness that cast a constant chill over them.

"About time."

Vance looked up from his thoughts. She stood by the steps of the restaurant in the same bomber jacket she'd worn for years, the one her father gave her. His own was similar, a gift from her for his thirty-fifth birthday.

Her hair was cut short, boylike except for the bangs that swept to the left, and her eyes blinked as if exhausted, but she still looked like Erin. Her cheeks still glowed pink, like she'd just come in from a brisk run. He wondered if he looked like life had beaten him down.

"Not my fault," Vance said, walking toward her. "If the cops in this city could get the traffic moving."

Her smile turned into a wide grin and then a laugh. She

approached him and pounded him on the back with a big hug. "Nice of you to come see me, loser."

Vance stepped back. "Looking good."

"You too. I'll remember these as the pre-salami days." She patted his belly and guided him toward the door of the restaurant. "Come on. I got us a spectacular seat. Not on the open deck, of course."

Their table sat against a window with a perfect view of the lake. The Chicago skyline almost looked like it was rising right out of the water.

Vance pulled out her chair, and she sighed as she plopped into it. "You've always got that gentleman thing going, don't you?"

"Most women appreciate that sort of thing, you know," Vance said. "I know, I know. You're not most women."

"Got that right. I'll never forget the time we were out eating and I ordered my steak rare. You couldn't even watch me eat it."

Vance smiled. "Yeah. It felt a little wimpy to order mine medium."

"That was the same night we caught Earl Stormand." She twisted the cloth napkin around her hand, then set it on her lap. "We'd been partners for what, three weeks?"

"Something like that."

Erin stilled as she looked across the table at him. "I'm sorry. I can tell that bothers you. It was a long time ago. I didn't realize it might, um . . ."

"I'm over it. Give me a break."

"Good." She grinned. "Because I still love telling the story about how I saved your—"

"I'm never going to live it down, am I?"

"Never! Now, let's order some expensive food neither of us can afford." She went on to joke about how she thought she might order a sandwich, in honor of him, and Vance played along with a wide smile. But trampling over any nostalgia were snapshots. Pieces, really. Fragments of the sniper's havoc.

He tried to focus on Erin's big-fish retelling of the day she saved his life. He'd been a cop for three years and had just been assigned a new partner, Erin Lester, when they got a call about a murder suspect they'd been hunting for a week, Earl Stormand.

They'd cornered him inside a warehouse, and Vance thought he caught a glimpse of him moving behind some crates. He followed what he believed to be Stormand's shadow, but it was a cat, and at the very moment he realized it, Stormand slammed him against a concrete wall, a gun pointed to his head.

Like it was yesterday, he could still see Stormand's face, blood red. Two veins in his forehead pulsing. Sweat shone on his skin, even in the dark. His eyes glowed with drug-induced rage, and the hand that held the gun at Vance hardly seemed steady enough to pull the trigger.

Lindy's face flashed through Vance's mind with such force that he thought she was there.

Then a loud pop, and Stormand collapsed, his head

cracking against the concrete floor and the gun sliding away. Stormand hollered like a caged animal, and Vance could see the blood oozing from his leg. The bullet was so close he'd even heard the sound of crunching bone as it ripped through Stormand's kneecap.

He dove for the gun as Erin approached, her gun drawn and her face flushed with adrenaline. They both pointed their guns at Stormand; then Erin kept hers on him as Vance planted a knee between his shoulder blades and cuffed him.

They'd celebrated by going for a steak dinner that night.

"Hey. You. What to drink?"

Vance blinked and found a waiter standing over him. "Oh, um, sorry. Water."

"Tea. The non–Long Island kind," Erin said with a charming grin, then looked at Vance as the waiter walked off. "Sorry. I keep forgetting how you don't find alcoholism jokes funny."

"Yeah, you saved my life. I may have saved yours, too. Just without a gun."

"I give you a hard time. But you know I mean it when I say I'm thankful." Erin looked contemplative as she leaned forward, her elbows on the edge of the table. "I always wondered if you were serious."

"Serious about what?"

"You threatened to turn that disc over to the captain."

"I had to get you to wake up, see what you were doing to your life."

"I know. I just always wondered if you'd really do it."

"Yeah, Erin. I would've really done it. And I would expect that you'd do the same for me. It's called tough love. Besides, we said we'd never talk about that again."

"It was years ago. Who cares now, right?"

Vance was silent as the waiter arrived with their drinks. He squeezed a lemon over his glass, the juice stinging his cuticles. He wondered if Erin had ever understood what he risked that day. For her. He'd never completely understood his motives for it, except that he figured he owed her one. A big one.

"I'm assuming you destroyed the disc, right?"

"Erin, the important thing is that you got your life on track. That woke you up, as it should have. And look at you now. You're thriving. Doing great. That's all I ever wanted for you."

Erin leaned back in her chair. She stared out the window. "Did you follow the execution?"

"Yeah. Told myself I wouldn't. But I did."

"Me too."

"I still have dreams. They're vivid." Vance paused before his next words. "I hear that rifle."

Erin looked away from the window, studied him.

"I just thought by now this would go away," Vance said, his gaze tracing the shoreline.

"I don't talk about it here," Erin said. "Nobody gets it if you weren't there."

The waiter returned to take their order, and they chatted

a little about how Chicago was working out for Erin. She seemed happy. When she talked about police work, her eyes brightened in a way that they never would otherwise.

"So how's it been living near your father?"

"I'm going to apply for lieutenant."

Vance couldn't hide his surprise. "You said you'd never do that."

"My dad wants it so badly for me, I guess. You know how I have to carry on the family name and all that."

They continued to talk while the food was served, and as they did, Vance came to a remarkable conclusion. He didn't know it before, but as he sat there with his former partner, he realized that he'd put more behind him than he'd thought. He didn't feel chained to Erin anymore. Didn't feel grief over their fallout. Still felt remorse over one of the greatest mistakes he'd ever made, but he could deal with that. He would deal with it. Maybe he'd even tell Lindy about it once they got settled in California.

Could she handle it?

He didn't know yet. It had taken him years to even face what he'd done. It was a long time ago. And as he listened intently to Erin tell some great cop stories from her time in Chicago, Vance couldn't help but smile to himself. He couldn't wait for lunch to be finished, to say his good-byes, and to get to California to be with his family.

He'd known seeing Erin would help him put his past behind him, but he hadn't realized it would show him he was well on his way.

* * *

"Get in the house! Get in there!"

"Mom?" Conner's voice snapped Lindy's focus back onto the road and away from memories that sometimes seemed a hundred years old. She slowly pulled to the curb and put the car in park. The shouting that rattled through her mind faded into the sounds of birds chirping in trees above her. The neighborhood road was quaint. Quiet.

"What are we doing, Mom?"

"Hold on." Ahead, a tidy-looking condo with a large, manicured front lawn boasted a small sign with red lettering that said For Rent.

She double-checked the address from the piece of paper she'd printed out with local houses and condos for rent.

She noticed a woman walk out with a broom. She started sweeping the front porch.

"Mom? What's going on?"

She was weary from the trip and Conner's inability to sleep well in a hotel room.

"Give me a sec, Conner."

After watching the woman for a moment, she got out of the car and looked the opposite way, down the adjacent sidewalk. A small storefront with dirtied windows and a large crack in the sidewalk out front also had a For Lease sign posted in its window.

Conner was now out of the car, hands on his hips, his brow furrowed just like Vance's. She put an arm around him and pulled him to her hip. "Look ahead."

"What?"

"See that condo?"

"What's a condo?"

"It's kind of like an apartment. Except it sometimes has a yard."

"I thought we were getting a house."

"Honey, we can't afford a house in this city."

"What city is this, anyway? Hollywood?"

"No, sweetie. We're in northern California. This is Redwood City."

It certainly lived up to its name, too. Majestic redwoods towered over the town, causing everything to look like a miniature village.

Conner watched the woman on the porch. "I don't like it."

Lindy sighed and let go of his shoulder. She squatted to his level. "Honey, I know this isn't like Maryland. I know you'd like a house. I'd like a house too. And someday we will have one. But we have to start small. Get our business going." She stood. "And see down this street? Look. See that sign that says For Lease?"

"Yeah."

"That could be our deli. We could walk there!"

Conner didn't seem to see the significance. He was now focused on an acorn on the sidewalk. He scooped it up and pretended to be a squirrel.

Lindy locked the car and walked across the street with Conner in tow. The woman with the broom noticed and stepped down the porch to greet her.

"Hi. Can I help you?"

"I'm interested in this condo."

"You're in luck! I'm one of the owners, Shirley Wright, along with my sister, Linda Beavers. Was just tidying it up. Want to take a look inside?"

Still holding Conner's hand, Lindy walked inside. The carpet, beige and soft, looked brand-new. The kitchen was smaller than she would've liked, but the large living room made up for it. Two bedrooms of equal size were separated by a decent-size bathroom.

"How long has this been for rent?"

"About a week."

"I'm moving here to start a deli. I noticed a small storefront over there."

"Oh, that's a wonderful place. You would love it. It used to be a newspaper stand and bookstore, owned for twenty-five years by Guy Clement. Wonderful, wonderful man. Passed away six months ago and his family closed the shop." She smiled as she looked out the window. "It would make a perfect place for a deli. This square mile is full of good people." Shirley patted Lindy on the shoulder. "Give me a moment. I'll go to my car and get the sheet with all the information on it, okay?"

"That would be great. Thank you." She turned to Conner, who was doing handstands in the middle of the room. "What do you think, buddy?"

"Microchip backyard."

"But a nice front yard."

RENE GUTTERIDGE || 37

"You won't let me play in the front yard."

Lindy sighed. It wasn't her rule. It was his father's, but she kept her mouth shut. She walked through the condo again, room to room. For no reason she could understand, her thoughts continued to roam back to darker times.

"You have to let me out!" Lindy had screamed.

"It's not safe! Don't you see it's not safe?" Vance's eyes were soaked with terror. His strong hand gripped her upper arm, squeezing it uncomfortably.

"You don't know what it's like to stay here. To not even go outside."

Vance let go of her and leaned against the doorframe, a hand combing viciously through his hair. "We're trying everything. Everything, Lindy. It's like a ghost. He comes and kills and vanishes."

Lindy took his shoulders. "Vance, listen to me. It's not a ghost. It's someone out there committing these horrible crimes for who knows what reason. You can do this. You can catch whoever this is." She placed a hand on his cheek. His skin felt flushed.

He put his hand over hers and closed his eyes, looking as if he might rest for a moment. "Just stay inside. And stay away from the windows. . . ."

". . . and this will show you the square footage. And the estimated cost of heating and cooling the place . . ."

Lindy looked up, just now realizing Shirley had walked back in. They stood by the kitchen bar, and Shirley busily talked about the condo. Lindy's attention darted to Conner, who had walked out the front door and was playing in the yard. She started to call to him, but Shirley said, "So what do you think?"

Lindy took in a breath and tried to focus. Was this the place? Was this where she was supposed to find her new beginning?

"Shirley, who used to live here?"

"A little old woman named Sue Smith. Ninety-four years old. Was supposed to be homebound. A shut-in, I guess you could say. But kept escaping." Shirley smiled. "She was quite a firecracker, let me tell you. Finally her family decided to move her to a home. But I suspect that hasn't done much to contain her."

Lindy squeezed Shirley's arm and offered a warm smile. "It's perfect. I'll take it."

"Wonderful! Let's get the paperwork started. I'll be right back."

Shirley went to her car and Lindy followed her out, watching Conner bounce around the front yard. She intended to get the number off the storefront. She also wanted to call Vance, tell him the good news.

Conner bounded up to her. "Where is Dad? Why isn't he here?"

"He's on his way," Lindy said, patting his head full of wavy hair. "He stopped off to see someone."

"Who?"

"An old friend."

"How old? Like a hundred?"

"I mean former friend. Former partner." Lindy sighed, exhausted at even having to explain it. "Anyway, he's coming. In fact, I'm going to call him now." She pulled out her cell phone and dialed Vance, but it went straight to voice mail. She absorbed the disappointment, but it reminded her of a night she couldn't get ahold of Vance. She'd called and called and nothing. It was her birthday, a little over a year after they'd married. They'd had plans to go out to eat when he got off work.

He arrived home at eleven. Lindy had fought resentment. "Where have you been?"

"Something happened at work," he said. Then the realization snapped across his face like a strong north wind. "Your birthday."

She couldn't control the tears.

"I'm sorry. I am so sorry. We had this thing happen. . . . We caught this man that we'd been looking for . . ."

"Why didn't you call?"

Vance didn't answer, and Lindy couldn't fathom what the excuse might be. She'd gone to bed that night without speaking to him anymore. The next morning he'd gotten up early and made her a big breakfast. He took off work, and they spent the day together.

It made up for it all.

Four years later, at some police banquet, Erin spilled the beans . . . that Vance was nearly killed. That she'd shot the guy. That they'd gone out for a steak afterward. Lindy smiled, pretending to know every detail.

"Did you get ahold of Dad?"

Lindy glanced at her cell phone. He was probably in a dead zone. She knew he wouldn't turn his phone off. She had to believe it.

"Not yet."

She spent three hours with the landlord, filling out paperwork and checking credit. By dark, she had the keys to the condo and had called the movers with the address; their things would be delivered sometime the next afternoon. She'd also heard from Vance, just briefly. He sounded excited, talking fast about the idea that he felt free.

And when she told him about the condo and the commercial space down the road, it seemed to send a shock of joy through him. "This is it, baby," he said. "This is our new beginning."

They worked out a few details. Then his phone went fuzzy again and dropped the call.

She took Conner out for a burger, and they drove around looking at their new city. For once, she started to allow herself to feel some hope.

*   *   *

Although he was making great time and had enjoyed the Midwestern scenery during the day, by now the Nebraska roads were getting tedious. And Vance had lost cell service again.

He was tired, but he wanted to push forward another few hours. Up ahead, a neon sign flashed Diner.

He could get a cup of coffee and a burger to go.

Suddenly his cell phone lit up. He snatched it off the passenger seat without even looking at the screen. "Hey!"

"Mr. Graegan?" The voice sounded husky.

"Yes?"

"It's Joe from Movers Unlimited."

"Hi. I'm sorry. I was expecting my wife." Vance pulled into the parking lot of the diner. Through lit windows, he could see patrons, mostly truckers, enjoying hot meals.

"I'm sorry to inform you, but we have a problem."

4

VANCE STOOD OUTSIDE HIS CAR, a driving north wind reminding him he was underdressed for the weather. Where was his jacket? He peeked inside his car but didn't see it. Maybe it was in the trunk or buried under something in the backseat?

He opened the car door, snatched the contract off the front seat, folded it, tucked it under his arm, and headed inside the diner. The warmth did nothing to soothe him, nor did the greasy smell coming off the grill. He'd lost his appetite, big-time.

He sat at the bar and ordered a tall coffee and a burger. He had to eat something because now he definitely wasn't going to be stopping for the night.

First, he had to stop shaking. Then he would call his wife.

How was he going to even be able to tell her this?

His phone lit up, surprising him again since he'd had such a hard time getting a signal. He looked at the number and didn't recognize it. He answered cautiously. "Hello?"

"Vance, it's Erin."

Vance let out his breath. "Hi."

"You okay?"

"Why?"

"You sound tense."

"No . . . I'm just . . . What's up?"

"You left your leather jacket."

"Ah. That explains why I'm frozen to the bone here in Nebraska."

"You're making good time."

Not good enough. A headache throbbed against his temples.

"I'll ship it to you. I know this is your favorite jacket from one of your favorite people. Glad to see you still have it. You got an address yet?"

"Yeah. Lindy found us a place. But I'll call you when I get there, okay?"

"Vance, what's wrong? You sound like something's wrong."

He stared at the burger that slid across the counter toward him. What was wrong? Just moments ago he'd felt free and clear.

"Can I get this to go?" he asked the waitress nearby, who

was swinging a dirty rag over what looked like a perfectly clean counter. He threw some money down.

"Vance?"

"Look, Erin, I'll call you, okay? I've got to get on the road, but when we're settled, I'd love that jacket back."

"Okay, sure."

"Thanks for calling."

While he waited for a Styrofoam cup and container, he flipped through the contract, trying to figure everything out. Joe had mentioned that the curb was over fifteen feet from the condo's front door and that the alleyway prohibited them from backing the truck any closer. Which meant there would be a fee.

Eight thousand extra dollars.

The words looked frantic on the page, like they danced around to avoid being read. Vance could hardly focus on what he was trying to find. He put his finger down, tracing a sentence here and there, but the document was so thick. Could it be true? A clause embedded in this document?

The waitress returned, and Vance dumped his burger and coffee into the containers. He tried to remember what Joe had said. From the point that he mentioned there would be a hefty fee for the curb distance, the rest of the conversation had been filtered through a lot of anger.

"It's in the contract."

"The contract."

"Yes. The one you signed, Mr. Graegan, right on your front lawn."

"But I don't understand. We couldn't have possibly known how far our home might be from the curb."

"Not my problem, sir."

"Where is this in the contract?"

"Page 11."

Page 11. Vance quickly flipped to the page and scanned the paragraphs until he found what he was looking for. There it was. Loud and clear.

If the distance from the curb is farther than fifteen feet, a fee will be incurred, up to eight thousand dollars.

"This is ridiculous," Vance groaned, grabbing his stuff and returning to his car. He threw his container in the backseat, situated the coffee, and stared at the contract. He wanted to light that thing on fire.

He knew this wasn't fair. How could they charge eight thousand extra dollars?

"It requires more time to unload, sir, and time is money for us." Joe's tone had seemed smug, like he was wearing a half smile when he'd said it.

Vance looked at his phone. No bars. Great. Man, it was patchy out here. He hit reverse and peeled out of the parking lot, gliding onto the smooth black road.

Maybe it was a good thing he didn't have bars right now. It wasn't Lindy who was going to get a piece of his mind. It should've been Joe.

* * *

"I like this place," Conner said. He'd hardly spoken as they drove around, and Lindy was worried about what was on his mind.

"When Dad gets here, we can go visit the ocean," Lindy said, smiling at him. She'd let him sit in the front seat, and he was hanging out the window, letting the wind bite his face. He ducked back into the car, and his hair was standing straight up. Lindy laughed. "We better head home. I haven't heard anything from the movers. They should be here sometime soon."

She'd turned off the GPS. She hated that woman's know-it-all voice. With a map in hand, she found her way back to the condo. The sun's fiery orange glow swam against the darkening sky. Her condo, perched atop a hill, would give her this view any night she wanted to take the time to look at it. And more than anything, she wanted time to see the beauty in everything around her. She checked her cell phone to see if Vance had called yet.

As she turned onto the street, the bright yellow truck came into view.

"There it is, buddy!"

"Our stuff is here? Can we hook up the Wii? I want to get that hooked up, Mom."

Lindy laughed. "Slow down. There's a lot of stuff to unload. And Dad will be here tomorrow to help us get it all organized, okay?"

She pulled to the curb behind the truck. The mover

named Joe was standing at the front door, looking as if he'd just rung the doorbell.

Lindy hopped out. "Hi! Sorry. We didn't get a call from you, so I wasn't sure when you were arriving." She smiled as she crossed the lawn toward him. He walked off the front porch. "This is our new place."

He nodded but remained expressionless. "I'm assuming you've talked to your husband?"

"About?"

"The distance your condo is from the curb."

"I don't know what you're talking about."

Joe's face, pleasant and cordial in Maryland, now looked congested with mistrust. "Your husband didn't call you about this?"

"No, I'm sorry. We haven't talked since earlier."

"Maybe he isn't taking this seriously." Joe's eyes sharpened.

"Can you please tell me what this is about?"

Conner blazed in a circle around them. "Mom, when can we get our stuff?" He jumped up and down like he was a human pogo stick.

"Conner, don't interrupt!" Lindy drew in a breath, immediately regretting barking at her son. She'd promised herself that this new beginning included not taking her frustrations out on him. "Conner, sweetie, just give me a second, okay?" She tried a smile again toward Joe, but he didn't return it.

"Your contract reads that the building we're moving your

stuff into can't be more than fifteen feet from the curb." He pointed to the front door. "It's twenty-nine feet. We can't get in the back way because the alley is too small."

"Okay, sure. I understand. So what does that mean?"

"It's an extra eight thousand dollars."

"Eight thousand dollars?" Disbelief prickled her skin, like bacon grease splattering out of the pan.

"Your husband should have called you about this."

"I don't know why he didn't, but I can tell you we are not going to pay eight thousand dollars. We don't have that kind of money. And why in the world would distance make that big of a difference?"

"It's in your contract. That your husband signed." Joe's tone was cold. There was no longer a customer service twinkle to his eyes. "Page 11."

Lindy crossed her arms. "I don't care what the contract said. You can't do this."

"I *can* do this because that's what the contract says." Joe began walking toward his truck.

Conner had stopped bouncing around and was now listening intently to the conversation. Lindy motioned for him to stay put as she followed Joe down the sidewalk.

"Sir! Wait right there!"

Joe kept walking. "Ma'am, you are contractually obligated to pay us what you owe us."

"We've already paid you over ten thousand dollars for this move!"

"That's right." Joe turned and Lindy almost ran into him.

"And if you want your possessions, you will pay us the rest of what you owe."

Lindy fought back tears. She wanted to push him in the chest as hard as she could. "This isn't fair!" She sounded seven years old, but it was all she could come up with. "I'm calling my lawyer!"

Joe's demeanor remained calm as he climbed into the truck. "That is fine, ma'am. Make sure you give the lawyer a copy of that contract." He cut his eyes sideways at her, making his point for a moment before starting up the truck.

"I'm calling the police!" she yelled over the truck's roar. Joe never looked at her again. Instead the truck rolled away from the curb and down the steep hill, out of sight. Lindy could do nothing but let the tears fall down her face. Eight thousand dollars? That was over half of what they'd saved to start this deli. She put a hand to her mouth, trying to hold in the sobs, but it was useless.

Conner came to her side. "Mom? What's wrong?"

She couldn't even pretend it away. She shook her head, not knowing what to say. Wishing Vance were here. Why hadn't he called her to tell her this?

"Mom, you're shaking." He put his hands on her. "I'm going to pray for you."

"It's okay. Mommy's okay." She handed him her keys as she wiped her eyes. "Can you go unlock the front door? I'll be inside in a second, okay?"

She brushed off the tears again, but they kept coming. She had to get a grip, for Conner's sake. How many times had that little boy seen her cry since he was born? Countless. This was supposed to be their new start, where Mom and Dad lived in peace. Where bad men were far away.

But bad men were everywhere. Sometimes they came with guns. Sometimes not.

And once again she was alone, and Vance was nowhere to be found.

5

VANCE TURNED the piece of paper over and looked at his bad handwriting, trying to decide if he'd written down a six or a zero. His eyes stung and felt heavy, like they were slowly being absorbed into his eye sockets. He'd pulled into a rest stop at 4 a.m. intending to take a fifteen-minute power nap. He woke up an hour later. But he'd made good time otherwise.

The conversation he'd had with Lindy late last night still swirled in his foggy mind. He'd hated how upset she was, but he'd finally convinced her that his patchy cell service was why he hadn't called.

He was furious that Joe had visited the house and talked

to her. Completely inappropriate. He had to figure out what to do, and quickly. But first, he just wanted to get to his new house, be with his family. Get some sleep.

A vague pain washed through his head. It would be a migraine soon if he didn't get real rest. But by his calculations, he was only fifteen minutes from the house, if he could find Stanton Street.

"There! Yes!" His hands did a little dance across the steering wheel. Now he was supposed to stay on this for three miles.

Already he was liking Redwood City. He'd rolled down his windows when he crossed the Bay Bridge. The salty smell of the ocean contrasted nicely with the woodsy scent of the trees and the clean, fresh air.

His mind wandered a little. Those days when fear masterfully played him like a puppet were long gone, but he hated himself for never getting the upper hand on it. For never being able to leave it behind.

With every bloodied body that he'd had to stand over in those weeks came a sense of desperation that he had never experienced before or since. He would stand at the crime scene, imagining those innocent people going about their everyday lives, death dropping them with one bullet.

The bloody concrete of the sidewalk, near the bus stop, had glistened in the October midday sun. He couldn't stop gazing at the tree line, wondering if he and his fellow officers were being watched. Taunted. Targeted.

A nearby car backfired. People screamed. Vance dropped

to the ground and pulled out his weapon. That day, October third, five people died by single bullets. At the end of that night he and his fellow detectives realized what they had on their hands. There were no connections between the victims. It was random, which was a conclusion that caused a dread so deep he didn't sleep for two days.

Then another one. A fortysomething woman was loading things into the trunk of her car. She lived, but they all knew: whoever was doing this wasn't going to stop.

And then October seventh came. They'd still been working the crime scene from three days before, wary and exhausted. The hunt was on for the killer, by air, by traffic stops, but the detectives knew he would more likely be caught in the details. They had to find something, anything, to lead them to the capture.

There was a white van spotted. Witnesses said they saw two men. Then someone saw a dark sedan. Roadblocks were erected. Task forces swarmed the hills and the roads. But the area was so expansive. It was like trying to find a button in a city trash dump.

He'd finally gotten some rest. Lindy had ordered it. He'd slept four hours, fitfully, but slept nevertheless. He arrived early at his desk, eager to see if anything new had come in. His supervisor, Detective Cantella, a veteran of twenty years, seemed like a rock. Vance had come off the streets only a year before, looking for a place he could find his footing. Lindy had suggested applying to go inside, and he'd gotten the job four months later when three other detectives retired.

It had taken some adjustments. He liked the thrill of the streets, the daily activity, and the sense that you never knew what was going to happen.

But he had a kid now, and the thrill was constantly coupled with the desire to give his son the very best in life, which meant keeping his danger level low.

Even beyond that, though, the real reason he'd left was Erin Lester. The nine-year relationship with his partner had grown complicated, and though Lindy would never believe it wasn't romantic, to keep his family intact, he had to make changes.

He'd found detective work partly mundane and partly challenging. Doug Cantella became a personal hero, and life behind the desk was more than tolerable. He was learning a lot about being a great detective. He was learning to follow the trail and pay attention to detail and get the guy at all costs.

Except the man with the rifle was like a phantom. Vance managed to keep his wits about him until October seventh. He had followed Cantella's instructions carefully and had pocketed his fears that whoever was doing this was going to open fire on all the police working a scene.

He was getting his third cup of coffee that October morning when his cell phone vibrated on his hip. He flipped it open.

"Vance?"

The voice was frantic. He recognized it immediately. Erin.

"Erin? What's wrong? What is it?"

She was crying. In all the years he'd known her, he'd never seen her cry. Not once. Not even when she broke her leg during a pursuit. The bone had slashed right through her skin and poked out of the leg of her uniform. All she'd said was "Did we get him?"

Vance set his coffee down and turned away from the noise of the office. It was 8:14 a.m.

"They got a boy," she sobbed. "We were the first to respond."

Vance motioned to his partner, Drakkard, waving his hand to get his attention. From where he stood, he saw Cantella's desk phone light up. Drakkard's phone lit up too. They locked eyes. They knew they had another one. But a boy? A *boy*?

"Where?" he asked Erin.

"Bowie. Get here, Vance. He's killing children now."

Vance hadn't hung up the phone when Cantella shouted from across the room, even as he grabbed his weapon and jacket.

"Graegan! Let's go!" Drakkard hollered.

But the chaos in the office was nothing compared to what he drove up on.

The kid had been shot right in front of his school.

Vance blinked away the images, straining his eyes to see street signs. He wondered if they'd ever leave him . . . the memories. They were so vivid. So much detail was still layered atop it all. He remembered the coffee being too hot to drink. He remembered the day being perfectly pleasant. He remembered Doug Cantella, who was calm in motion, pointing, and his hand was shaking.

He glanced ahead, trying to read the upcoming street sign. He'd gone at least three miles, hadn't he? Sometimes when his mind drifted, time did too. He'd given Lindy the GPS. He hated that thing. It was like a rude relative, always interrupting the conversation.

He slowed down and squinted. That was it. Mistletoe Street. He turned right and drove three blocks. Up ahead he saw a condo on the corner, perched on a hill. That had to be it.

He could see why Lindy liked this street. As he topped the hill, a magnificent view spread out below him. Homes and businesses lay quietly beneath the shadows of the trees. And he quickly found the place she was thinking of for the deli. It was right across the street.

And then he saw Conner, running around the front yard, his arms extended like an airplane. Vance pulled to the curb. As he got out, Conner turned and spotted him.

"Dad!" Conner jumped into his arms and hoisted himself up, where he wrapped his arms around Vance's neck and nearly choked him with a hefty hug.

"Hey, buddy!"

"You're here! You're here!" He dropped to the ground and pointed. "That's our new home. You want to see it?"

"Of course!" Vance followed him up the sidewalk. The condo looked tidy. The bushes were neatly trimmed, the sidewalk weed-free and nicely swept. "Where's your mom?"

"Inside."

"Inside?" Vance tried not to react, but they had an agreement about Conner playing outside by himself. Today, though, he had to let it drop. Or try to. He opened the door and saw Lindy at the kitchen bar, just hanging up the phone. She saw him and her expression lit up. Momentarily. Dread diminished her normally sparkly eyes. But she still smiled.

"Well? What do you think?"

"Looks perfect," he said, pulling her into a hug. She felt tired in his arms.

He kept an arm around her as Conner tugged at him. "Come on! You gotta see my bedroom!"

The place looked like it had potential but felt especially cold without their belongings. The short hallway led to two bedrooms and a bathroom.

"This is going to be my bedroom," Conner said, pride stretching its way across his grin. His backpack and Etch A Sketch sat in the middle of the room. The tent was by the window. "And Mom says I can arrange it however I want. I'm going to put the bed there, by the window, and I'm going to make a secret hideout in my closet." His shoulders suddenly slumped. "When is the TV coming? And I want my video games."

Vance ruffled his hair. "Soon, buddy." He guided Lindy out of the room, and they returned to the empty living room. "Are you okay?"

She shook her head. "Joe called again."

"What?"

"I just hung up with Karen Kaye. She's an attorney here. She had left a flyer on the windshield of my car." Lindy was talking fast, breathing hard.

Vance put a hand on either shoulder, glanced over his own shoulder to see if Conner was still in his room. He was. Watching. And his hands were squeezed together like when he prayed. "Okay, talk slowly. Tell me what Joe said."

"He said we're up to nine thousand dollars."

Vance wanted to gasp, to strike something, to kick something over, except there was nothing in the room to kick. He let go of Lindy's shoulders, trying to compose himself.

"He said that each day he has to hold our stuff is an extra thousand dollars. Each day, Vance!" She started crying. "We only have fifteen thousand dollars. That was for the new deli. What are we supposed to do?"

"What did this attorney say?"

"She said that it sounded like a scam. She said to contact the police."

Vance nodded, but inside he knew how useless that was going to be. At least in the short term.

Lindy put a hand on his arm. "Vance, I think we should go to the police. Make a report now." She smiled a little as she wiped her tears. "And I know what you're thinking: this isn't going to help what's going on. But we've got to do something and at least get the ball rolling."

Vance felt helpless.

Conner bounded into the room. "Do I have to sleep in the tent again tonight? I want my bed."

"What do we tell him?" Lindy whispered.

Vance walked to the front window of his new home and stared at the redwoods. So much for new beginnings.

6

"So you were with the police force in Maryland?" Officer Hill, chubby and unenthusiastic, asked as he worked on the report, printing as slowly as if he were just learning the alphabet.

"That's right," Vance said.

"Well. Welcome to Redwood City."

"Do you think we'll get our stuff back?" Conner asked.

"We'll do everything we can." Hill's answer was flat and rehearsed and not the least bit convincing.

Conner's voice quivered. "He stole everything I have."

Vance pulled him onto his lap, squeezed him tight. "I'm sorry this is happening, buddy."

Conner turned to him. "You're a cop, Daddy. You're supposed to stop people like this."

"I'm not a cop anymore," Vance said, glancing at Lindy, who only looked away. "But I'm sure the police officers in Redwood City understand how big of a problem this has caused us." He shot Hill a look.

"I only have the five toys I brought in the car. That's it. Mom doesn't even have anything to cook with. We don't have anything." Conner broke down and buried his face in Vance's chest.

Lindy looked like she was about to do the same. "Sweetie, come on. Let's see if we can find a vending machine. You want a soda or something?"

"Down the hall in the waiting room, ma'am," Hill said.

Conner nodded and climbed off Vance. Lindy took his hand, and they disappeared down the hallway.

Vance caught Hill's attention. "You understand what a nightmare this is."

"Sure. We'll get this over to our property crimes unit and see what we can do."

Vance leaned forward. "What would you do if you were me?"

"Sir, you've done the right thing by coming in and filing a report. We'll do everything we can to figure this out. The contract that you signed makes it more difficult, and you may find yourself in court. But we'll investigate this to see if there is a crime being committed here."

Vance searched the officer's eyes to see if underneath the

compliant facade there was another message he was trying to convey. But the only thing returned was the blank stare of a man who loathed desk work and couldn't wait to get home to his TV dinner.

The fifteen-minute drive back from the police station consisted of their eight-year-old throwing a temper tantrum like a four-year-old. Vance's patience grew thin with each raging bark that came from the backseat. Yet really, could he blame the kid? He'd promised that their stuff would arrive safely, and now it not only wasn't safe, it was very possible they might not ever see their things again.

Finally Conner settled down a little, distracted by a cough drop that Lindy handed to him. That was the great thing about having an eight-year-old with a slight case of ADD. He had very little focus, even on important things.

Lindy touched Vance's arm, lowered her voice. "I've been thinking. Maybe we should just pay it."

"What?"

"Even if we did have a case, it could be tied up in the courts for months. Years. Is it worth it?"

"Lindy, we can't let this guy win. Give up half of our savings to this rodent?"

"I'm just saying, let's get this over with."

Vance didn't say anything. He squeezed the steering wheel to keep himself from saying what was really on his mind. There was no way he was going to let this happen to his family. There was no way this was going to be the beginning of his new beginning.

His cell rang. "Hello?"

"Vance, it's Andy."

"Andy, hi. You got my message?"

"Yeah. Listen, with what's at my disposal, I couldn't trace that number. It's locked down. If you had more, like an address, that would help."

"I'll see what I can do," Vance sighed.

"Man, sorry to hear about this. Unbelievable. You got a lawyer?"

"Yeah."

"Let me know if there's anything else I can do to help you, my friend."

"Thanks." Vance slowly shut his phone. He couldn't believe what he saw coming up on the horizon as he approached the house. "Look who is at the house."

Like a small building, the yellow truck towered atop the hill, parked against the curb. Vance slowed the car and pulled behind it. "Stay in the car." He looked directly at Lindy. "Do you hear me? Do not get out."

She grabbed his shoulder. "What are you going to do? Don't do anything crazy."

"Just stay in the car."

He got out and walked swiftly into his front yard. The door to the cab opened and Joe hopped out. He looked so unassuming, like a good ol' boy. But Vance immediately noticed his eyes. The whites were dull and yellow, like smokers' teeth.

His irises, a light green, were shadowy from the trucker's hat he now pulled low on his head.

"Mr. Graegan."

Vance trembled inside. He wanted to punch this guy out, right there on the front lawn. But there was probably someplace in the contract that stated if you punched out a moron, you owed ten thousand more dollars.

"Your wife told you I called."

"I told you to deal with me, not my wife."

"I can't deal with you, Mr. Graegan. You're not taking this very seriously."

"You are a scumbag. And this is a scam. If you think you'll get away with this, you're seriously mistaken. I will personally make sure that you don't."

"The problem is," Joe said, his voice low and calm, "that you don't understand the power I have in this situation."

"I know—the contract."

"I'm not talking about the contract." His eyes drifted toward Vance's car. He settled an uncanny stare there for a moment, then returned his attention to Vance.

And with one swift right hook, Joe fell to the ground. Vance's knuckles stung like they'd been struck by a match. He shook it out while watching Joe stagger to his feet. He didn't look back at Lindy. He already knew this was the thing she didn't want. But there was no way this man was going to imply he had power over Vance's family.

Joe stood, pressing the back of his hand to a bloody lip. He didn't look terrified, as Vance had hoped. He didn't even look stunned. A measured calm steadied him, and he glared directly at Vance.

"You can threaten me if you want. But that is only going to make things worse. Now, you have twenty-four hours to get me the money. We are up to ten thousand dollars because I am going to have to hold your possessions for one more day." Joe's eyes hardened to a cold stare. "I know you have the money. This is your last chance. If you don't pay up, you will lose everything." He took a step backward. "And I mean *everything*."

Joe returned to the cab. It took everything in Vance's power not to tackle him to the ground. All the old feelings were rising up. That anger at injustice.

Joe opened the cab door, took one step up, and looked at Vance. He smiled as if they were good friends and he was about to give a friendly wave good-bye. Then he said, "And if you go to the police again, Mr. Graegan, there will be consequences. Besides, you and I both know the police can't really do much, can they?"

He climbed into the cab and started the rig. Black smoke puffed from its exhaust pipe. Lindy got out of the car, but Vance held a hand up at her. He turned his mind into a camera, taking as many snapshots as quickly as he could. The license plate was unreadable, intentionally splattered with mud. The flaps were distinct, though. Both mud flaps were the same, and as Vance got a better look at them, a chill shot through him. They appeared to be hand-painted, almost like a childish drawing. A sick feeling rolled against his stomach.

He jogged forward, trying to get a better look. It looked like the Death card that was found in the woods near the school where the boy was shot in Maryland.

It was a tarot card with a distinct design of a skeleton in armor riding a white horse and carrying a black flag. Printed on the bottom was the word *DEATH*. Neatly handwritten across the top of the card, in blue ink, had been the words *Call me God*. It was the first time the snipers had communicated with police.

On the flaps of the bright yellow moving truck was the same image of the skeleton and the horse.

The truck pulled away, rumbling and grumbling, letting out large sighs when the air brakes were employed.

He couldn't catch his breath. What did it mean? Was it a coincidence?

"Vance?"

Lindy's voice startled him. He turned to find his wife's expression frantic and Conner standing behind her, grasping her arm.

He swallowed the fear and anger that was starting to consume him. He had to hold it together for his family. He offered a small smile.

"Okay, so I punched the guy. He kind of deserved it, right?" He grinned at Conner and winked.

Conner smiled. "You got him good, Dad. Is he going to give us our stuff back?"

Vance looked at Lindy, hoping for help, but she still looked frightened. "Yeah, buddy. He's going to give us our stuff back. I think he just needs some time to think about it." Vance put an arm around each of their shoulders. "Why don't we go inside. Figure out what we're going to do for dinner."

He let Lindy and Conner walk ahead. He needed air, needed to think, needed to decide whether what was on those mud flaps was going to change this game, permanently.

"Vance?"

He smiled at his wife. "I'll be there in just a second. Go on in. Just need to get a little more fresh air."

She nodded, understanding the underlying desperation in his eyes, and they disappeared into the house. He turned to face the great view of the city below the hill. No matter how many deep breaths he took, though, he couldn't shake the feeling that whatever was going on here went way beyond a scam for money.

"Vance! *Vance!*"

Vance turned at the sound of his wife's screams. He bolted to the front door, flung it open. Once inside, he first noticed Lindy, crying near the kitchen. His eyes darted to Conner.

Then he saw it. Their dining room table—the one that Lindy had been so careful to instruct the movers about— sat in the middle of the floor, splintered and crushed into pieces.

7

So THIS WAS their new beginning. Lindy stood in the kitchen, without utensils, cookware, or even a towel. There was hardly anything in the fridge . . . a gallon of milk, some yogurt. In the pantry were things that could be eaten easily without the use of a stove. Peanut butter and crackers. Raisins. She grabbed a Dixie cup and turned on the tap.

She'd wanted some time alone. But Vance had refused to let her stay at the condo by herself. So they'd all made their way out to the Target together for blow-up mattresses and paper goods. Lindy wandered the aisles to find a few essentials and to think. Vance took Conner to get two mattresses and then pick out a few toys, including board games to pass the time. Before they left, Vance purchased a bar lock for the back door and a dead bolt for the front door.

The whole time she had been trying not to cry. After Vance punched Joe out on their front lawn, there was something different about him. It felt like they were reliving the sniper nightmare all over again. She sensed him withdrawing the same way he did after that boy had been shot.

Before that night he'd been panicked, hustling her in and out of the house, on edge about everything. But then it seemed he vanished right before her eyes. He wouldn't talk about it. He wouldn't talk at all.

There was that same sense of vagueness in his eyes now. He smiled. He assured. But something wasn't right. She'd always been able to read his eyes. He'd taught her that . . . to always look someone in the eyes and let your gut tell you their intention.

Conner's laughter in the other room brought her back to the condo. She walked quietly to her empty bedroom and shut the door. Why was it so hard for them to find their happiness? Their peace?

Lindy stared at the package of toilet paper sitting by the wall. Her suitcase, with only five days' worth of clothes in it, sat against another wall. She plopped down on the carpet, lay on her belly, and put her face down. Tears streamed out and there was nothing she could do about it. There was nothing she could do about any of it.

Except pray. It felt uncomfortable, though. Especially since she was always telling her son to stop it. But he'd do it anywhere—the grocery store, his school. His two little hands would squeeze together as tightly as his eyelids. Sometimes he looked like he was about to burst. His face would turn red. And then, if he was really getting into it, his hand would fly up into the air and he'd start praying out loud.

So far, the few prayers she'd tried hadn't done much good anyway. She'd prayed for a new start, for family unity, for safety and protection.

The bedroom door opened and Vance peeked around it. He smiled a little when he saw her sprawled on the floor. "Meditating?"

She laughed. "Trying to bury myself."

He came in, shut the door, and sat by her. She turned over and looked at him.

"It's going to be okay," he said. "I give you my word: we are going to be okay."

Lindy looked away, toward the window that was now dark with the night sky. "I can't believe this is happening to us. It's like we're not supposed to make it."

"Don't say that. This is where we're supposed to be. We're going to be okay."

"We have our family. That's what counts." She sat up, curled her knees to her chest, and laid her head on them. "Vance, what if this is part of our new beginning? Maybe we're supposed to let it go. Let it all go."

"What are you talking about?"

"I mean, yeah, this place feels empty. But why don't we fill it up with us?" She paused, trying to read him. "I know it sounds corny, but maybe our new beginning means just that. We start completely from scratch."

"You mean, just let this guy walk away?"

"I mean, not let him have power over us."

Vance stood and walked to the closet, where he'd put the bags he'd carried with him. He took out his black bag and pulled out a small revolver, the one he'd taught her to use years ago.

"You remember how to use this?"

"Vance . . ."

"Lindy, this guy is not messing around. He got into our house." Vance checked the gun over. "You remember?"

"Yes, Vance. Of course I do. You took me to the gun range four times in one month. I know how to use it. You made sure of it."

"You keep this with you. In your purse."

"I don't have a permit in California."

"Just make sure this is with you at all times."

Lindy stood and went to him, lowering his hands as he fidgeted with the gun. "Let him have it all. Let's walk away from it."

"It's not going to happen." He snapped the barrel of the .38 Special closed and handed her the gun. "It's loaded."

Lindy stared at it in her hands. It still felt heavy to her, even though it was one of the lightest and smallest Smith & Wessons.

"Vance, listen to me. I don't care about all of our stuff. I

RENE GUTTERIDGE || 75

care about us." She looked him in the eye. "There's something you're not telling me."

His wandering gaze darted to her.

"I can see it in your eyes. I don't know what's going on with this Joe guy and this scam, but there's something that you know."

"What I know, Lindy, is that this guy is dangerous. He's threatening us. He's breaking in to our home. I don't know what he's capable of, but I have a bad feeling."

"I get that." She sighed, her fingers massaging the cold metal of the gun. "Then let's just pay him. Get it over with."

"I can't believe you're giving in to this guy." Vance walked to the door. "I am going to hunt this man down. At all costs."

* * *

"This guy's a pro," Andy Drakkard said.

Vance cradled his cell phone as he stood at the corner of the yard, his other hand stuck in his pocket. He'd slept only about four hours last night, partly due to an air mattress that wasn't holding its air and partly due to the fact that the air mattress was the best thing he could hope for at the moment.

"So you found nothing." Vance took a deep breath. If nothing else, he could enjoy the fresh morning air. He hated standing out in the open, but their yard had no trees. He had to get over it. He'd tried in the past, but again and again he returned to safe cover.

Gas stations were the worst.

"Nothing at all. I asked the IT guys, and they said they

might be able to find it, but they're buried in a high-profile political scandal right now. You would love this one."

Vance closed his eyes. He wondered if there would always be times when his heart ached for the job. "Thanks for trying."

"Dude, I'm sorry this is happening. I'd kill this guy. I swear I would."

"Listen, call me back if something pops up, okay?"

"All right. Enjoy that California sunshine."

Vance slid the phone into his back pocket and stared at the sky. That famous California sun was hidden by a heavy gray cloud. Vance looked for the silver lining but saw only whispers of sunlight fighting to dominate the sky.

An apple-red Cadillac, shiny and quiet, suddenly pulled to the curb of his condo.

Vance bristled but kept his cool as he watched the car idle there for a moment. A sleek tinted windshield captured the sky like a photograph but stopped him from seeing the driver.

Vance knew where his gun was, but it was inside. Should he go in? Or knock on the window?

Then the driver's-side door opened, slowly. A woman emerged, decked out in chunky costume jewelry and looking like Phyllis Diller's more eccentric sister. She noticed Vance and her face lit up with an expression so wide and frantic that Vance wondered if maybe she thought he was someone else. Her hand shot into the air and she waved like that crazy relative everyone tries not to invite to family events.

"Hi!" she sang, quickly shutting her door as she heaved a shiny red leather purse onto her shoulder. "Hi there! Hi!" She tiptoed across the grass like she was walking across hot coals. Then Vance noticed her three-inch high heels and realized if those things sank into the ground, she might not get them out. Well, at least he'd have an escape if he needed one.

She managed to get herself back onto the sidewalk and approached with an arm stretched out in front of her. Vance smiled. It was like she was walking an invisible dog.

That smile might've been a mistake. The arm retreated, and the next thing he knew, he was suffocating inside the enormous hug of a 110-pound woman. "You must be Mr. Graegan!"

Vance stepped back, took a breath. She smelled like perfume mixed with smoke. "You are?"

"I am so sorry. Your wife didn't tell you I was coming? Also, I'm Southern, so excuse me if I come across that way. I've been trying real hard to blend in with the West Coast folks."

Vance glanced at the house. "I didn't, um, know. . . ." They hadn't really talked much this morning. Lindy had emerged from the bathroom twice, obviously having cried. Vance didn't know what to say. But he knew he was going to make things right for her. Whatever it took.

"Your name?"

"I'm sorry. How un-Southern of me." Her hand shot out. "Karen Kaye. So glad to meet you."

Vance shook her hand, trying to figure out who this woman was.

"I'm your lawyer."

Dread stung his heart. She seemed more like she might be selling cosmetics.

"'Bout that problem you're having with the movers."

Vance folded his arms. "Okay."

"Yes. Terrible thing, Mr. Graegan, but I am prepared to help you fight for your rights."

"You do get that this is a scam."

"A good one, from what I understand. They certainly have all their ducks in a row, with that contract and all."

"What, exactly, do you plan to do about it?"

"That's what I wanted to discuss with the two of you. We do have quite a bit of legal recourse."

"Assuming you know where to find this man."

"I have a private investigator. He's real good. He caught my third husband cheating on me. No easy task. Howie was a sly son of a pistol," she said with a wink. She cleared her throat. "I understand you're new to California. Me too."

"How did my wife find you again?"

Vance's cell phone rang and he pulled it from his pocket. Karen motioned that she'd make her way to the front door by herself.

Vance watched her tiptoe across the lawn again as he answered the phone. "Graegan."

"Vance, it's Erin."

At her name, Vance sucked in a deep breath. He turned from the door just as Lindy opened it. He could hear the two women talking.

"You there?"

"Hey, uh, yeah. Sorry. Was just talking to someone." He stepped closer to the curb. Looked back to see Lindy and Karen still talking at the door. "What's going on?"

"Your jacket."

"What?"

"Your leather jacket. You left it here. You were going to call me with the address."

He rattled off the address information, watching Lindy and Karen disappear into the condo. The front door shut.

"You okay?" Erin's voice lowered as if she knew this was a delicate question. "You don't seem right. Did the rest of your trip go okay?"

"Yeah. Fine. I'm just tired. Busy moving in. And we had some, um, trouble with the movers." His words felt as hollow as the empty condo he stared at. The image of the tarot card on the mud flaps shoved its way forward through all his other thoughts.

"Vance?"

He couldn't get it out of his mind. It was all he'd dwelt on the night before. It couldn't be a coincidence, could it?

Maybe.

He wondered if he should tell Erin. Maybe she'd have some good ideas, be able to give him some advice. She was one of the best cops he'd ever met. Back in Maryland, the captain had asked her to come inside, but she never did. She always liked the thrill of the streets. He understood that.

"Yeah, I'm here. Sorry. Just absorbed in the whole moving thing. You know how it is."

"Well, not really. I sold nearly everything I had to move to Chicago."

"You wouldn't believe the cost of living here," Vance said.

"I believe it. Chicago's the same way. At least you get an ocean. I just have a lake. A big one. But it's still a lake." She paused. Sounded like she was sipping something. "So have you found a place to open this deli of yours? What's the name?"

"Ernest and Annette's. After Lindy's grandparents. There may be a place right down the street from us."

"Convenient."

"Yeah."

A long stretch of silence was filled by some birds melodically singing in the redwoods nearby. Vance hated the awkwardness. But it was what it was. He couldn't change the past. He wished it were different, but wishing wasn't going to change anything. He'd said good-bye a long time ago to what they shared. He missed it, but he knew it was what he had to do.

"I better go. Help Lindy figure out what's going on with these movers."

"Right. How is Conner?"

"Adjusting well. Thanks."

"I'll stick this in the mail. You should get it in a few days."

"Thanks, Erin. I really appreciate—"

The phone went dead. He decided to walk back inside,

see what this Karen Kaye had to say about things. Get out of the openness. He began to turn toward the house, then spotted something.

It looked white and it hung off one of the two mailboxes that sat at the edge of the curb. The first one belonged to his condo. He liked the fact that they still had a mailbox by the curb and not a metal box crowded in a block of dozens of other metal boxes.

Upon examining it, he found a clothespin holding a white envelope to the handle of the mailbox. How long had that been there? He ripped it off and examined it. Nothing written on it. Sealed. Maybe it was some documents for the condo.

The flap unstuck easily. He felt the glue. Still slightly damp. Inside was a single piece of paper. A short, typed letter started at the top.

You have secrets that I am willing to expose. $15,000
by tomorrow or you will lose everything.

8

LINDY WISHED she had some hot tea and fancy cookies to serve. Her dad's side of the family was from the South, and she knew there should always, always, always be refreshments. And polished silver.

All she had were paper plates and some Ritz crackers. Karen, with her long, neon pink, manicured fingernails, politely declined them. Instead, she was busily chatting about her legal career, how she'd been a stay-at-home mom for years, got divorced from three husbands by the age of forty-five, put both her girls through college, then went back to school to become a lawyer.

Lindy tried to look attentive, but all she really wanted to

know was whether or not she'd be able to get her belongings back. Karen eventually returned to that topic, rattling off some legal jargon that seemed to indicate it was possible. At least that's what Lindy hoped when Karen slapped her hand on the counter and said, "Come hell or high water!"

Her focus continued to shift between Karen and Vance, who was out on the front lawn, talking on the phone. It was unusual to see him standing in an open space.

"So when is the last time you heard from this fella?"

"We haven't heard from him since yesterday, when he crushed our table right here in the middle of the house." Lindy glanced to where it had been. They'd moved it outside against the house but hadn't thrown it away. "Do you think this man is dangerous?"

"Honey, this guy is a big bully with a moving van. Don't let him intimidate you. That's what he wants, for you guys to be scared witless and willing to do whatever he says." Karen reached across the kitchen bar and patted her arm. "Oh, sweetheart, don't cry. It's all going to be okay." She opened her purse and handed Lindy a tissue, another staple of a Southern woman. "Now, you do have a gun, don't ya?"

Lindy blotted her face, but she couldn't hide the surprise. How did they go from it all being okay to *do you have a gun*?

"Nothin' to be ashamed of. We Southern women all know how to use a gun. I got mine BeDazzled." Karen smiled, revealing a smudge of red lipstick across her overly large white teeth. She nodded toward the front window. "Your husband seems a little high-strung. I probably wouldn't give him a gun. We women are far better candidates for guns, let me tell you. Sure, a high-powered rifle can blow us as backward as Arkansas, but we don't go aiming the thing at everything that moves. Also, I don't have anything against Arkansas people. My daddy's veterinarian was from there. It's just a sayin' we like to use." She leaned forward and whispered, "Personally, I think New Yorkers are the weird ones."

Lindy had managed to get her tears under control. Karen, in her goofiness and warmth, made her feel at ease. At least temporarily.

The front door opened and Vance stuck his head in. He smiled, but it was tense. "Hey. Just wanted to let you know I was going to run up to 7-Eleven. Get some gas."

"You've met Karen, right?"

"We met," Vance said, not looking at her. "I'll be right back, okay?"

Lindy offered an apologetic smile as Vance disappeared again. "I'm sorry. This has been really hard on my husband. He's normally not this rude."

"No apology necessary. I did a stint at the local federal prison as a public defender for a while, so there's not much that's going to shock me."

Lindy tore at her tissue. "My husband and I moved here to get away from everything. To start over. Part of me wants to just leave this mess, you know? Just let the stupid guy have everything."

Karen's frown deepened. "Honey, I am assuming there

are quite a few things that are important to you in that van. Keepsakes and whatnot?"

"Sure. Of course. Tons. But what good does any of that do us? I mean, look at us. My husband and I are hardly speaking. So we get our stuff back. But our relationship is devastated?"

Karen reached across the bar and took her hand. "I know this sounds impossible right now. But I am not going to rest until I get you your stuff back. I even canceled my vacation."

"Oh no. That's not necessary."

"It's okay. I was planning on going to see my aunt in Georgia, and she's sometimes very hard to be around. She's pushy. Talks a lot. Wears makeup like she's trying out for the circus."

"Honestly, Karen, I'm not even sure that we can afford a lawyer. With things so uncertain."

"You don't pay me until I win this case for you, okay? And by that time we will have sued this cockroach every which way and into Friday. We'll even own his shoelaces."

"This seems like it could take such a long time."

"Honey bear, sometimes the best things in life, like real, sun-soaked iced tea, are worth the wait. I won't make you admit it, but I know you want this foot fungus to suffer." She smiled. "Speaking of iced tea, you should always have it on hand. This is sun-soaked California, after all!"

* * *

Vance parked his car in one of the few spaces in front of the 7-Eleven but didn't get out. Now he knew . . . this was more than your run-of-the-mill scam. But what *was* it? Something personal? Something connected to the sniper case?

He opened the letter again, rereading the words *You have secrets*. He'd buried those secrets a long time ago. At least he'd tried to.

He slid down in his seat, trying to think, trying not to let his emotions get the best of him. He remembered Cantella pounding that into their skulls.

"I know this is emotional," he'd said as he gathered them all together in the office on the seventh day of the sniper case. "But you have to leave it checked at the door. If you get emotional over this, you're going to miss something important. You may miss the one thing we need to solve this case."

Vance had checked his emotions at the door. Every emotion but one. Fear. And unfortunately, he let his emotions get the best of him at home.

He squeezed the steering wheel as his gaze bounced from one person to another. Someone could be watching him. Someone had gotten the edge on him. Someone knew too much about him. And someone was willing to do anything for money.

How was he supposed to protect both his family and himself?

He closed his eyes, breathing deeply, feeling very small on the planet. Even when the snipers were on the loose, there was always a sense around the department that they'd be caught, eventually. Nobody ever lost hope. Nobody knew how long the shooters were going to wreak havoc, but eventually they knew they'd catch them.

Vance didn't have that same sense now. It felt like everything in his world was about to crash down on top of him.

On most days during the sniper case, Vance never let on that fear was getting the best of him. The only person who really knew was Lindy. And unfortunately, she'd gotten the fallout from a lot of it.

Which was why it seemed so hard to talk to her now.

A strong urge swept over him to call Erin back. She would understand. She would talk him through it.

Vance slid his cell phone out of his pocket and stared at the numbers on the keypad. He used to have her on speed dial. Now he only had her in his call history.

Lindy would have a cow if he called her.

But that would be nothing if she found out everything he'd tried to hide. He turned on his phone.

Suddenly, though, another person came to mind.

* * *

Karen stayed and talked for another thirty minutes. But what else did Lindy have to do? Lindy talked a little about herself, at Karen's prompting, and about her hopes and dreams for the deli. Karen seemed interested in it all. She said it was hard to start your own business, and she'd had her ups and downs in hers, but ultimately it was really satisfying.

Finally, Karen said she had another appointment and left. Lindy spent some time playing with Conner, though she'd been pleased with how resourceful the kid had become. He'd made a small fort out of sticks in the backyard and then made a house, out of random materials he found around the condo, for the hamster he was hoping to convince his dad to buy. Then he'd spent an hour or more drawing on his Etch A Sketch.

She'd become pretty resourceful too, heating up a cheese quesadilla for Conner's lunch by putting it directly on the burner of the stove.

These things kept her temporarily busy while her mind wondered and wandered. She wondered what was taking Vance so long at 7-Eleven. Then her mind wandered to the idea of handing over their savings and what that meant for their future. And then she wondered about starting completely over, with nothing.

It would be like a house fire, wiping everything out but the clothes on their backs. People had survived that and were better for it.

The front door flew open as Lindy was cleaning up the kitchen, startling her. It was Vance. He was out of breath.

"Are you okay?"

He nodded. Smiled. But he didn't look good. He hadn't looked good since this whole ordeal started.

"Sweetie, what's wrong?"

"I'm okay." Another smile. This one wider, she guessed, for more emphasis. "I need you to get your stuff together, get Conner. We're going to Foster City, north of here."

"Why?"

"There's a detective who lives there—Doug Cantella. He moved here to retire. I want to talk to him about what's going on."

Outside she could hear Conner making airplane noises. "Why do we have to go?"

"I'm not leaving you here. I'll drop you off at a park or something."

"Vance," she said, setting the paper towels down and walking toward him, "I'm not going with you."

"Look, maybe we could find a mall while I go talk to him. Get you out of the house to go do something."

"The mall is no fun when you don't have any money."

"I'm not leaving you here. And I don't want Conner scared. I don't want him to hear me talk to Cantella. The guy's old and crusty and doesn't like kids, anyway."

"I know you mean well. And I get it. But I'm not going to let this guy bully us, dictate our lives. He's not going to have me scared to stay in my own house."

"This isn't an option."

"I'm not going. I have the gun. I know how to use it."

They stared each other down for a few seconds. Lindy searched his weary eyes. He was taking this thing so hard. He seemed to be withdrawing into himself. Again.

"Okay." His eyes passively blinked, then wandered to the back window, where Conner could be seen digging in the dirt. "But Conner stays indoors. The whole time I'm gone." His gaze snapped back to Lindy.

"All right," she sighed. "Maybe I can get him interested in chess."

"I have to go. He's waiting for me."

"You think this guy can help us?"

"He's as good of a shot as anything. You know what to do if Joe comes to the door."

"Lecture him and give him a stern look?"

That quip managed to get a small smile from him. "Funny."

She put a hand on his shoulder. "I will call the police after I pull the trigger."

"That's my girl."

Vance walked out the door and to his car, which he'd parked at the curb. She watched him drive away as she deadbolted the door, then went to the window to watch her son. He chipped away at the dirt with a thin but sturdy-looking stick, caught up in his own world. His imagination seemed to have blossomed since they'd arrived in California, out of pure survival. She hoped he could meet some new friends once they got him in school. She hadn't seen any kids out playing in the neighborhood, but she hadn't made an effort to find any either.

Maybe they could find a good park. She didn't want to bring him in; he was having such a good time.

Suddenly the doorbell rang. Lindy whirled around, her back against the window she had just been peacefully staring through. In an instant she realized there was no peephole. She was going to have to look out the side window, which meant alerting whoever was out there that she was home.

She calmed herself, rationally thinking through the fact that anyone in the world could be behind that door. A neighbor. The mailman.

It rang again. This time twice, with urgency chiming through the electronic bell.

Lindy hurried to the bedroom and grabbed the shoe box with the gun from the closet shelf. She took off the safety and felt her pocket for her cell phone.

The doorbell rang again, angrily repeating itself. Lindy hurried to the door, her left hand squeezing the gun tightly, her right hand shaking as she tried to get the phone out of her pocket.

She was just about to find the nerve to peek out the window when she heard, "Linda Michaela Webster, open this door this instant!"

Lindy unlatched the locks and pulled open the door.

Joan Webster loomed six feet tall without heels. Her sharp green eyes, small like they'd been pinched into her skull, seemed unaffected by what must've been a shocked expression on Lindy's face.

"Mother! What are you doing here?"

"Are you going to invite me in, or am I going to have to sit out on this dusty porch and get a sunburn?"

9

VANCE KNOCKED on what looked like a freshly painted front door. It was baby blue and so was the porch. The house looked awfully small, but it sat on the bay, so the size didn't matter. The salty, heavy smell of the water saturated the air. The sound of waves spilling onto the rocks caused a deep sense of relief even as he held his breath, waiting for Detective Doug Cantella.

The door opened, and there the man stood, a plaid cotton button-down shirt tucked neatly into tan pants. A nice leather belt was cinched tight. Vance figured that was exactly what he'd look like one day. And maybe he'd have a beachfront house, too. He'd always wanted one.

"Sir, it's Vance Graegan. I used to work for the Montgomery County Police Department."

Doug's eyes lit with recognition even as he took a skeptical glance around and then focused on Vance. "What's your business with me?"

"My family and I just moved to Redwood City." Vance paused, trying to figure out how to word it. "We're in a situation, and I'm not sure how to handle it."

"How'd you find me? I moved out here so I wouldn't ever have to think about that police department again."

"I understand, sir. I'm kind of in the same boat."

"I suppose you are a detective—and apparently a decent one, if you found me. You worked the sniper case. I barely remember you."

Vance smiled with relief. There were rumors that he'd had a nervous breakdown after retiring from the department. "I was a rookie then. Had just come off the streets."

"That case made us all feel like rookies, kid." He took one more look around, then waved Vance in. "Enter."

The house was small, tidy. Everything had its place. Ocean-view paintings and nautical decor crowded the living room walls. In one corner sat a TV with rabbit ears that had been unhooked. The side wall of the house was taken up mostly with a large plate-glass window holding a breathtaking view of the bay.

It smelled like he'd just microwaved lunch.

"Have a seat," Doug said with a short gesture toward an old-looking couch.

"What a view."

"Had to have something to remind me there are things to

live for." He limped toward a recliner like he had a bad knee. Easing down into it, he still looked skeptical.

"I know it's strange that I'm here. But I wasn't sure who to turn to. We don't know anyone in the area."

"We?"

"My wife. And I have a son, Conner."

"How long were you with the department?"

"Twelve years on patrol, then eight years inside."

"Retired at twenty years, huh?"

"Yes."

"Losing a lot of benefits."

"My wife and I moved out here to start a deli. It's a dream of hers."

"I bet there's more to the story than that." He smirked. "Instinct."

Vance laughed. "Yes, there's a lot more to the story."

"I retired early, too, you know." His gaze was set at the view of the bay. "Could've had thirty years."

"Why'd you leave?"

"You saw the madness, didn't you?"

Vance nodded. "I still can't stand in open spaces."

Doug briefly looked him up and down. "If that's the worst of your problems, you're doing okay, kid."

"The problem is that it isn't."

A knowing expression softened the lines crisscrossing Doug's rugged features. His eyes narrowed suddenly. "I remember you now."

"You do?"

"You were in that shoot-out." He fingered the edges of his recliner. "Yes. Earl Stormand."

"Earl Stormand."

Doug began rocking slightly in the recliner, seeming to relax a little. "If I recall, your partner took him down."

"She saved my life." The sounds of the bay washed over his words.

"It is a debt you can never repay. You can only accept it. Or you'll drive yourself crazy."

"I tried to repay it. And I made a terrible mistake."

"Is that why you're here?"

Vance took the paper Joe had left on his mailbox out of the pocket of his Windbreaker. He unfolded it and handed it to Doug. "This is why I'm here."

Doug slipped reading glasses out of the front pocket of his shirt. He held the paper close and read it. Then he peered at Vance. "Secrets."

"Secrets."

"All right." He refolded the paper. "This is going to require a cup of coffee."

* * *

Lindy's grip on the doorknob was causing the blood to drain from her hand. Joan's stoically cold expression never faltered even as wave after wave of awkwardness washed between them. Lindy stared out the door like she might just make a dash for freedom. It had taken years to unlock all the chains her mother had put around her.

She released the doorknob and stepped out of the way. Joan strolled in, her long, shapely legs a reminder that Lindy never got the glamour gene.

Joan stopped, putting one hand upside down on her hip, striking a pose like she'd just stepped out of a 1940s movie and needed a cigarette and a stiff drink. "You've yet to unpack, dear?" she asked, swiveling on her three-inch heels. "Where is all your furniture?"

Lindy sighed. She'd hoped her mother's first question would be *Where is my grandson?* But Joan was not one who liked children very much, though she seemed to tolerate Conner more than most. Still, even as a child, Lindy had sensed her mother was not fond of children.

"It's a long story," Lindy said. "We've got two lawn chairs over there."

"That's all?"

"That's all."

"I drove all the way from Guerneville to see you, Linda. You are telling me that you can't offer me a couch?"

"That's what I'm telling you." Lindy pulled at the bottom of her shirt, just like she used to when she was eight. "And it's Lindy. Please."

"Lindy never suited you. It sounds like you never reached maturity." Joan walked to the back sliding-glass window. "There's Conner. He is growing fast."

"I'll call him in so you can say hi."

"No. Not now. Let him play outside. He's got muddy hands." She turned around, her fist again planted sharply on her bony hip. "We have things to discuss. I hoped I might come help you unpack. Where are all the boxes?"

"They haven't arrived. We had a slight delay." The words sounded weary on her tongue. "But it was nice of you to drive all the way here just to help me unpack. How'd you find me?"

"So you weren't going to let me know you moved to California?"

"Of course I was. But we don't talk often. I figured we could catch up once I was in your home state. I thought it would be a nice surprise."

"Hmm. Surprise indeed." Joan fluffed her hair with her fingers. A heavy pearl bracelet draped off her tiny wrist like it was a necklace. Blue veins swam under her translucent skin—particularly in her hands, which had been pasty and frail-looking even when she was younger. Lindy used to spend hours watching her mother tap her fingers against her cheek or pull at her dangling diamond earrings. Her fingers always seemed freakishly long, especially with the fiery red fingernail polish. Joan's nails had not been naked in decades.

Lindy sat in one of the lawn chairs. Joan stood.

Joan. Lindy wasn't sure, but she thought it was around college when she stopped calling her mom *Mother* and started calling her *Joan.* At least in her head. She still called her *Mother* to her face, when she called her anything at all.

"Where is that husband of yours?"

"Vance."

"Yes. That's the one."

"He's out."

"Working?"

"He retired."

"Oh?" This actually caused an expression to flicker across Joan's face.

"You know how I've always enjoyed catering?"

She nodded even though she didn't seem to know that.

"We're starting a deli. Just across the street if I can get that storefront."

"A deli."

"It's been a dream of mine."

"And your husband went along with this?"

"Vance. Yes, he's very supportive."

Joan shrugged her shoulders as she found interest in the ceiling. "Hmm. Surprising."

"Which part?"

"Well, I harped enough, didn't I, about your marrying a cop?"

A weariness crawled over Lindy's skin. Indeed, she had. She had been relentless. It was what had broken an already-rocky relationship.

Lindy tried to relax in the chair. It had taken years, but she knew she was capable of not letting her mother get to her. She had few memories of nice, normal conversations with Joan, but she clung to them anyway. She remembered being awed by her presence as a child. Joan could walk into any room and immediately dominate it. As she grew older, she wondered what her mother was like as a therapist. Could she set anyone at ease, or did she simply scare them into spilling out all their feelings?

The older she became, the less she feared Joan. But she never understood her either, and that's what she wanted most as an adult. What made Joan Webster tick?

Joan had dropped in every now and then when they lived in Maryland. She never stayed long and always wreaked a little havoc—either intentionally or unintentionally—while she was there. Yet Lindy always longed to see her. There was something that connected a mother and daughter. She never could put her finger on exactly what that was.

"I know you never approved of me marrying Vance," Lindy said, suddenly wishing she weren't sitting below Joan. "But everything has turned out well. He's a good husband and a good dad."

Joan's sharp eyes cast their shadow across Lindy. "That didn't seem to be the case the last time I saw you. You weren't well. You looked horrible, like a ragged housewife who'd stopped taking care of herself."

"You don't understand what we've been through. That sniper case took a toll on us."

Joan fingered the scarf around her neck. "Don't you see, Linda? There is always a case. Always a reason. Always something that makes them not want to come home."

Lindy sighed, looking out the back window to watch Conner. "You'll just never understand. Besides, we came through it. We're okay now."

"Did your home get foreclosed on? Is that why you have nothing?"

"I told you, the moving van is late."

"I know what you told me. I'm only wondering if you would tell me the truth." Joan's eyes flashed with fierce mistrust, then softened. "Lies only lead to terrible things, Lindy."

"Our house was not foreclosed on. In fact, we made good money on it, which is what is going to help us start our deli." Lindy looked away again, fearful Joan might see right through her . . . see that they were in a heap of trouble.

To Lindy's surprise, Joan suddenly sat in the lawn chair next to her. Lindy wished she could serve her tea or biscotti. Her mother liked fine things and believed that riches made the world go around.

"Darling, I only wanted to protect you." She shifted in the chair as if she were having to endure pine needles.

"I'm sorry Dad left, but it doesn't mean all cops are like that."

"I was the chief of police's wife, Linda. For twenty years. I saw what it can do to a person. I saw what it did to your father. So few of them can bear the scars."

"Then Vance is the exception."

"You think so?"

"I know so. Yes, the sniper case was difficult. It was horrible on everyone. But Vance got the help he needed."

Joan only stared at her watch, twisting it around her wrist, zipping her fingernail along its gold band.

"I'm glad we're closer now. Maybe we can see each other more." Lindy looked at her, unable to hide the hopefulness she knew had latched onto her expression. She'd always wanted a normal relationship with her mom, but this was what she had. Maybe she could build on it, one small step at a time.

"I told you I was here to help you unpack," Joan said, her voice low, like a purr. "But I lied. There's another reason. And I will tell you what it is." Her gaze fixed on Lindy. "But I want you to prepare yourself for what you are about to hear."

10

THE SMALL DECK creaked slightly against the strong breeze gliding off the ocean's surface. Supported by two wooden beams erected on the sand, it seemed unsure of itself, but Vance figured it had outlasted many storms. He wondered how old the house was. The railing looked freshly painted, but the deck wood had been lightened by the sun. The deck was so tiny it held only a hibachi, two wicker chairs, and a short table in between, but what else would you need with this view?

Vance had just started to relax a little when Doug returned with coffee. He set down a small serving tray between them. "Cream and sugar? I take mine black. Real black."

Vance laughed. "Me too."

"I always told my boys they should stop drinking all that sugar. I'd watch 'em in the afternoon. They'd about be asleep at their desks. Nobody listens to old guys on the force, though. See? It was good that you got out when you did. You'll never be that old guy."

Vance nodded, watching the waves roll in and out. Sometimes he couldn't help but think about what his last years might have been like. The glimpse he saw caused him to lose sleep. But he would go there to remind himself what he had to fight for in the present.

Doug listened intently, occasionally asking questions as Vance told the story of the move, how Joe had held all of his belongings for ransom, and how he felt like there might be some connection to the sniper case.

When he got to that part, Doug turned quiet. His expression looked mildly reflective, but in his eyes Vance recognized horror, because the eyes always told the real story. That's what they taught at the academy, anyway. Vance had seen that horror duplicated many times in his own mirror.

"I thought it would never end," Doug said, his finger tracing the rim of his mug. "I remember that first day. Do you remember it?"

"October third."

"Five of them."

"We didn't even know for sure it was the same shooter."

Doug nodded, finally taking a sip of his coffee. He continued to stare out to sea. "We first thought the victims were connected somehow." He rubbed his fingers over his brow, pushing his thumb hard against his flesh. "It didn't occur to us that this was random. That he was picking and choosing people at will. That we had a real-life sniper on our hands." He blew out a breath and leaned forward like he was mesmerized by a crime scene in front of him. "Snipers. One of them just a kid."

"I thought that day would never end. When Chief Moo—"

"Don't say his name. His name is never to be uttered in my presence." Doug's tone turned sharp, and he set his coffee down. Then he stood and went to the railing of the deck. His wispy gray hair parted as the brisk wind captured it.

Moose had been a central but controversial figure in the middle of the chaos. The public counted him as a hero and a reason to hope. But inside the police force, many believed he made some vital errors that caused them to miss Muhammad on several occasions. Vance closed his eyes, trying to shut out his thoughts. But he knew . . . he always knew . . . there was never a way to run from what was in the mind. It relentlessly haunted him, which was why he found himself in this place.

"What sucker punches me to this day," Doug said, drawing Vance out of his dark thoughts, "is how many times we had them. They were right there—right in front of us—the whole time."

"You're talking about the pizza delivery guy?"

"I could talk about all of them, but don't get me started."

Vance knew Doug was thinking of all the times that

Muhammad and his sidekick, Malvo, had been stopped by police. Their dark blue Caprice always raised suspicions. It had black-tinted windows—a red flag for cops, especially when coupled with the kind of car. Criminals love retired police cars. The old Chevy Caprice police model was a popular car among the low-rider crowd because of the heavy-duty suspension components and its ease of conversion.

The pizza delivery guy, just a few doors down from Michaels craft store, where the first shot was taken the day before the massacre began, described to police a suspicious blue car with two men in it.

The report was discounted because they didn't believe the car could've been in the right place to make the shot.

Other officers over the coming days would stop the Caprice or run its tags, but they were always cleared because nothing came up on the computer.

Doug said, "It taught me something. Taught us all something. We cops depend too much on computers. We should go with our gut. Always."

Vance was suddenly overcome by nausea. He hunched over, afraid he was about to hurl.

"Are you okay?"

Vance nodded, but he wasn't. The guilt of the entire case crushed his lungs and squeezed him from the inside out. He was shaking, but he couldn't stop.

"You sure, son?"

No matter how much he tried, he couldn't have stopped the sobs that seized him.

Doug sat back down. "We have hit a nerve, then." He put a hand on Vance's shoulder.

"I can't live with this secret anymore," Vance said. He couldn't even uncover his face.

"Whatever it is, it has consumed you."

"I just wanted my life to be lived out normally, but that will never happen. Not after this."

"Son, tell me what's wrong. Tell me what happened."

The sobs faded and numbness spread over him. "I should've seen the car."

"What car? The Caprice?"

"I missed it. I was assigned to surveillance tapes. I was supposed to be looking for . . ." A sharp pain splintered through his head, pounding behind each eye. "Only one soul on earth knows about it. And she will never tell. And if I ever tell, it will change both our lives forever."

Doug picked up his mug again, sipping as if they'd been talking about an upcoming sports event. "So all your possessions are missing and you need to get them back."

Vance looked at Doug, unsure what to make of his comment. "I guess so."

"You guess?" Doug raised an eyebrow at him. "You're going to let this guy get away with this?"

"I don't know what to do. He's got the upper hand."

"Only because you're letting him have it."

"I don't know how to find him."

"A good detective always finds a way."

"I'm not sure I'm a good detective."

"Of course you are."

The headache worsened. He could barely focus on anything, so he closed his eyes.

"You fight for what is rightfully yours."

"How do I fight against this?"

Doug set his coffee down. "Let me see the note that was left to you."

Vance handed it to him, then watched as Doug carefully opened it, turned it back and forth, held it up to the light, looked it over like he was trying to find something very tiny on it. Then he set it down on the table, secured it with the sugar, and folded his hands together.

"Lots of things can kill the body. But guilt can kill the soul." He glanced at Vance. "You have nightmares?"

"Not as many anymore. But some."

"At least once a month I dream about Maiden Choice. I used to drive by there every week to remind me what had been at stake. The unimaginable horror that none of us could have comprehended was even a possibility."

"What is Maiden Choice?"

"It's a school for severely disabled children. It was written on a note found in Muhammad's car, under the headrest of the passenger's side. Along with Maiden Choice were three other schools and a preschool. Those were their next targets." He let out a long sigh. "There is always a next phase. Higher stakes. You have to stop it at all costs."

"Why can't I just let it go? Just let this guy win, go on with my life, take my wife and kid, and—?"

"Because that's not in you. And whatever mistakes you made in life? There can sometimes be restitution. But you have to seek it out. Now," Doug said, tapping his finger against the note on the table. "The first clue you need is right here on this paper."

* * *

The smooth, rehearsed tone in her mother's voice caused Lindy to shiver. What in the world could she mean by "prepare yourself"?

"What are you talking about?" Lindy asked.

Suddenly the back door flew open. Conner said, "Grandmother?"

Joan smiled and cringed at once. She hated to be called *Grandmother* and had asked to be called *Mama Joan* instead, but it never stuck with Conner. And *Grandma* certainly wasn't appropriate. It didn't even sound close to right.

As Conner stood at the door, his eyes flickered with hesitation. He didn't run to her. Or even smile.

"Conner, dear. Come over here and give me a hug."

Conner walked slowly, glancing at Lindy for assurance. Lindy smiled and nodded and tried to encourage him on with what was surely a tense imitation of what he was seeking—approval from her.

"Surprise!" Lindy grinned. "Mama Joan came for a visit."

"Hi," Conner said, reaching in for an awkward, sideways hug.

"My! You've gotten so big since I last saw you!"

Lindy wanted to say, *Yeah. Two years is like an eternity in a kid's life.* Last time Joan saw Conner, he was six and still dragging around a blanket. Thank goodness he'd traded it in for an Etch A Sketch.

"Does Grandmother live in California?" Conner asked, breaking away from her hug.

"Yes, I do," Joan said. "About two hours to the north, when the traffic is tolerable. We're practically neighbors now, aren't we?" She looked at Lindy. "I drove all that way to see your mother. It is such a long drive for a woman my age."

Conner glanced between them. "I get it. This is an adult conversation and you're going to need me to play outside."

Lindy pressed her lips together, trying not to wince. The poor kid had probably heard that more than a dozen times since they'd arrived in California. Lindy was unsure how to respond. Obviously there was something her mother needed to tell her, and by the tone of it, she didn't think it was going to be something she wanted Conner to hear.

"Don't worry," Conner said, patting her shoulder. "I'm having fun outside. I'm playing with sticks and rocks and stuff." He bounded back outdoors.

Lindy hesitated once again because she knew Vance didn't want him outside by himself. But Vance didn't see what she saw . . . a kid enjoying his freedom. He was eight now. They couldn't keep him in the house forever. Besides, they were three thousand miles from Maryland. That was like another world.

She let him go and decided to keep an eye on him through the back window. She could see his head bobbing around.

"He gets more and more handsome, doesn't he?" Joan asked. "He really reminds me so much of you. His eyes."

Lindy nodded, even though he was really the spitting image of his father. She lowered her voice. "So what is this thing that you have to tell me?"

Joan drew in a long breath, as if all this might cause her to faint if the day were a little bit hotter. She studied the cuff of her navy blazer, probably because there was nothing in the house to fix one's eyes on.

"Your father and I went bankrupt before. You never knew. You were just a baby."

Lindy sucked in a breath, slightly, trying not to gasp. "You did?"

"The higher your father climbed in the ranks, the more disgruntled he became. He'd go buy all kinds of things. Boats. New cars. Jewelry for me. Anyway," she said, "not important. It was a long time ago."

"That's what you came all the way here to tell me? Dad drove you into bankruptcy?"

"Sweetheart, there is a sense of disillusionment that every wife of every cop seems to have to endure. Their own disillusionment and that of the marriage."

"Look, if you've come to lecture me on how disillusioned you think I am about my marriage, save it. Yeah, we went through some rough patches. This is our new beginning."

Joan suddenly rose, gliding across the carpet as if she'd been walking in heels since the day she was born. She twisted her bracelet around and around her wrist, staring out the front window for a long moment. Then she said, "I received a phone call."

Lindy waited, listening to every breath she took.

Joan continued to keep her back to Lindy. "It was a woman. She said she had information that would help save my daughter."

"Save me?" Lindy rose from her chair. "Save me from what?"

"She didn't say, but I know. Disillusionment."

"What did she *say*?"

"She said one sentence and then hung up." Joan turned. "'Vance never got the psychological help he claimed he did after the sniper case.'"

Lindy planted her hands at her waist, staring hard at her mother. She tried her hardest not to have a reaction. She kept her tone neutral. "That's preposterous."

"I am only telling you what she told me. That's all she said."

"Maybe you're making this up. You've never really liked Vance."

"That's untrue. But, my dear, a mother's greatest hope for her daughter is that she doesn't make her same mistakes. I stayed with your father far too long. There were all kinds of warning signs that things were not right, except I chose to ignore them."

"Who would call you and tell you this?"

"She didn't give her name."

"I don't believe it."

"So you are choosing to ignore it, like so many other things, Linda."

Lindy turned away, willing herself not to cry. Was her mother so against the marriage that she would make something like this up? Vance had promised her he'd get help, and he did. He even gave her the name and number of his therapist. It had worked, too. He'd changed. Not overnight. But it had seemed like one day he came home from work and there was a smile on his face. And he played with Conner. And the world wasn't sitting so hard on his shoulders.

"My dear," Joan said, spinning out her words as if Lindy were hanging on them, "I am not a religious woman, as you well know. But I've heard of generational curses, and not to sound overly dramatic, but you may be living in the middle of one."

11

Doug handed him the paper. Vance looked it over, but he wasn't seeing anything. He looked at the lettering, the way it was written, the words used . . . but none of it was giving him any clues. He hated that he was already failing his first test.

"I'm sorry. I'm not seeing it," Vance said.

"Then close your eyes."

"Close my eyes?"

"Yes."

"But how am I supposed to—?"

"Just do it."

Vance sighed and closed his eyes. He sat there for a moment, trying to figure out where Doug was leading him.

He listened to the waves. He felt the wind against his face. He smelled the saltiness of the air—

"Smell . . ." Vance brought the paper close to his nose and took a deep breath. "What is that? Gasoline?" He opened his eyes.

"Oil." Doug stared intensely at him. "What does that mean?"

"He was maybe changing his oil or messing with his rig?"

"But there are no smudges of oil on the paper, are there?"

"No. It's clean."

"But smells of oil."

Vance tried to think it through as Doug watched him carefully. He looked away, trying to concentrate. "The air." He smiled, looking at Doug. "It's in the air. The air is so saturated with it that it soaks into the paper."

"Well done. So that would say to me that this guy is staying somewhere that works on cars. A mechanic shop maybe. Or someplace that runs machines."

"He's got to be hiding the truck somewhere. It's bright yellow, easy to spot."

"Now you've got the upper hand. He can't be far from you. He wants his money and he wants out."

Vance folded the paper and put it in the front pocket of his shirt. "What do you make of it being connected to the sniper case?"

"Vance, the case made us all a little crazy."

"You think I'm crazy for what I saw?"

"What do you think?"

Vance stood this time. He walked to the railing, wanting to lay into Doug for even suggesting it. He couldn't really wrap his mind around it all.

"You know," Doug said from behind him, "people used to think I was crazy. I'd hear them talk about it around the office. I guess it's no secret that I was critical of the department. Critical of how they handled the sniper case. Critical of the chief and all the red tape that made a hundred men lose their minds with anger."

"It was unprecedented. We'd never dealt with something like that before."

"Doesn't matter. Our very basic police skills should've gotten these guys long before we did. How many lives could we have saved?"

"There's no use thinking about it now. It will just drive you crazy."

"So maybe I'm a little crazy. That's all I do in this little house . . . think about all the ways we failed."

"We didn't fail."

"Then I guess I can only speak for myself."

"Do you have a family?" Vance asked without turning around. He liked the view of the bay. It calmed him down.

"Used to. They're gone now."

"Gone?"

"My wife left me. Took my kid. Haven't seen them in years. My boy's twenty now. I can only imagine what he looks like."

"Why didn't you fight for them?"

"I did. I tried. But at the end of the day, my wife gave up on me. Gave up on us. Didn't want me to see him. And let me tell you, when a mother makes a decision like that, there's really no hope."

"I'm sorry, Doug."

"It's probably for the best. I live by myself. Mind my own business. Dwell here, waiting to die."

"You can go on living your life, you know. A fresh start."

"I got a fresh start all right. A fresh nightmare that never ends." Doug paused, and the bay's noises drifted lazily over them both.

Vance finally sat back down. He didn't want to leave this place. He didn't want to face what waited for him—the possibility of failure, of losing what he'd worked hard for. He didn't want to disappoint Lindy. She'd already gone through enough.

"Now," Doug said, "I am going to go get us more coffee. And when I return, we are going to talk about this secret that is eating you alive."

* * *

Joan had backed off her doomsday predictions for Lindy's marriage and somehow managed to turn the entire conversation into chitchat. She was notorious for being unable to keep an in-depth discussion going unless she was paid by the hour for it.

But Lindy could barely follow even the light conversation. Although she refused to show it, distractions kept tangling up in her mind. She needed to get rid of her mother. But how?

". . . so I told the tailor that it just wouldn't do, and then she rambled on and on about something. I couldn't even understand her, and—"

"Listen," Lindy interrupted, "you've traveled so far, I hate to hog all your time here. Why don't you go outside and play with Conner for a little while? I know he'd love it."

Joan raised an eyebrow, and her normally less-than-enthused eyes lit with a startle. "Play?"

"Dirt is completely removable with dry cleaning."

Joan rose from her lawn chair. "Dear, I'm sorry, but I must go. I'm having dinner with friends. I need to go freshen up at the hotel."

"You booked a hotel?"

"Of course. I wouldn't want to drive home tonight. That's a lot of driving for one day, don't you think?"

"Sure. I want you to be safe, of course."

"Breakfast in the morning at the hotel? Bring along the family." She handed Lindy a card. "Here's where I'm staying. Say around ten o'clock?" She smiled mildly. "My treat."

Lindy shrugged. What else did she have to do around here? "Sure."

She let Joan out but didn't bother walking her to her Mercedes. Instead, she locked the door and ran to her bedroom, scrambling through her suitcase to find her directory. She'd grabbed it out of the truck, figuring there might be some numbers that would come in handy. Her husband's former therapist was not one she'd predicted she might need.

She flipped through the pages. She couldn't even remember this woman's name, but she thought she remembered writing it in bright blue ink.

It took several passes through the book, which was in desperate need of purging, before she found it. Dr. Nancy Sullivan. She dialed the number.

"Dr. Sullivan's office," a friendly voice said.

Lindy took a breath. She hadn't even thought through how she was going to pursue this.

"Hello?"

"Um, hi. I need to speak with Dr. Sullivan, please."

"I'm sorry. She's in session. I'd be happy to book an appointment for you."

"I don't need an appointment." Though she could probably use one, in all reality. Lindy took another breath. "But I am needing some information regarding my husband. He's a former patient."

"I'm sorry, ma'am. Unless your name is on the file as a person we can disclose information to, then I'm unable to give you any information."

"I understand. Could you please check his file? I'm his wife. I'm certain my name is on there."

"Ma'am, almost nobody gives permission for their file to be disclosed. Even to their closest family members."

"If you could just check . . ."

A long pause was followed by "Certainly. Let me get your name and number and have someone call you back."

Lindy knew that routine. "No. Please. I need to know now. This is an urg—" She squeezed her eyes shut and hoped she didn't sound too crazy. "We've moved to California, and we're just needing to get his medical records for his new doctor."

"I see. Well, your husband will have to fill out a form for us to release those to him."

"Of course. That's no problem. Can you just make sure you can find those records before I hang up? I am honestly not entirely certain I have the right doctor. It's Sullivan, but not sure if it's Nancy. Also, it was a long time ago—2002 through 2003."

"We have it all stored in computers, so it's no problem, even if it's archived."

Lindy could hear typing.

"What did you say your husband's name is?"

"Vance Graegan." Lindy spelled it for her.

"Hold on for a moment." More typing. And then more. "Ma'am?"

"Yes?"

"You must have the wrong doctor. We have no record of a Vance Graegan."

"You're certain?"

"Yes."

"Oh. Okay. Thank you for your time." Lindy hung up. Her hands shook like she'd downed a couple of espressos.

At the time, Vance claimed to have gone through the

channels of the police department, which was offering to pay for counseling for any officer who needed it. She'd never even seen a bill.

Vance had lied to her? Could she really get herself to believe this? Lindy leaned against the kitchen bar, putting her head down, trying to think inside the darkness.

"Mom?"

Lindy's head popped up. She'd entirely forgotten about Conner, he'd been playing so quietly in the back.

Lindy blew her bangs out of her face. "Hi. How was outside?"

"Is Grandmother gone?"

"Mama Joan, and yes. I'm sorry, sweetie. She had to go in kind of a hurry. She told me to tell you—"

"It's okay," he said with a relieved smile. "I've been busy outside."

"What have you been doing?"

"Building a fort. With sticks."

"That sounds awesome."

"It is awesome. It looks really cool. The lady even told me so."

"The lady? What lady?"

"She told me I'm a good builder."

"Who was the lady?"

"I dunno. It was earlier. You want to come see it?"

Lindy tried to calm herself. When she got stressed, she tended to verge on hysterics. Yes, she was processing that her husband had lied to her about something monumentally important, but she couldn't let Conner see it. This little boy had been through enough.

"Of course I want to come see it." She followed Conner out the back door, cautiously scanning the nearby redwoods for a sign of anyone. The alleyway that ran behind the four condos was quiet.

"See?" Conner beamed as he pointed to his little fort, which actually looked very well constructed. It was out of the line of sight of the back window.

"Was it Shirley?"

"Who?"

"Our landlord, Shirley. You know Shirley."

"No. It wasn't Shirley."

Lindy squatted, feigning continued interest in the fort. Her mind spun with rage. How could Vance do this to her?

"She was nice," Conner said, adding a stick to his fort. "Real nice. She even knew my name."

Lindy stood, the hairs bristling on her neck. "She knew your name?"

"Yeah. So she wasn't a stranger, right?"

"Come on, let's go inside," she said, widening an already-tense smile.

"But I want to—"

"Inside. Now."

12

ANOTHER WAVE CRASHED onto shore, spraying his face lightly. Perched on large, jagged rocks, Vance was far enough back so he wouldn't get soaked, but close enough that he could feel like he was part of the bay. There was something about the water that caused him great peace. Maybe because he always knew, somehow, he'd end up here.

Sunny California.

Except it was dark now. It had been for an hour. Maybe three. He was losing track of time. The moon was full, round, with crisp edges. The water was washed in its wafting light. And the smell. It was an endless symphony of purity. He crossed his arms and tried to keep warm. He didn't want to leave. It seemed, for now, he couldn't. So he stayed.

"You've been here for some time."

Vance turned, startled. He'd thought he was alone. Not even a dog had wandered by. He jumped up from the rock, trying to see the shadowy face of the person standing nearby. She stepped lower, onto a rock a few feet above him.

"Erin?"

"I know. Shocking, right?"

"What are you doing here?"

"Watching you. What are you doing out here all by yourself?"

"How did you find me?"

"I wouldn't be a very good cop if I couldn't track somebody down, now would I?" She stepped forward, the bay breeze blowing through her short hair. "I could tell you were in trouble. We know each other well enough. I heard it in your voice. So I jumped on a plane."

Vance wasn't sure if he should feel alarmed or thankful.

"May I join you here in your fancy bungalow?"

"Funny."

Erin sat down next to where he'd been sitting before. She leaned back, watched the moon for a moment. "It's been ages since I've been on the water. I used to surf, back in the day. Long time ago. Now I bet I couldn't even run three miles on the beach." She closed her eyes. "It's perfection out here."

Vance slowly sat next to her, still shaken by the surprise. It had been perfection moments before. But now, here he sat, with his former partner by his side like she'd appeared out of nowhere.

"What are you doing here?"

She sat up, looked at him, pulled her knees to her chest, and laid her cheek against them. "I could ask you the same thing, Graegan. You've been out here forever."

"You've been sitting here this whole time? Watching me?"

"Over there, in the car, trying to figure you out. You looked like you needed some space. I went and got a burger, came back. Went and got a coffee, came back. You're still here."

"I'm just trying to work through some things. Sort some things out in my head. You still haven't told me why you came all the way from Chicago."

"Sounded like you needed my help. Sounded like a bad situation." She grinned and returned to reclining against the rock behind her. "Plus, you left your coat."

"You could've just mailed it."

"Yeah. I guess I could've. Your coat is the least of your problems, isn't it?"

Vance lay back also. The night breeze was topped off with a slight chill.

"All I want is my family. Safe. Sound. Happy. And no matter how hard I try, I can't seem to give them that. Now I've got this guy who is trying to take everything else away from me. Holding all our stuff for ransom. And maybe I should just let him have it. That's what Lindy says. I guess it gives a whole new meaning to 'starting over.'"

"Vance, I can't even believe you'd contemplate something like that."

"Like what?"

"Just letting it all go."

"Why not? I've got what's most important to me."

"You've got to catch this guy. Or did you leave behind your sense of justice, too?"

Vance stared at the stars. They dotted the darkness like freckles splashed across the universe.

"Look," Erin said after a little while of silence, "you and I have been through a lot. I mean, we've got history, you know? We've got a lot of baggage. I get that. But we're cool, right?"

"Erin, you haven't been in my life in years. Now, suddenly, you're back. And I'm not sure it's a good thing. Yeah, we've got baggage and that baggage concerns more than just you and me."

"You've gotten yourself into a real mess. I'm here to help you. That's it. Unless, of course, you're sitting on this beach because you've got everything worked out, have all your belongings back, and have nothing better to do with your time."

Vance sat back up, crossing his arms. It seemed to be getting colder by the second. "You want to know what a real mess is? I saw the tarot card on the mud flaps."

"What tarot card?"

"What tarot card? The card of Death. The one we found after the kid was shot."

"Okay, well, there's lots of people into tarot cards. At least it wasn't a naked lady. Those drive me crazy."

Vance felt himself getting angry. She didn't seem to understand how complex this was.

"He knows."

"Knows what?"

"He knows our secret."

Even in the moonlight, Vance saw fear flash through her eyes.

"Yes. That secret."

"How does he know that?"

"I don't know, Erin. I don't know anything." Vance stood, shaking the bitter cold off him. "I don't know what any of this means."

"How could he know that? Nobody knows that," Erin said, jumping to her feet, grabbing Vance by the arm.

Vance shook her away. He maneuvered around the rocks, heading toward the water.

Erin hurried after him. "How does he know?" she repeated.

Vance didn't answer.

"You never threw it away, did you? I can't believe it. You never threw it away. You lied to me."

"I never told you I did," Vance said, turning toward her. "You are the one who lied to me!"

"How do you figure that?"

"Because you said you were done with alcohol. And you weren't."

"I had some slips."

"More than slips. As usual, you're delusional about the reality of your situation."

Erin's glare pierced the darkness. "What's it feel like, Vance? What's it feel like to be able to hold something over someone?"

"You don't know anything about what I feel. The guilt about what happened. The guilt that I have to wake up to every day."

Erin's voice softened. "Vance, we talked about this. It wouldn't have made a difference."

"Yeah, well, I never bought into that theory."

Erin walked a few paces away, and Vance was thankful for it. He felt like knocking her into the sand. After a few moments, she returned. "So it's all there. In that van. For this guy to go through."

"Apparently. He's had to rummage through a lot to find it. It was buried in a box somewhere. And now he's holding my darkest secret for ransom."

"Look," Erin said, breathing deeply, "we can figure this out. We can get this guy."

"I don't know. He's smart. He's cut off his cell phone—prepaid with cash, by the way. He's communicating through notes."

"We can find him. I can find him."

"I don't want you involved, Erin. You shouldn't have come out here. Lindy would freak out if she knew."

"Lindy rules the world, I guess."

RENE GUTTERIDGE || 131

"Shut up. Just shut up."

"I'm not trying to be hard on your wife, even though she's been a real pain in—"

"I said, shut up. You've got to leave."

"There's a lot at stake here."

"No kidding."

"And not just for you, Graegan." She stepped closer to him. "If you're thinking about walking away from this, think again. I won't let that happen. Do you know what would happen to my career if that disc ever came to light?"

"The mistake we made was covering it up. We should've just come clean."

"Yeah. Easy for you to say. You weren't going to lose your job."

"I could've been demoted."

"Yeah, well, I would've been out. Permanently." Her voice sounded weak. "Do you know how many times I've imagined how I would tell my father that I've been dropped out of the force? I never can find the right words. I never will be able to." She focused her attention on the sea. "Police work is all I have, Graegan. I don't have a family. I don't have a life. I just have the force. Generations of cops to let down."

"That's your fault. You're the one who buried yourself in work."

"I see. You kept everything well-balanced, did you?"

"You shouldn't have come here. I want you to leave. I will handle this however I need to handle it. But however I choose, it will be what's best for my family, because I am not going to be a man who lives alone, with only his memories as his companions. I've got everything I want."

"Good for you. Glad the universe offered you the luxury."

"You never took care of your problem. You never faced it, Erin. There's nobody to blame but yourself."

"You're so superior. You've got your home, your family. You've done something right in life. I must not have, since I'm alone."

"I never said that."

"You implied it."

"No. All I said was that you never took care of your problem. And you should have."

"I'm sober now."

"Good."

Erin bit her lip like she was trying to keep a mouthful of hate from spilling out. Her nostrils flared. She popped the knuckles on both hands. "So. You kept it all these years. Did you ever intend on using it?"

"I just kept it, Erin. It seemed like I should. Maybe as much for my own guilt as anything else. I've never been able to reconcile myself to what I did."

"I sleep fine at night."

"You always did." Vance finally turned to her. "Go home. I'll handle this. Just go home."

"I'm glad I saved your life that day so you could toss me aside, without any regard to what's at stake for me."

Vance watched Erin tread through the sand and up the rocky hill, her body lumbering with anger. His resolve suddenly shuddered with indecision. He owed her so much. More than he could ever repay.

She had asked him to keep her secret.

It had been at such a great cost.

He stepped forward, wanting to shout out her name, but it only sounded like a whisper against the force of the waves.

"Erin, wait. . . ."

She didn't hear him.

And he was glad.

* * *

Lindy managed to get through three games of Sorry! trying to keep herself and Conner occupied. She really just wanted to go to the bathroom and cry.

But having a child cured her of having a breakdown anytime she wanted.

She continued to feel shaken by the woman who'd approached Conner outside. She'd thought Vance paranoid for all his insistence about Conner and the outdoors. Now she had something to worry about, though Conner said the woman wasn't scary. He couldn't give a good description, but he'd never been that observant about people. He could identify any species of bug, but the day Lindy cut off ten inches of her hair, he didn't even notice.

She tried to put the incident aside. She had other things to worry about, like the fact that she couldn't get ahold of her husband.

And night had fallen.

Where could he be? Still talking with this detective? Then why didn't he answer his phone?

She'd gotten one text from him. All it said was *I will be home late.*

What was late?

And why wasn't he answering his phone, for crying out loud?

These questions and more continued to distract her. She found herself standing in the kitchen with the refrigerator door wide open and no idea why.

From his bedroom, Conner shouted, "I miss my TV!"

Yeah. Lindy did too. As bad as it sounded, she wished she could stick him in front of some mindless cartoon so she could try to get a grip.

"Mom? Where's my milk?"

Milk. That was it. She pulled the carton out and found a plastic cup. Everything felt like slow motion right now, and she was afraid at any moment she might burst into tears.

The last thing Lindy wanted was for Conner to feel afraid. He'd been adjusting fairly well to the situation. She wanted that to continue.

But she couldn't do it alone.

And alone was where she was at the moment.

On top of that, she was still processing the fact that Vance had lied to her about going to therapy.

A sob from deep within bubbled up, sticking in her throat.

Then a knock rattled the front door. Lindy gasped, spilling the milk. It splashed over the counter and dripped onto the tile floor. She left it and grabbed her gun, which she'd stashed on top of the fridge—just while Vance was gone—for easy access.

Her hand trembled, but not the one with the gun.

She stepped lightly toward the front door, keeping the gun low, just in case Conner came to see who it was. But he probably didn't even hear the knock in his bedroom. The air conditioner made a racket most of the time.

On her toes, she peered through the side window, hoping for a solicitor. But these days she couldn't trust anyone to say who they really were.

Joe.

Lindy lost her breath, turning her back against the door. Her heart raced and she gasped for another breath. And another.

What should she do?

It was obvious they were home. All the lights were on. But she didn't think he'd noticed her through the window. He'd turned and was looking over his shoulder.

Tears that she'd managed to hold in most of the day dribbled down her cheeks. Her nightmare just wouldn't end.

And then, as fast as the dread had coursed through her veins, a strange uprising filled her. She snatched the doorknob and pulled the door open so fast that Joe stepped back, his eyes wide.

"What do you want?" she hissed. Every moment of

disappointment, discouragement, and sorrow collided with anger and frustration. Whatever expression she was wearing, it was doing a number on Joe. The gun probably helped too. "I said, *what* do you want?"

"You know what I want," Joe said, his voice slick and his eyes quickly recovering from shock. He shifted his gaze toward the gun. "You really know how to use that thing? Doesn't matter. You ain't gonna shoot me."

"Don't be so sure about that," Lindy said. She kept her tone cool.

"I'm going to give you one more chance. Your husband doesn't seem to know what's at stake here."

"Just leave. Take it all and leave."

Joe's eyes narrowed. "It's that easy, is it?"

"No, it's not easy at all. You're wrecking our life. For money."

"Sweetheart, your life was already wrecked. Or didn't your husband tell you all his dirty little secrets?"

Lindy held steady. Barely. "Yeah. I know all of them." *Don't blink.*

Joe smirked. "Then you're as guilty as he is."

"You're the guilty one. And you're not going to get away with this. You may take every possession we own, but those are just things. And we can live without things."

"He never told you." Joe's eyes flashed like he'd just glimpsed into her soul.

Lindy's breathing turned labored, but she wasn't going to back away from this fight. She stared him down.

"What I know is worth a lot of money," Joe said. "Tell your husband *that*."

"Get out of here before I call the police."

"The police," he laughed. "They've been real helpful, have they?"

"The police aren't typically thrilled when a man threatens a woman. We are, after all, rather helpless." But her eyes, she knew, said otherwise. And maybe they told a story—that at this point she really didn't have much to lose by going crazy on him.

Joe backed down off the porch. "Just give your husband the message."

Lindy stood in the doorway of her home, the gun dangling by her side. Joe walked away, around the corner of the next block. She felt a little like a woman of the prairie, except she needed a shotgun and livestock to defend. Relief finally took hold, and she found herself able to breathe again.

"Mom?"

Lindy whirled around, stumbling against the doorframe. Conner stared at the gun.

"It's okay, sweetie."

"What's that gun for?"

"Honey, it's nothing." She grinned. Wide. Too wide. "Bath time, okay?"

"Where's Dad?"

"He just had a lot to do today." She hated those words. She must've used them a hundred times, back in the days when Vance couldn't find his way home. She stared at her little boy's face. He was growing up and, by his expression, wasn't buying the same old story. "I actually don't know what time he will be home. I really don't know where he is."

Conner blinked. "You don't?"

"I don't. But I know he'll be home. He always comes home."

Conner smiled a little. "Yeah. Dad always comes home."

"Go start your bath, okay? You look like you rolled in dirt!"

"I did!" He laughed and disappeared down the hallway.

Lindy looked at the gun in her hand. She'd forgotten it was there for a second. She put it back on top of the fridge. As soon as she let go of it, her whole body started shaking.

Was this what a nervous breakdown felt like? She'd always imagined it would start deeper, like in the soul. But right now, her body felt like it might just get up and go and never come back. Leaving her soul on its own.

She needed to talk to someone. She closed her eyes. She didn't have many options.

But she had a couple.

And one kind of made sense.

13

"THANK YOU SO MUCH for coming," Lindy said, pushing her hair out of her face and trying to seem pulled together. "I know it's late."

Karen walked in, looked her up and down. "We haven't known each other long," she said, her accent strong and a little loud, "but I heard it in your voice. Something's wrong."

Lindy bit her lip and looked away.

"Where's that precious boy of yours?"

"He's asleep. He had a long, hard day of playing."

Karen smiled. "And where is that high-strung husband of yours?"

Lindy laughed. "High-strung. That's good." The laughter

faded and her heart felt heavy. Her whole body felt heavy. Even her words. "Come on. Let's sit on the back porch."

They both carried the lawn chairs that were sitting in the living room to the back porch, which was only one small slab of concrete with two steps leading to the lawn. It wasn't much of a view. There was a dilapidated old shed that leaned sharply to the left. Still, the beautiful redwoods towered everywhere. Even in the darkness they seemed mighty. Through them were glimpses of a dark sky and bright stars.

"It's a nice evening," Karen said, adjusting herself in the lawn chair.

Lindy sat where she had a full view through to the front door. She kept the screen door open so she could hear everything inside the house.

"I filed the paperwork," Karen said, "and everything is in motion. We're doing some research on the company to see what their past is."

"That's good."

"How about the business? Any luck moving forward with that?"

"Haven't heard from the real estate agent yet. Hopefully I will soon. Truthfully, it's been a little hard to wrap my mind around it."

"I understand. You've been through a lot."

"Karen—" And it was that single word that opened a floodgate of tears. The sob roared out of her and she covered her face. It seemed her cry filled the entire night air. She tried to quiet herself, but the more she tried to hold it in, the angrier the tears became.

"Oh, sweetheart," Karen said. She knelt beside Lindy, rubbed circles on her back.

"I'm so sorry," Lindy whispered. From nowhere, shame cloaked her. "I just needed to talk. I just wanted to talk to someone."

"I'm here," she said. "I'm right here."

Lindy managed to stop crying. She wiped her tears and blotted her face with her shirtsleeve.

Karen returned to her chair but gave Lindy her full attention.

"It's just that Vance . . ."

"What is it, honey? You can tell me."

"He doesn't know this, but I fell in love with him the first time I saw him."

Karen smiled. "Well, he is a cutie."

"He was kind of cocky back then. He'd just come out of the academy, and he was on the streets. He was sort of an adrenaline junkie, and I wasn't sure I was exciting enough for him."

"Turned out you were wrong, huh?"

"No. I was right. Just turned out that he was growing tired of adrenaline."

"You settled him down."

"Yeah, I guess so," Lindy said. "He found more purpose than just being a cop. But I always let him be a cop, you know? It was who he was. And he was good at it. Really good at it. He never gave himself enough credit when he became a detective. The D.C. sniper case caused him to doubt himself."

"Boy, that was a horrible time."

"It was beyond imagination," Lindy said. A picture flashed through her head. It was of Vance standing over a body, hands on his hips. His holster barely showing. A newspaper photographer had taken the picture and it landed on the front page of the paper. Only Lindy would notice, but Vance's eyes had held a fear that to this day she'd never seen again.

All the guys had been flustered. They started bringing in the FBI, the ATF, the marshals . . . anybody. There was such a sense of desperation. It seemed endless.

"We had some marriage trouble," Lindy said. "I guess it was expected. Vance was very concerned about our safety. It's all he could think about, day or night."

"Understandably."

"I lost him for a while," Lindy said, her mind drifting to thoughts of all the nights alone, the hours she spent worrying about him. "And there came a point when I wasn't sure I wanted to find him again."

Karen's eyes glistened with tears. "Relationships are difficult, aren't they?"

"I'm sorry. I didn't mean to upset you."

"You didn't, sweetie. Go on. Tell me more."

Lindy rested her head on the back of her chair and gazed upward. In a weird way, the expansiveness of the sky made her feel peace. It was too large for man to take any credit, and that meant it had been created with painstaking detail—by God, if Conner had anything to say about it.

"I have loved that man fiercely," she said. She blinked slowly, afraid if she closed her eyes longer, she'd fall asleep from sheer exhaustion. "I love him so much it hurts."

Karen was quiet for a moment. "That is some kind of love."

"I watched him fall, and there was nothing I could do but watch and hope that he'd make it back to us."

"Where'd he go?"

"Inside himself. And that's the hardest place to reach. It seems the farthest away. But I begged him to come back. Told him that we were safe for him."

"And what happened?"

"Finally he did. He came back. It was gradual, yeah, but one day it was really apparent. I remember it like it was yesterday. He walked through the front door and he was different. It was like this giant dark cloud had lifted away from him. He picked Conner up in his arms. He hadn't picked him up in over a year. He kissed him. He kissed me. He said, 'I'm sorry I was gone. Now I'm back.'"

"And he stayed?"

"Yes, he stayed. He'd been in therapy . . ." Her words trailed off into the dismal reality of what she'd since learned. "I thought he had. He told me he had."

"And then what?"

"And then we settled back into marriage. And work became hard for him. The red tape, the politics of police work. We tried our best to overcome it, you know? But he was unhappy and so was I. So we decided the best we could do was start over." Lindy looked down at her hands, traced the bones and the veins with a fingernail. "And . . . there was another woman."

"Vance cheated on you?" Karen's eyes widened.

"No. He never cheated on me."

"Then what do you mean, another woman?"

"His partner. Erin Lester. She saved his life once." Lindy paused. "And the thing that always stung was that I couldn't. I couldn't save him." She sighed.

"I guess the saving of his life came at a price."

"He tried to repay her. And there was always this line and he never knew if he was crossing it or not."

"It's complicated."

"Yeah. I'd watch them sometimes, at Christmas parties or whatever, and they had this unbelievable chemistry. They'd finish each other's sentences. They'd tell stories and they'd have everybody captivated. They seemed like the perfect fit."

"But he stayed with you."

Lindy's voice grew soft. "Yeah. I guess he did." She smiled.

"He chose you."

Lindy glanced inside the house, listened for Conner for a moment. "That's why he became a detective. He got off the streets to put some distance between them. And it worked. For a while."

She looked at Karen. Her bright eyes, overly made-up with blues and yellows and clumpy mascara, blinked willfully.

"What's the matter?" Lindy asked.

"Nothing, sweetheart. I just think you've got a great love story there. You two have been through a lot. He loves you. I could tell that the first time I met him. There's something in the eyes of a man who loves his wife. You can't explain it or put your finger on it."

A lump swelled inside Lindy's throat. She sat up in her chair, fixed her gaze on Karen. "So I have a question for you."

"Shoot."

"If he lied to me, what should I do?"

Karen smiled a little. "Depends on how big the lie was."

"Big enough."

Karen straightened her back like she'd dispensed this kind of wisdom over and over again. Except then she looked away. "You got a good man there, Lindy. A real good man. He treats you right. He takes care of you. Sometimes, darlin', you just gotta look the other way."

14

THE NIGHT HAD BEEN nearly sleepless. Lindy heard Vance come in—after 2 a.m.—but pretended to be asleep. She still hadn't decided what she should do. Was it worth all the emotional energy to confront him? Even if she did, could her heart take watching him lie right in front of her?

The lie was in the past, she reminded herself as the clock turned the corner to 5 a.m. And maybe she didn't have the whole story. Perhaps there was a reason he didn't go to counseling. Maybe it didn't really matter because he came home changed.

And their ups and downs, she decided at 5:45, were all part of marriage and the particular challenges of being married to a cop.

Maybe Karen was right. Maybe she should look the other way.

After only about an hour and a half of sleep, she got up, thankful to have her family together at least. The house was quiet. The glow of the sun peeked through the limbs of the redwoods. She fixed herself a cup of coffee and opened the front door, standing on the porch in her robe and admiring the city below. She liked mornings here.

Soon enough, the boys were stirring, so she came inside and got out the cereal and Styrofoam bowls. She couldn't look at Vance as he came into the kitchen looking like he'd spent a hard night with the badge.

Before a conversation could even get started, Conner bounded in and tackled his dad from behind. He squeezed his little arms around Vance's waist, and Lindy savored the moment. Just for a second, things seemed normal.

Vance sent Conner to brush his teeth, then wrapped his arms around her waist from behind. "I'm sorry I was so late."

"I was worried about you," she said without turning around. She poured cereal into a bowl.

"I know. I needed to think."

"You needed to think." Lindy turned and moved out of Vance's arms, that nagging mistrust she'd fought for so long starting to bubble to the surface. "Why wouldn't you answer your phone?"

Vance blinked. "I never heard the phone."

"I called at least a half-dozen times, if not more."

"I'm sorry." He sighed. "I was by the ocean. It was loud. I'm sorry. But I figured some things out. And I made a promise to myself. I'm going to find Joe. I'm going to hunt him down and get our possessions back."

"Well," Lindy said, crossing her arms, "if you'd been home last night, you wouldn't have had to look far. He came here."

Vance, who'd been leaning against the counter, shot upright. "What?"

"Stood right there on the front porch and threatened me."

"*Threatened* you?"

"That's right. And I told him to get out of here. I didn't even have to use my gun. But I would've. And I think he knew that."

Like a welding torch, white-hot rage glowed in his eyes.

"Don't worry about it," Lindy said. "Really. Obviously I can take care of myself. But he did have a message for you. Something about secrets. Something he knows about you that he says you're willing to pay a lot of money for."

Vance turned away, walked to the front window of the condo, stared out with his hands on his hips.

"How'd he get here?"

"Excuse me?" Lindy asked.

"Was he driving?"

"Not that I could see. He walked around the corner, so maybe he parked his car there. I was too busy protecting our child to be a good eyewitness."

Vance glanced at her, then away. "I can't believe he showed up here."

"I guess we're going to have to decide whether your secrets are worth our life savings."

Lindy could tell he was trying not to glare. This was not how she'd hoped the conversation would go, but here it was. As usual.

"I'll tell you," he said.

"Maybe I don't want to know."

"I don't think you do. But it's what happened. And you're my wife."

"Maybe I already know your secret."

Again, he was caught off guard. His face twitched like a feather had just run across his skin.

"And no, I don't think it's worth our life savings." She walked toward him. "I don't know why you lied to me about going to the therapist. But it's in our past. It was a tumultuous time for all of us. I just want to move forward, Vance. Just forward. I don't want to look back."

Vance started to say something, probably in defense of the lie she'd uncovered, but she softened her voice and took another step toward him. "Let's walk away from Joe. From everything. Let's start over. For real."

"What exactly did Joe say?"

Lindy sighed. As usual, he was missing the point. "I don't know, Vance. I was too busy deciding whether to shoot him or not. But it was something about a secret. Something you knew. Something you'd pay for." She tried to calm herself down, talk the way she'd seen Dr. Phil counsel on his talk show. She put a gentle hand on his arm. "See? Joe has no power over us. I already know your secret."

"How?" His voice was barely audible.

"Someone called my mother."

"Joan?"

"Yes. She's here. In town. Came to help us unpack." Lindy laughed. "Horribly ironic, isn't it?"

"I don't understand what this has to do with Joan."

"I don't either. Someone called her. Presumably someone working with Joe. Told her you'd never been to therapy. And you know what a grand fan she is of you. She sped two hours to break the news to me."

Vance stared at the ceiling. His fingers tapped against his belt like they played the ivories. "This is getting more bizarre by the minute." He looked at her. "Who would call your mother? Who would *know* your mother?"

"She said it was an anonymous call. A woman."

"What good would it do to tell someone that? What is the angle here?"

"Maybe you should stop thinking like a detective and think more like a husband." Lindy tried not to but teared up anyway.

Vance's shoulders slumped and his expression softened. "I'm sorry."

"I was scared last night," Lindy said, wiping her tears. "I mean, I stood up to him and everything, but I was really scared."

"I should've been here."

"Where were you?"

Vance paused for a moment. Lindy searched his eyes for any untold answers. Finally he said, "Ever since the snipers, I've been different, Lindy. You know this. It changed my life forever. And I've learned to live with it. But sometimes it's unbearable. I grieve. I panic. And then I get over it."

"Was that what happened yesterday? Was that why you disappeared?"

"Sometimes it takes a glimpse of what your life would be like, without all that you love, to help you regain perspective. That's what I got yesterday. Perspective. And a new will to fight."

"Fight for what?"

"For us. For our new beginning. I'm going to find Joe and I'm going to get us our possessions back."

"I don't care about those."

"I am not going to let a guy like that take away your dream." Vance's eyes glistened. "I took years away from you, Lindy. It's your turn to live like you've always wanted. I am going to make sure that happens."

"Aren't you hearing me? Everything I want is in this house."

"You've always been there for me. You never gave up on me." He pulled her into a hug.

Lindy buried her face in his chest. This was it. This was all she wanted. Why couldn't he accept that?

He lifted her chin. "If today were a normal day and we'd moved out here with no problems, what would you be doing?"

She tried to stop her tears with a finger under each eye. "I don't know."

"Come on. Tell me." His voice had turned playful.

She shrugged. "Maybe scouting out more places for the deli. I like the one down the street, but the lady hasn't called me back yet. And maybe I don't want to look out the window every morning and see it." She smiled.

"I'm going to take Conner for a few hours. The kid needs to get out of the house. We'll go to a park or something. I want you to go find your perfect place."

Lindy drew in a breath. She wanted to get out of this craziness. She needed to. But could she really play make-believe for a day, wandering Redwood City in search of property for a deli that was most likely not to be?

"We're not going to be victims, Lindy. Not again." His jaw tensed, but inside his stern gaze she saw his vulnerability. Lindy knew instantly that perhaps what had caused the most damage to him in Maryland was the idea that he, like each body he stood over, had become a victim.

Conner returned, grinning widely like he always did after he brushed his teeth, hoping they sparkled and shined like in the toothpaste commercials.

"Cereal again?" he lamented. "What about a cheese omelet, Mom?"

Vance cupped her shoulder. "You need a break. You know you do." He smiled and brushed the back of his hand against her cheek.

"Yeah. I guess so," she sighed. "Just for a little while. I want us together tonight. Let's order out. Play a game."

"Sounds awesome. Now, get dressed and go find your dream shop."

She got dressed, put on makeup and even some jewelry. But she had no intention of scouting out shops.

15

"DAD, WHEN ARE WE GOING to the park? This place doesn't look like a park."

"In a little bit, buddy. Just hang with me, okay?"

"Does Mom know you let me sit in the front seat?"

"No. And don't tell her, or you'll be in the backseat *with* a booster."

Conner nodded, rolling down his window. "That would be horrible. Luckily I have no friends here to see that."

Vance smiled. "School will start and you'll have plenty. We'll go to the ocean soon. I went there yesterday and it was beautiful. You'll love it. We'll build lots of castles."

"You were gone all day, Dad. You don't even have a job

anymore. You can't be gone all day. Unemployed people stay at home in their pajamas."

Vance cracked up. "Yeah. Well, we can have a pajama day later. Right now, I'm looking for something."

"What? The park? I'd say head toward the trees and the fresh air, Dad."

"Let's pretend we're on a stakeout."

Conner raised an eyebrow. "Really?"

"Sure."

"Who is the bad guy?"

"A thief."

"Cool. Can I have a weapon?"

"Sure. All good detectives carry a weapon. And a badge." He pretended to hand them over.

"And handcuffs?"

"Sure. Take mine." He grabbed the key out of the console and handed it to Conner, who unlocked the glove box and took them out. Conner's grin nearly fell off either side of his face.

While Conner toyed with the cuffs, Vance kept an eye out for any sign of that bright yellow truck or Joe.

While Conner and Lindy were getting dressed, Vance had told them he was going for a short walk. But instead he rounded the corner where Lindy said Joe had disappeared, looking for any and all clues he could find.

He didn't expect much.

But he found something. It was a heavy oil spot, still fresh, just out of sight of their condo and right against the curb. And a line of spots continued down the street. He'd followed it on foot for two blocks, then went back for Conner, and now they were fresh on its trail.

Sort of. He kept having to get out of the car at stop signs to look and see where it went. Told Conner he was checking the air pressure of a tire. It was nice to have an eight-year-old who believed everything he said.

If he could just catch a glimpse of something, he could come back later, sans Conner, and investigate.

He figured the oil trail would run dry once it led to the highway or a major street. But instead they were only eight blocks from the condo in a pseudo–industrial park that looked mostly abandoned. Junkyards. Tire yards. Warehouses. Mechanic shops that looked to be in business, barely.

This made sense. A good place to hide. The smell of oil.

And then, like that, the trail ran dry. He pulled the car to the side of the road and backtracked. It was hard to tell now, with so many oil slicks on the road, what was fresh and what was not. Or what was even from Joe's truck or car, whatever he may have used. Lindy said she didn't remember smelling the exhaust or hearing the roar of the truck engine. And if he had to guess, Joe had probably acquired a car and didn't want it identified.

He wondered if Joe had known he was gone that night.

He hopped back in the car, took one more good look around, then drove away. He couldn't do anything anyway. Not with Conner in the car.

"Off to the park, buddy." He smiled.

"Dad?"

"Yeah?"

"I know you're lying to me."

Vance glanced at him. "What do you mean?"

"Our stuff is gone, isn't it? And it's not coming back."

* * *

Of course, the hotel was Redwood City's finest. Lindy was glad she had some slacks and a blouse handy. She'd packed them in case she needed to meet hastily with a real estate agent or a banker.

The morning was perfect in temperature. They sat at a small table for two, with a white umbrella shading them from what was not yet a hot sun.

Nearby, crystal blue water glistened inside the pool. But the smell of chlorine, mixed with sunscreen, caused her to wish she were elsewhere.

But if she had to be honest, it was another smell that bothered her more.

Chanel No. 5. Always. Just enough to taunt, to make a statement, to remind Lindy of a childhood she wished she could forget.

"Egg white omelet?"

"Sure," Lindy replied and watched her mother order for her like she was a small child. She didn't have the stomach to tell her no—or even to eat. She wasn't here to cause an argument, so she just let things roll as her mother wished.

"And where is Conner?"

"With Vance."

"Hmm."

"I wanted to talk to you. About Vance."

Her mother's penciled-in eyebrow, the left one, rose a half inch on her Botoxed forehead. "Oh?"

"Don't you think we should?"

"Naturally, but you've never seemed to want my advice."

"It's not that. It's that I've lived this, you know? I watched you and Dad. I watched him walk out the door. I didn't want the same for me."

The sharpness in Joan's eyes shrank. "I didn't want that for you either."

"I never told you this," Lindy said, "but I understand now how hard marriage is. You can't possibly know until you're in it. There are a lucky few who dance through it. The rest of us have to crawl."

Joan's eyes, nearly always dull thanks to the colored contact lenses she insisted upon, shone with tears. She reached her hand across the table, her long fingers beckoning for Lindy's. Lindy hesitantly slipped her hand into her mother's, which was cold as ice. But her eyes, for once, were warm.

"Darling, all I ever wanted was for you to be happy. Perhaps a mother's worst trait is the instinct of wanting to keep her daughter from her own mistakes."

Lindy wanted to say she knew Joan meant well, but that wasn't always the case. Besides, she was about to be vulnerable enough. She withdrew her hand.

"I wish I could say we moved out here and everything

has been fine, but it hasn't." She sipped her coffee, hoping to appear like she wasn't falling apart inside. "The news you told me—that Vance had never seen the therapist—is apparently true. I called the doctor's office."

"I'm so sorry." Joan leaned over the table, unmannerly in a way she normally wouldn't be. The waiter returned with their meals, but Joan didn't sit upright.

"He disappeared all day yesterday. Wouldn't answer his phone. But then this morning, he seemed fine." Lindy struggled with the next words. "Is it okay for me to accept this? To understand that maybe a little piece of him died years ago?"

Joan took a moment to answer, her long fingernails gliding over the tablecloth, the motion so fluid it seemed she might be cutting right through it. "You were five when your father worked a case involving a six-year-old girl. She was kidnapped right out of her house at night. The parents were poor. The dad had a history of drinking and had a domestic violence charge against him ten years before. They kept interrogating the father. A day and a half later they found her mutilated body on the side of the road. Turned out it was a pedophile who'd made parole a month earlier."

"I never heard that."

"You wouldn't have. Your father never spoke of it again. Not once."

"Did you ask about it?"

"No. I could see it in his eyes. He would not talk and never would." She sighed and regained the composure she loved. "Anyway, it was to his demise. I told him once that if he didn't talk about it, it would eat him alive from the inside out. Turns out I was correct."

The eggs, which hadn't sounded appetizing to begin with, started to make Lindy's stomach turn. She pushed them out of the way. Sipped her coffee.

"My dear, I will tell you something, and they don't teach this in the psychology books. But a wife has an instinct. Perhaps it's given to her on the day she weds. But she knows."

"Knows what?"

"Knows."

"That's the whole problem. I don't know. I don't know at all."

"Yes, you do."

"Mother, please. Don't play head games with me."

She leaned in. "You know." She set her napkin on top of the table. "If you don't, then someone does."

"What does that mean?"

"There's a reason I got an anonymous phone call. There's a reason someone felt compelled to call. Not only that—to call me. Not you."

Lindy threw her own napkin on the table.

"Linda, you may think of me what you will, but I came here to speak the truth to you. And I am still speaking the truth to you."

Instead of retorting, as she so often did, Lindy kept silent. She tried to ponder what Joan was saying. If there was anything she knew about Joan Webster, it was that she was not one to say anything but the truth, even when the truth was perfectly inappropriate.

The waiter came, filled their orange juice glasses, and left.

"If that's his only secret," Lindy finally said, "maybe I should just live with it."

"But I sense," Joan said, "that it is not."

* * *

"Dad, I'm hungry. I thought we were going to the park, anyway."

"Yeah. Okay. We can go." On their little adventure down the side streets of Ghost Town, Vance had ended up telling Conner the truth. Or at least the partial truth—it was unlikely that they'd get their stuff back.

"But I'll try my best, kiddo," Vance had said, grinning as he tried to believe it himself. Conner stuck his head out the window of the car, and it'd been out there since. Until now.

He ducked in and Vance laughed. His hair was sticking straight up like he'd been electrocuted.

The street on which they drove was empty. No tumbleweeds, but lots of trash blowing against the curb. A couple of abandoned or dilapidated shops were there, but not much else. Except a few bums.

"What do you feel like—?" Vance quickly pulled the car to the curb.

It was just a glimpse, and he couldn't be sure of what he really saw. These days he knew reality often betrayed him.

"Dad, what are you doing?" Conner asked as Vance threw the car in reverse. His years driving patrol cars on courses gave him an advantage, although there wasn't another car around to dodge.

"Just a second," he said. He stopped the car right in front of what might've been a mechanic or tire shop. Peeking around the corner of the building, between two air-conditioning units on the side, was a slice of yellow.

"Stay here," he instructed Conner. "Lock the doors."

"But—"

"Just do it!"

Vance got out of the car and Conner obeyed. Vance had no intention of letting Conner out of his sight, but he thought he could at least snoop around a little. See if it was indeed the truck.

An old El Camino sat out front, rusty and looking utterly exhausted. Didn't look like it could even get its motor started. He peered in its windows, seeing nothing that indicated it was often or recently used.

He wanted to go around back, but then he'd have to leave Conner alone. He glanced at the car. Conner stared through the driver's-side window, his nose pressed against the glass.

No, he wouldn't leave him. He'd snoop around, look through the shop's front windows, and then leave. He'd drop Conner off and come back without him.

Vance stood by the El Camino, trying to take in everything. The windows of the shop were covered with something that looked like soot, probably not even clean enough to see through. He noticed a flimsy chain-link fence with an even flimsier double gate locked only with wire.

But wide enough to drive a truck through.

Vance walked to the gate, keeping his attention focused, alert to sight and sound. Even smell.

Oil. Gasoline. Rubber from tires. It smelled like a junk-yard.

He squatted, keeping Conner in sight, and examined the tire tracks in the thick dirt. Large. Semitruck large.

Even from the gate, he couldn't get a good glimpse of the back of the building, where he suspected the truck was. But there was that strip of yellow. It could be anything. But it could also be a truck. Behind the building were train tracks, so nothing else backed up against the property.

The park was going to have to wait. Conner needed to be safe before Vance did what he needed to do.

He was walking toward his car when he heard a sound: metal scraping against metal. The front door of the old building was slowly opening, like it weighed a ton or maybe didn't fit the frame anymore.

Vance reached instinctively but knew immediately that he didn't have his gun. It was in his car.

And then Joe appeared, his attention focused on the door and nothing else. He wore a trucker's hat with a John Deere logo. He cursed as he kicked the door, trying to get it to shut again.

Vance was only about five yards away, unsure what he

should do. But he knew he had to do something. And he had to do it before Joe knew what hit him.

It ended up being quite a hefty tackle. Vance ran fast toward him, and Joe glanced up, his face lighting up with fear just as Vance threw a shoulder into his stomach, sending them both hurtling to the ground. They rolled once and Vance landed on top. He gave him a good punch across the cheek, just to make sure Joe knew he was in no position to fight. Joe tried to squirm away, and Vance decked him again.

With blood trickling off his brow, Joe finally lay still, staring at Vance. "You gonna kill me?"

"Only if I have to," Vance said.

Joe glanced to his left, where the shop was. "You think this is about your stuff, don't you?"

"I don't know what this is about. You're going to tell me." Vance grabbed him by the collar of his shirt and lifted him up several inches. "Yeah. I've got a few questions for you."

Joe glared at him, his nostrils flaring with each labored breath he took. "The ball's in your court, buddy."

"Shut up. First of all, why did you put the tarot card on the mud flaps?"

"What are you talking about?"

"I saw it. The Death card."

"I don't know what you're talking about."

Vance threw him against the ground. "Start talking."

Joe glowered. "You don't want me to start talking."

"What's that supposed to mean?"

"I didn't realize what a treasure I had. I figured it was

usual business, but turns out you've got a lot stashed away, don't you."

"Spit it out," Vance said, raising his fist.

"Is that what you really want? You want me to start talking? Start telling everyone your secret?"

Vance climbed off him but put a knee on his forearm. Joe lay still.

"It was so nicely typed out, too," Joe said. "You're covering up an enormous misdeed."

Vance tried to take in a deep breath, but air wasn't reaching his lungs. "I guess it's no surprise you went through our belongings."

"So what's this misdeed worth to you?" Even though his face was bloody and he was flat on his back, Joe spoke in a cocky, menacing tone.

A terrifying anger seized Vance, so fast and furious that it jolted his body. He hated this man. He wanted to see him suffer.

Joe turned his head, like he was expecting another punch, but said, "It was an interesting read. I especially like the three-page letter detailing all of your misdeeds, though it did kind of seem like you threw your partner under the bus. Maybe that's just me. Sounds complicated. I mean, it's not complicated to me. It's simple. I can expose something that would ruin your reputation forever. But for you, I understand that it's complicated." He smirked. "I had no idea what was in the back of that truck when I loaded it all up for you. Not a clue." Then he winked. "Saw the disc too. Compelling evidence. Man, if it were me, I would've burned it all. But I understand. There was a lot at stake. For you and for her. I'd say more for her. But you're all twisted up in it, so that makes you guilty too."

"Shut up."

"I'm simply asking, what is it worth to you? We can all walk away from this deal, nice and unscathed." Joe took his free hand and wiped his brow. "Other than, of course, this nasty cut on my eye."

"I could kill you in an instant, right here and now," Vance said. "Nobody's around. They probably wouldn't find your body for weeks."

"Except," Joe said, his eyes cool and fixed, "I'm guessing that you're morally opposed to murder."

"You've seen the disc. You don't know what I'm morally opposed to."

Joe's eyes flickered with a hint of desperation, but it was gone as fast as a flame vanishing in the wind.

Vance drove his knee further into Joe's muscle, and the man winced. This had consumed him for so long, and here he was at a crossroads. He was having to face it again, even though he'd tried to bury it over and over.

He could bury it again, along with this lowlife.

But he knew it would never stay buried. And no matter how much he wanted it to die, it never would. Not until it came into the light. Light was going to be its stake through the heart.

Vance stood, dusting off his jeans. "I'm done. This isn't going to have power over me anymore."

Joe sat up. "What are you talking about?"

"Take it. Take it all."

"Do you know what would happen if I released this disc to the media?"

"I can only imagine," Vance said, his voice quiet. "What will be will be."

Joe stood, then took a cautious step away from Vance. "So this is how you want to play the game, huh? I'm calling your bluff."

"Do whatever. I'm done. I'm walking away from it all. I've got my family. But I will tell you this: if you ever come near my wife or child again, I will kill you."

"Daddy?"

His little boy's voice pierced the air. And what he saw next was more than he could bear.

Conner stood on the pavement, near the curb, pointing Vance's gun at Joe.

"Conner! Put that gun down now!" Vance said, trying not to sound frightened or urgent—except he sounded exactly that way.

But Conner wasn't looking at him. He was looking at Joe. And he simply answered, "No."

16

"Conner, listen to Daddy. I want you to put the gun down." Vance's hand trembled as he tried to wave the weapon down.

Conner pointed the gun at Vance as he turned to him. It overwhelmed his little hands. "No, Daddy. No."

Vance froze and glanced at Joe, who looked equally worried. "Do what your dad says, kid. Put the gun down."

"No! You're a bad man!" The gun was now pointed again at Joe, who took a step away.

"Conner, please, listen to Daddy."

This time Conner kept the gun pointed at Joe, but his eyes darted between them both. "It's okay, Dad. I already have the safety off."

A cold chill shot down Vance's spine. How did he get the safety off? How did he even get the gun? It had been locked in the glove compartment . . . but Vance had given him the key so he could get the handcuffs.

Conner took a step forward. Then another. Vance had let him shoot his BB gun back in Maryland. He was a pretty good shot. But this was no BB gun. The force of the blast could send Conner flying backward.

Joe stood motionless, hands in the air, his expression way more desperate than when Vance had him on the ground. "Kid, for crying out loud, put the gun down!" Joe shouted at him.

Vance pointed at Joe. "You shut up! Or you're likely to get shot!"

"I want my stuff back!" Conner yelled. Tears streamed down his face. "I want it back! You're a thief!"

Joe managed a small smile. "Okay, sure, kid. Yeah. You can have it all back. Sure thing."

"Conner," Vance said, trying to redirect his attention. "Look at me. This isn't the way. Okay? This isn't the way. Shooting someone doesn't solve anything." Vance glanced at Joe with a look that said *usually*.

"Daddy, this is a bad man. And that's why you have a gun, right? For bad men?"

"For protection, Conner." Vance hated this. Everything he was saying to Conner was everything he *didn't* want Joe to believe about him. He needed Joe to believe he was capable of just about anything. And maybe he was. But he was not capable of watching his son shoot someone.

Then, without warning, Joe took a step toward Conner. Conner's arms snapped straight and his eyes filled with more tears.

"What are you doing?" Vance shouted at Joe. "Do you want to get shot?"

"I think this kid is like his daddy. I don't think you'd shoot me and I don't think he will either." He took another step.

"Listen to me. He has the safety off. Do you get that? He could accidentally shoot you, if nothing else."

Joe smirked at him. "Chances are he'll miss."

"I know how to shoot! I'll do it!" Conner yelled.

"No, Conner! No! I am telling you to put that gun down!"

Joe took another step forward. Vance wanted to run and tackle him, but he was unsure what that might cause Conner to do.

"But you said for protection, Daddy."

Vance couldn't grab more than half a breath at a time. Something was going to have to give here, and he wasn't going to let it be his son.

"You're right, Conner." Vance squeezed his eyes shut for a moment, trying to decide if he was about to make the dumbest move ever. "If he takes one more step toward you, you can shoot him, because that means your life is in danger."

Joe balked. Midstep, he stopped and slowly put his foot down. "I'm not going to hurt you, kid. See? Look. I'm stepping backward."

While Conner watched Joe, the gun still sticking out in front of him, Vance made his way over, slowly and cautiously.

He didn't want to get shot in the process. Once next to him, he delicately removed the gun from his son's hands.

He couldn't believe it. The safety *was* off. He'd thought maybe Conner was bluffing.

Vance lowered the gun to his side and looked at Joe, who was covered in a layer of sweat. "I am coming back to get my belongings. They better be here."

"Don't threaten me," Joe said. "I still have way more leverage than you do. I don't believe for one second that you don't care what happens to the information I found."

"You can believe what you want. But I'll say it again. Stay away from my family because I meant what I said about this gun and what I'd use it for." He nudged Conner. "Get in the car."

Conner raced to his door and climbed in. Vance slowly backed away and got in the car. He reached for the keys in the ignition, but they were gone. "Conner, where are the keys?"

"Here," Conner said, handing them to him.

Vance started the car with shaky hands and burned rubber as he left the curb. He couldn't breathe until they were two blocks away. He looked at Conner, who seemed to know he was about to get in trouble.

"I know how you got the gun. But how did you get the safety off?"

"Dad, I've seen you do it before. I've known since I was like four."

Vance tried to compose himself. He wanted to yell at Conner, but he knew that wasn't going to solve any problems.

And frankly, that was the least of his concerns right now. He had to talk to Lindy.

And confess the deepest secret of his life.

* * *

She'd been driving in circles for an hour. She didn't want to go home. Vance and Conner were at the park, hopefully getting their minds off things. But she couldn't get her mind off anything. Her mother's words had always had a particular talent for nagging her, even when she was a kid, long after they were spoken. They were often biting. Condescending. Critical.

But this time the words were haunting. After circling Redwood City a third time, she knew that the reason her mother's words haunted her was because they were true.

Lindy *knew*. She knew something was wrong. She could sense it. Things weren't adding up. Lies weren't put together well. Vance couldn't answer simple questions. He'd stopped looking her in the eye.

It seemed different from before, when Vance was always angry and controlling and freaked out of his everlasting mind. This time it wasn't obvious. It was just off center. And that was hard to peg.

Except in her gut, something just didn't feel right. But *what* exactly? Did any of this stem from the phone call her mother had received? Who would call her *mother*, of all people? Why?

And if it was true that Vance had lied to her, what did that mean for them now? They'd overcome a lot, it seemed. Should she go back and revisit it all? Or just let it go? Move on? Live with a little ding in the side door of their marriage?

Little dings tended to rust. And rust would spread.

For all the years she'd known Vance, more than all his training, he'd talked about his gut instinct. When he was on patrol, he would talk about how he could drive this street or that street and then turn onto another street and feel like something wasn't right. Hairs on the neck. Chill bumps on the arm. Mouth going dry. Skin tingling with adrenaline. "They can't teach you that in the academy," he would say.

No. She supposed they couldn't. It was human nature to know when something wasn't right.

She pulled her car over to a little ice cream shop that sat at the end of a busy outdoor marketplace. She got out and walked the sidewalk, stuffing her hands deep in her pockets and trying to make the most of the fresh Pacific air.

She needed a clear head to think.

It took over an hour. Vance called her twice, but she didn't pick up. Finally she decided she needed some answers. And there was perhaps one man who could help her. Detective Doug Cantella. Vance seemed to have put a lot of stock in this man. There weren't too many people Vance Graegan would confide in.

Maybe he'd offer some advice at the very least.

Yeah, it wasn't exactly forthright sneaking in a phone call to a man she'd never met, behind Vance's back.

But her gut told her that the rules of the game had changed.

First, she had to find him.

She could probably go through the call history on Vance's cell phone. But she could just as easily call the Montgomery County Police Department. She still knew a lot of the dispatchers and personnel there. She had no doubt they would give her his contact info.

She already had the number in speed dial.

"Montgomery County Police Department."

"Adelle?"

"Yes? Who's this?"

"It's Lindy. Lindy Graegan."

"Lindy! Girl, how are ya? We sure do miss you here. How's that husband of yours? He slicin' ham okay?"

Lindy smiled. Just the sound of Adelle's voice brought her comfort. Adelle had worked for the police department for over thirty years. Lindy guessed she was in her seventies by now, though she looked no older than fifty last time Lindy saw her. Her husband had been a motor jock and was killed in the line of duty while chasing a bank robber. During the sniper shootings, she'd been more than the department secretary. She'd been a grief counselor too. And a mother. Some of them even called her Mama Adelle.

"We're still getting adjusted. We ran into some snags. But we're making it okay." She put a little ring in her voice so she hopefully wouldn't sound like she was about to fall apart.

"If I ever make it out to California, I'm coming for a club sandwich, girl. I want some California avocados!"

Lindy laughed. "Oh, Adelle, you make me laugh. Stop! I am going to want to come back!"

"I was hoping that was why you were calling. To tell us you're bringing that sweet family back where you belong."

"No," Lindy said, stopping at a rack of silk scarves. She mindlessly stroked a few as she tried to figure out how to smooth-talk her way through this. "I was actually calling to get some information."

"You know I'm the woman for that, though they don't tell me nothin' that's goin' on here—you know what I'm sayin'? But how can I help you?"

"I know there is a former detective from County who moved out here. We thought it'd be nice to get together for dinner with him. But we couldn't find him in the phone book and wanted to see if you had contact information for him."

"I am sure I do. We keep up with all our people. Who is it?"

"Doug Cantella."

"Come again?"

"Cantella. Doug is his first name." A long stretch of silence was louder in her ear than all the noise from the market. "Adelle? Are you there?"

"Honey, did you say Doug Cantella?"

"Yes."

"Sweetheart, I think you are mistaken."

"Mistaken?"

"Yes."

"Well, maybe I have his name wrong."

"No, you have his name right. Detective Doug Cantella worked for the police department for twenty-five years."

"Then what's the matter?"

"He died, sweetie. Of a heart attack."

"He died? When?"

"Two years ago."

17

LINDY SAT IN HER CAR at the curb, with a view of the house. Night was falling and she knew the fading sunlight made it hard for her to be seen out the front window of the home.

Inside all the lights were on, and she watched Vance and Conner move from room to room. Vance fed him a snack. They wrestled. Everything seemed normal.

There it seemed normal. Here she was in turmoil. She couldn't even get out of the car. She'd texted Vance, told him she was looking at some property, would be home later. He texted her back that he wanted to talk to her this evening. Important things.

She blinked tiredly. She wasn't sure she could handle a

talk. She wasn't sure she could handle *him* anymore. She'd been through his ups and downs, his mood swings, his desperation and confusion. And now . . . he was lying to her?

Why would he tell her he went to see a detective who was dead? And where had he been?

How could she face him?

Lindy put her head against the steering wheel and wept. Maybe for minutes. Maybe it was an hour. Time was so inconsequential right now. She just wanted peace in her life.

"Peace, God. Just peace . . ." It wasn't a tidy, pulled-together prayer like Conner was used to saying. His had a beginning, a middle, an end. It had praise, thanks, confession. Hers was messy, just like her life. It was desperate. She begged, like God might be a tyrant and her life was in His angry hands.

But then she softened. She knew God was no tyrant. Life was her tyrant right now. She was being squeezed from all sides. She needed to know the truth. She needed some assurance that she wasn't going down with the ship.

Lindy rolled her head to the side, looked out her window. She loved that man. With everything in her. But she wasn't sure how much more she could take. She needed to be a good mom to Conner, and right now she was not a good mom. She was a woman on the edge.

At the time, it had seemed so right . . . to move out here, make a fresh start. But really, can you run from yourself? Changing geographic locations never solved a human problem. She couldn't totally blame Vance. She had enabled him for years, making excuses for him, trying to see his situation from another perspective . . . trying to hold on to a life she desperately wanted. But it was like a mist. It always disappeared. Just out of her reach.

"God . . . God . . . ," she cried again, grief washing over her. She had now lost nearly everything. Her family was not what she thought it was, and her husband was not who she thought he was. There was no reasonable explanation for why Vance had told her he was going to see a detective who had died two years ago.

Adelle told her that Vance had been at the funeral. Lindy vaguely remembered him talking about a former detective who had died of a heart attack and how he thought the job had killed him.

There was just no reasonable explanation.

Her phone rang. It was Vance. Again. She could see him through the window, pacing in the kitchen. She wiped the tears and tried to take a breath. "Hello?"

"Hey, babe. Just checking on you. Are you okay?"

Lindy couldn't answer that.

"Lindy?"

She swallowed. She had to be okay, at least in the short term, to try to figure this out. She had a little boy who needed at least one stable parent. But which one of them was stable? "Yeah. I'm here. Sorry. Bad connection."

"When will you be home?"

"Soon."

"You sound . . . strange."

"Just tired."

"Listen, Lindy, some things happened today. And I need to talk to you, okay?"

"Sure. I'm about thirty minutes away." That should give her enough time to get herself pulled together. She couldn't be falling apart. She wasn't sure how she was going to confront him. If she even should. Her confidence rose and dove with every other breath.

Why had she walked her tumultuous marriage alone? Why hadn't she asked for God's help before?

Maybe it was pride. Maybe it was shame. She didn't know. All she knew now was that prayer was the only thing she could cling to.

Things were making less sense by the minute.

Or by the second. Because as she glanced up, she saw a car pull to the front curb of her home. A woman got out.

Lindy leaned forward, gripping the steering wheel.

It was Erin Lester.

* * *

Conner had drained Vance of nearly all his energy. The kid was bored out of his mind, and his favorite play toy right now was Vance. He tried his best to focus on his son. He knew Conner needed him. But his mind kept wandering back to Joe, Conner with the gun, the whole incident. It incensed him. Joe was a thug. That smug look he kept giving Vance. Taunting him. Taunting his son.

Finally Conner rested a bit, engaged with a cardboard box,

tape, scissors, and four rocks he was calling Rock Men. Lindy was always concerned when Conner used scissors and would hover over him. But the kid had held a loaded gun today. Vance could live with a little unmonitored scissor time.

He wondered when Lindy would be home. He was anxious to talk to her. He had a lot to get off his chest, not the least of which was Conner's foray into firearms. She was not going to take that well. But the question was, which bomb should he drop first? Or maybe he should wait and go get their stuff.

He was unsure what Joe's next move would be. He hoped he'd made it clear enough that he wasn't messing around anymore. Yet even as he knew where his possessions were, he didn't feel an urgency to get them. Right now he wanted to make things right with Lindy. Tie his family back together. Balance things out.

Yes. Balance. That's what he craved. That's why he'd moved out here in the first place.

A knock. Vance instinctively reached for his weapon, which he was keeping on his belt at the moment. His hand stayed on the gun as he rushed to the door and opened it.

"Erin?"

"Yeah. Erin. Surprise."

"What are you doing here? I told you to go home."

"I know what you told me." She swept past him and into the house. Vance followed her, not even shutting the front door.

Conner raced around the corner, then stopped, observing

Erin. Vance didn't feel like making the polite introduction that he normally would. They'd been trying to teach Conner how to shake hands and look people in the eye. But right now he wanted him to be rude and go back to his room.

"Hey, buddy. Just some business stuff. Go play, okay?"

"Hi," he said to Erin, smiling.

Now the kid decides to use his manners?

Erin smiled back. "How are you?"

"Good! I'm playing with some rocks."

"Okay, Conner, back to your room."

"I like her, though."

"That's very nice. I'm glad. But we need to talk. Adult talk."

"Fine," Conner said, rolling his eyes. He gestured toward the open door. "But we don't live in a barn, Dad." He disappeared around the corner.

Vance turned to Erin. "*What* are you doing here?"

"I never left. I can't leave. There is a lot undone here."

"There's nothing undone, Erin. I don't know why you're struggling with this. We were partners. We went through a lot together. I get that. But that doesn't chain me to you."

"Wake up, Graegan. I'm not here for that. You've got something that I want."

Vance sighed loudly like a large tire deflating. "You've got to get over this. We had a deal." His voice started rising, but he couldn't help it. "The deal was that you stop drinking. The deal was that I had to do what I had to do so I could sleep at night."

"It's not my problem that you're led by your guilty conscience."

"Besides, I don't even have the disc." He gestured dramatically toward the living room. "I don't have anything, as you can plainly see."

"I don't get it. You don't want my help finding your stuff? You're just going to let it all go?"

"I found it, okay? Behind a building in an old industrial park near here. I'm going back to—"

With no warning, pain splintered through Vance's skull, so sharp that it caused him to squeeze his eyes shut. It felt like he'd been slammed by an axe. He opened his eyes. Erin was blurry. Another migraine. He'd had them off and on in Maryland. Migraine medicine never worked.

"What's wrong with you?" Erin asked, peering at him.

"Erin, just leave, okay? Just please leave. I made a promise to you. I'm holding on to my side of the deal. Hold on to yours, and we're fine. But I need you out of my life right now."

Vance closed his eyes again. The pain was about to bring him to his knees.

"What's going on here?"

Vance and Erin both looked toward the doorway. Lindy stood there, arms crossed. Vance glanced at Erin, who didn't hint at being surprised. Vance was sure he looked both surprised and guilty even though he wasn't doing anything wrong.

"Hello, Lindy."

"Erin, why are you here? You live in Chicago."

Erin's voice was smooth. "Just trying to help Vance out. Get your things back. Right, Vance?"

"You told her? When did you tell her?"

Vance held the side of his head, trying to ignore the pain, but it was nearly impossible. "Look, Lindy, Erin was just about to leave."

"I'm sure she was," Lindy said. "Where's Conner?"

"Mom!" Conner burst around the corner, into her arms. "I missed you!"

Vance looked at Erin. "Let's go." He took her by the arm and nearly pushed her to the door.

Erin wiggled away from him. "I'm pretty sure I can find my way out."

"Can you find your way home?"

Erin walked to the front porch and turned to him. Vance stood in the doorway, the crushing pain sending waves of nausea through him.

"You never fully appreciated me, did you?" she said, her eyes hard, cold.

Vance closed the door behind him. "Erin, there is nothing I can do to repay you for what you did for me."

"I'm your friend, Vance. I will always be your friend. That's why I'm here. To try to help you."

"I don't think your motives are as pure as you're making them out to be."

"I'm trying to help you get your life back. That's it."

Vance pitched a thumb over his shoulder. "That's my life. Everything that matters to me is in there."

Erin suddenly teared up. It took Vance by surprise. She wasn't the overly emotional type. "You possess more in that room than I've had in my whole life."

"Erin, listen to me. You have a great life. You're a great cop. Yeah, you put a little too much into your work, but you don't have to. Your whole life doesn't have to be police work. Believe me, I thought I'd never say that, but I realize now how much—"

"Just stop, okay? Maybe you could walk away from it, but I can't. And you shouldn't have. You're pathetic now, you know that?"

"*I'm* pathetic? Take a good look in the mirror."

A vein pulsated in Erin's neck. It always bulged out of the skin when she was angry. They had nicknamed it the Blue Snake.

Vance regretted his words. He wasn't trying to make a bad situation worse. He just wanted her to go away.

And his head hurt like crazy.

She walked to her car without another word. Vance quickly turned to go inside. He found Lindy in the bathroom, running water for Conner's bath.

"She dropped by, unannounced."

Lindy didn't look at him. Her expression remained strangely neutral.

"We've got a lot to talk about tonight. There are things I need to say. To get off my chest." Vance tried as best as he could to fight off the pain fracturing his skull, but it was hard to even talk. He hadn't had this kind of headache in a long time. He touched her shoulder. "Let's get Conner in bed first, okay? And then let's talk."

Lindy gave a short, nondefinitive nod. Vance went to the bedroom. He lay down on the blow-up mattress, which was quickly losing air. He sank into it like it was a half-rate water bed. If he wasn't careful, he might roll right off.

He listened to Conner splash in the bath. The condo was filled with his lighthearted giggles. He'd told him not to mention the gun incident to his mother until after Vance had talked to her.

He closed his eyes, but when he did, the only images that filled the darkness were of the bleak days of his former life. It seemed like ages ago, except he could see everything with such clarity. The blood. The chaos. The fear in his fellow detectives' eyes.

Intermingled with the pictures he would give anything to forget were Conner's giggles. Those giggles gave rest to his soul.

18

PARENT-WISE, THERE WEREN'T too many things worse than having gone a sleepless night only to be confronted with a well-rested kid. Conner was up at the crack of dawn, chattering on about the park and the trees and the ocean.

Vance had fallen asleep last night flat on his back with his arm across his face, which meant he'd had another migraine. Back in Maryland, they had been somewhat crippling to him for a while, but as distance grew from the sniper case, the migraines became less frequent.

Lindy let him sleep. She wasn't sure she could handle what he was going to tell her. And whether or not it had anything to do with Erin Lester.

She didn't want to admit it because she disliked the idea of hating anyone, but she hated Erin. She hated how intrusive she'd been in their lives, in their marriage. How Vance ignored all the warning signs, dismissing them or making excuses. And now she showed up? Lindy knew it couldn't have been out of the blue. There were pieces missing to the puzzle.

Vance was still asleep at 8 a.m., and Conner had already eaten breakfast and played outside a little. Inside the condo Lindy felt suffocated, so she took Conner and decided to go to the library.

On the way there, Conner was jabbering in the backseat about whether redwoods could reach heaven, when chills washed over her for a full minute without relief.

Something nagged at her conscience and hammered at her emotions. It was like she'd walked into a tunnel and the only thing to see in the dark was the light ahead. It felt like someone was speaking to her, except nobody was around. There was a voice, but it was indistinguishable. So quiet she had to strain to hear, though she wasn't listening with her ears.

"Mom?"

Lindy blinked. She was at the library. She had parked. She had no recollection of even turning in.

"Mom?"

"Sorry. Yes, honey?"

"Can we get out?"

Lindy nodded. She got out with him, locked the car.

Watched him run across the parking lot to the sidewalk, but there were no cars. Looked like they were the first ones at the library this morning.

Normally she would lecture Conner on library manners, reminding him to be quiet, to not bounce around, to treat the books like they were people, etc. But the doors swooshed open, and Conner hurried in. Lindy didn't rush after him. She gave a polite nod to the stern-looking librarian who was eyeing Conner as he perused the bookshelves.

Near the kids' section was a computer and Lindy sat down, putting her purse next to her. She took a deep, settling breath. The tips of her fingers rested gently on the keyboard. She navigated around a little, finding where she could type in a topic.

She set the parameters and then typed four words.

They were the words she'd heard not in her ear, but in her soul. They were altogether confusing and confirming. They were like the light of a lantern, illuminating her path only enough so she could take another step. But right now that was all she could hope for.

She looked up, made sure she'd spelled it right, then slid her finger over the Enter button. She reread the words one more time.

Post-traumatic stress disorder.

* * *

Vance awoke to a quiet house. He got up to look for his family and was shocked to see what time it was. He never slept until nine. He'd always been an early riser. He must've fallen asleep while waiting for Lindy to finish up Conner's bath.

A note on the counter said they were at the library. He sighed. Lindy was avoiding him. He could feel it. And he didn't blame her. Erin's showing up was just another blow to an already-dicey situation.

His head still ached, but it was tolerable. Tolerable enough to come up with a game plan. And that included getting his stuff back.

If he could just do that, perhaps it would send them back toward normalcy. He had no doubt that Joe had already taken the disc and the information out of the truck. But Vance knew exposing his own secret would take the power out of Joe's threats. And he knew it was time. Holding on to it for so long had its costs. He wasn't willing to pay anymore.

At some point he was going to have to weigh the consequences regarding what was on that disc. In that letter. He was off the force now, but there was a chance they would cut off his pension. They probably wouldn't prosecute him, but who knew? For Erin, there could be ramifications for her career in Chicago. If her chief found out, she could get fired.

He rubbed his eyes. Memories wanted to flood his mind. They often did when he was tired or stressed. Sometimes he could see nothing but a sniper victim lying in a pool of blood.

Today, though, he had to focus.

He needed to go secure their things. Or at least see if Joe

had moved them again. He got dressed, grabbed his gun, and was out the door in twenty minutes. In another five he was at the old mechanic's yard. The El Camino was gone. But he could see the truck.

He took a moment to look around, notice his surroundings. Joe was expecting him back, and Vance didn't want to be surprised. But everything looked quiet.

Vance emerged from the car, his hand near his gun, but no badge to flash. The morning air cooled his skin, caused his shirt to breathe a little. He approached the double chain-link gate, which was wired shut. Easily breakable, but he jumped the fence instead, even though that left him more likely to pull a hamstring. The day he couldn't jump chain-link fences, he'd always joked, was the day he'd retire his badge.

With cautious steps, he walked to the back of the building. The ground was littered with oil cans, old mechanic tools, rusty engines. With each step he could see more and more of the yellow truck. It was like a giant square highlighter. Joe should've picked a color that wasn't going to stick out like this.

He pulled his gun, just for his own peace of mind. Behind the building were trees and a lot of places to hide . . . even what looked like an outhouse.

He took his time looking around, making sure he was alone. Then he approached the back of the truck. A padlock was the only thing that secured a rod running through the metal frame. Vance got on his knees. He needed to know one thing.

What was on those mud flaps?

As Vance stooped, he couldn't believe what he saw. Nothing.

Not even mud flaps. There were no mud flaps?

Vance stood and stared at the ground for a moment. He knew he'd seen them. He knew it. And he knew he'd seen the tarot card. He could never mistake it.

"Just get your stuff," he said, trying to refocus. He could figure the other thing out later. Right now, he had to find out if his belongings were actually in the truck.

He could've broken the padlock with his gun, but no cop would ever risk scratching or harming his gun to break a lock, no matter what the movies showed. Instead, he found a good-size rock. With two decent blows, the lock fell off.

Inside it was dark, musty, strangely pungent. But there they were. All his belongings. Even in the shadows, he could see his bed. Their bedside lamps. Conner's toy box. Vance relaxed a little. He holstered his gun and climbed in.

As his eyes focused in the dark, he began to make out in detail even more things. Conner's bed. Boxes of clothing marked *Winter* or *Coats*.

Then he noticed a pair of shoes right in the middle of the crowded stacks. His eyes focused more, and he thought he could see pants. Maybe Joe had strewn clothes about when digging through the boxes?

Then a shirt . . . Vance stepped closer and covered his mouth to keep the gasp in. It was a body. Hands. Hair. He pulled his gun and glanced over his shoulder. Everything was quiet behind him.

He took a few more steps in, and as soon as his eyes re-adjusted to the dark, he could clearly see.

It was Joe.

A dark, bloody bullet hole was centered right between his eyes. He'd been shot at close range. Execution style. Vance glanced to his hands, which were bound with duct tape.

Joe had been executed, but why? For what? Everything seemed to be here.

Vance stooped for a closer look, his heart rattling inside his chest. By the way the blood had dried around the wound, he thought Joe had been dead for a while. There wasn't enough light to see whether there was an exit wound or a pool of blood. Vance stood, turned, grabbed a nearby box to steady himself. He was flashing back, and he didn't want to. But streams of images wound through his mind like a ticker tape.

He stumbled to the opening of the truck. He squinted as the light hit him, then closed his eyes and let it wash over him. The warmth penetrated him. Shivering, he stepped off the truck, walked to its side, and planted his back against it, trying to catch his breath.

Joe was the bad guy. That's what he knew. That's what he believed. But now there was somebody even worse. Somebody willing to kill.

* * *

Conner returned with an armful of books. Lindy wasn't sure how much time had passed. She'd been immersed in the computer, wandering the pages of cyberspace, trying to look for answers. The answers were coming, but they were not ones she wanted to see. Vance had many of the symptoms of PTSD. Most of them. And if Doug Cantella was any sign, he had some psychosis, too. Was he seeing things that weren't there? Or was he hiding something and lying to try to get away with it?

"How many books can I check out, Mom?"

Lindy glanced at him. "What?"

"This many?"

Lindy kept a neutral expression. If she looked the way she felt inside, she'd scare Conner to death. "How about five."

"Seven?"

"Six."

"Oh, all right."

"Go over to that table and pick out your favorites."

Conner took his books, dumped them out, and began looking through them. Her phone vibrated in her purse and she pulled it out, expecting Vance. She couldn't talk on her cell at the library, but she could at least see who was calling.

Karen?

She let it go to voice mail, then texted her: @ the library. Can I call you in a bit?

A text was returned almost immediately. Please call ASAP.

Lindy pushed the phone into her pocket as she grabbed her purse. "Conner, hurry up and pick, okay?"

"Hold on, Mom."

Lindy went to the front desk and filled out the form for a library card. Finally Conner decided on his books and brought his armload to the counter. The librarian here was younger, seemed a little less uptight. She engaged Conner in conversation about books and reading, which ordinarily would've delighted Lindy, but today she was heavy with thoughts of Vance. How could she have missed the signs?

He didn't sleep well. He'd had mood swings, but those had leveled off in the last few years. The migraines were back, though.

And he was visiting dead detectives.

She watched the librarian laminate the card and vaguely kept an eye on Conner, who had wandered to a nearby jungle display. Inside, deep inside, she prayed. It wasn't a prayer with words. And it was desperate and unorganized. She wavered between clinging to a God she had barely believed in to raging against Him for the mess they found themselves in. Then she'd start over with an apology. Then desperation. Then anger. This cycle continued until she was interrupted by Conner, who stood next to her with two more books. On the jungle.

"These look good," she said, pressing that mommy smile onto her face. She wondered what age kids started looking at the eyes, not the mouth. Conner seemed unfazed and was drawn to a life-size cardboard cutout of a giraffe.

She checked out the books, and they walked outside. Lindy felt like she was suffocating a little. She gasped for air, then tried to take some deep breaths. Maybe Karen had some good news. If they could get this thing settled with Joe, they could start the process of healing.

Even in the midst of the chaos and this new revelation of what might be going on with Vance, she found within herself a resolve that wasn't there before. She wasn't angry with Vance, and that had to be a minor miracle. She felt sorry for him and wondered how long he'd been suffering without any support from her. It brought tears to her eyes, imagining him wandering this hot, desolate desert by himself.

That was going to change.

She unlocked the car and motioned for Conner to get in as she dialed Karen's number.

"Hello?"

"Karen, it's Lindy."

"Thank you for calling." She sounded different. Tension weighted each word.

"Is everything okay?"

"Yes, why?"

"You sounded like it was urgent."

"I just have some things I need to discuss with you. It is urgent. But I can't talk by phone. Can you meet me at your house? I'm just a couple of miles away."

Lindy stood outside her car, her hand on the door. "Karen, is everything okay?"

"Yes, sweetheart," she said, that Southern accent smooth as butter. "I'm sorry. I probably am sounding stressed, aren't I? Don't worry about me. I got a million and one things rolling through my mind. See you in a few minutes?"

"Okay, sure. I'll be there."

19

VANCE PULLED OUT his phone, started to dial 911. But stopped. Was that the right move? Of course it was . . . except this was complicated. And he wanted to know more before the police arrived. Would they go through his things? Would they find the disc? Maybe it was hidden among the rest of his belongings.

He hated that disc. He had been ready to tell Lindy everything. But was he ready to tell the police if they asked? This would be a murder investigation, and that meant they'd investigate everything. Even him.

He, after all, had motive.

He could walk away. Let the police eventually find him. But that wouldn't solve the problem of who killed Joe. And why.

Was his family in danger?

Vance dialed Lindy's number. She picked up on the first ring. "Hey," she said. She sounded tired.

"Hey." He didn't want to alarm her. But he didn't want to take this lightly either. "Where are you?"

"Driving back to the house."

Vance closed his eyes. What should he tell her?

"Karen's meeting me—is she there yet?"

Okay, that was better. Someone would be with her, at least, until he could figure out what he was going to do.

"I'm not sure. I ran out for a minute. But I'll be home soon, okay?"

"We need to talk." Her voice, for the first time in weeks, sounded soft. It took him by surprise.

"Yeah. Sorry about last night. I was so tired. The next thing I knew, it was morning."

"You needed to sleep." The brief silence was filled with traffic sounds through her phone. Everything was quiet around him. "I'll see you in a little bit, okay?"

"Okay."

Vance hung up the phone and then dialed the one person who could help him figure this out. Only a fellow cop would know for sure.

*   *   *

Lindy arrived home. The drive seemed instant, as she was lost in her thoughts most of the way. Conner was in the backseat, immersed in his books.

At the curb was Karen's dazzling red car, looking like a cherry on top of the dark fudge of the asphalt. Lindy parked in the driveway and got out, expecting Karen to emerge from her car, but she didn't. Conner struggled out of the car with his books, insisting on carrying them himself. Karen still didn't get out of her car. Her windows were reflective, like aviator glasses, and Lindy couldn't see inside.

She walked across the lawn, waving a little. When she got up to the car, she had about decided Karen wasn't in there. She leaned forward, peering in, with her hands shading her face from the sun.

No Karen.

She looked up and down the sidewalk, wondering if she'd decided to take a little stroll. But the sidewalk was mid-morning quiet. A car drove by slowly but didn't stop, and it seemed like the driver was looking for an address.

Lindy pulled out her cell phone and dialed Karen's number. But before it even rang, she turned to find Conner and saw him hurrying inside the house.

The door was unlocked?

Maybe she'd left it unlocked and Karen had somehow found her way inside. Lindy's feet carried her swiftly across the grass, up the porch, and into the house. "Conner?"

No answer.

"Conner!"

Her eyes scanned the room. Karen was nowhere, and everything was quiet. Except it shouldn't be because Conner was never quiet.

"Conner!"

"What?" He came around the corner from the hallway. "I was just putting up my books."

"Was the door unlocked?"

"I guess." He shrugged, going to the fridge. "Do we have any Kool-Aid?"

Lindy took a deep breath and nodded to him as she passed by the kitchen. She glanced out the back window but didn't see anyone in the backyard.

"Mom, I'm hungry."

"It's an hour until lunch."

"Please. A snack. Please, please, please."

Lindy sighed, trying to get back into mommy mode. She had so much on her mind, and it was hard to be a good mom when dread filled her. A big part of her just wanted to curl up on the bathroom floor. She and Vance had a lot to talk through, and she could only wonder about how he was going to take it. Before, in Maryland, discussions about how he was doing never went well. He always felt like she was blaming him, and fights would ensue.

Nasty fights.

They still caused a lump in her throat, just thinking about them.

She would approach it differently this time. With more care. Because she felt more care. Before, she just wanted him to get well for the sake of the family. Now she saw the man, all his hurts, what he'd endured and tried to endure on his own because he wanted his family more than anything. He didn't want to burden them—her—with it all.

She hated herself for it. But she was going to make it right.

"Mom? Hello?"

"Sorry," Lindy said, again with the smile. She hoped he wouldn't grow up hating that smile. "Graham crackers with peanut butter?"

"Lots of peanut butter."

"All right. Go get some good reading time in, okay?"

"I got a book on dinosaurs." He grinned and pretended to superhero-fly into his bedroom.

Lindy found the graham crackers and peanut butter and grabbed a paper plate. If she never saw another paper plate in her lifetime, she'd be okay with that. She just wanted stainless steel forks and cute ceramic plates that matched something. Anything.

She got out the milk. He always wanted milk with peanut butter.

Her thoughts on where Karen might be pervaded her worry about Vance momentarily. She'd left the front door open so she could see the car better, and she was enjoying the evergreen smell wafting in on the air of a distant ocean.

A scratching noise bothered her back into the here and now. She was living a lot inside her thoughts, and she couldn't quite leave their grip, even for a few moments.

"Conner, what are you doing?" she called, standing at the door and staring at Karen's car, still looking for her.

"Reading!"

"Stop making that noise."

"What noise?"

"Whatever you're doing. Scratching the wood."

"I'm not doing anything. Can I have my snack?"

Lindy sighed. *Focus. Get the kid his snack.*

But that scratching noise. She knew she wasn't hearing things. It was like a kitten clawing at a door or something. Light. Barely there. But noticeable in the silence. Maybe she hadn't gotten used to all the new-house sounds.

Focus.

She took out the graham crackers and slathered some peanut butter on, then poured the milk and took it to Conner's room, where he lay sprawled out on the floor with three books open. Ordinarily she made him eat his snacks at the table, but ordinarily was gone these days.

The scratching noise was a little louder in Conner's room. "Do you hear that?"

"Hear what?"

"You don't hear that scratching noise?"

Conner listened but the noise stopped. He shrugged and went back to his books.

Lindy stepped into the hallway and heard the noise again. She followed it carefully, with light steps, and found herself in front of the hall closet, where they kept their coats and some board games.

She stood there for a long moment, waiting for the sound. It didn't come again.

But then, right as she was about to step away, she heard it very faintly. She wasn't even sure it came from the closet.

It was probably a squirrel. Or a mouse. She shuddered. She didn't need to be facing a rodent right now. She hated them, and she was the quintessential screamer-with-the-broom lady.

The broom. They'd bought one to try to keep the floors clean until they got their vacuum cleaner back. She hurried to the kitchen to get it. She needed something to fight it off, because as far as she was concerned, squirrels, rats, and other horrible little creatures always came flying out of closets with their fangs exposed.

Back at the closet, she tried to calm down, but her heart was pounding so hard, she couldn't even get half a breath in.

"Come on, Graegan. Get a grip."

Talking to herself wasn't helping. She gripped the broom with both hands and held it out like it was a medieval weapon.

But she just couldn't get herself to reach for the doorknob.

She lowered the broom. Vance would be home any minute. That was one of the perks of being the wife. The husband was expected to do these things, even if he was equally as terrified.

She took a step away and laughed. She was pathetic.

Then she heard another sound.

It was her name. Being whispered.

* * *

"He's dead," Vance said. He'd moved around the side of the mechanic's shop so he could keep an eye on the street to see if anyone was coming or going.

"Where are you?" Erin's voice sounded strained, urgent.

"I'm safe. I'm fine. I'm in this old industrial district. At an abandoned mechanic's garage. The truck is here. Joe was inside the truck, shot dead. In the head. Like he was executed."

"How'd you find out where the truck was?"

"Part investigation. Part luck. The truck was yellow. Easy to spot. I had a confrontation with Joe yesterday. I told him I would be back to get my things. I had Conner with me at the time." There was a long silence. "Erin?"

"I'm here. Listen, just stay there, okay? I'll be there. We'll figure this thing out. Just stay right where you are, and I'm coming to get you."

"I'm worried. I don't know what to do. I don't even know what this means."

"Vance, we'll figure this out. We always do. I'll be there in a minute."

"It's right off the highway, on Duncan Street."

"You caught me just in time. I was leaving town. On your orders."

"Look, Erin, we have to put that aside. For now."

"It's lonely in a new place. Not knowing anyone. No one to call on for help."

"Don't rub this in. Not now."

"Just stay put. Everything will work out how it is supposed to." She hung up the phone and Vance sighed in relief. He hated calling Erin, but there was nobody else. He had thought he was too late, that she'd already left town. He was glad she hadn't.

He wasn't sure how long she'd be, so he decided to go back to the truck. He wondered again if Joe had removed the disc and the evidence he'd planned to blackmail him with.

His feet felt heavy, weighted down with concrete guilt. He'd run from this for so long, and it still had come to hunt him down.

But now that he'd lost everything he thought was important to him, he realized the only thing that really mattered was his family. And that was all he cared about.

Protection was everything.

He took out his cell and texted Lindy. **Will be there soon. U OK?** He tucked the phone into his back pocket and climbed into the truck. He'd been around enough bodies to recognize the smell. Decomposition would start soon, even more so in a warm truck. He put his arm over his mouth and let his eyes adjust to the darkness again.

He knew which box the disc was in. It was red. They'd had the box since their wedding day. A blender came in it, from Lindy's mother, and Lindy had always loved how sturdy and pretty the box was. It had held various things through the years but ended up in the attic, dusty and old. He'd asked if he could use it to store some of his police work, and she said that it was fine.

There were a lot of boxes in here, but only one red one.

He scooted past furniture and climbed over other boxes, making his way to the back as he tried to not think of the smell.

A small piece of light seeped through a tiny crack where the roof of the truck met the side. It amazed him how it could pierce the darkness. So small, but mighty in its effect.

It set aglow the back half of the moving truck, and with it he could make out color. He spotted the red box. It had been set on top of some furniture. Opened.

He cleared the way and got to it. Inside it was totally empty. He pushed the box away in frustration. What had Joe done with it? Had he given it to somebody? Who?

He checked his phone. Lindy hadn't texted back. Maybe she was still on the road. She never texted when she was driving. Both their rule.

Pulling out the phone, he decided to call her, just to make sure everything was fine. But then something caught his eye. It was in the far corner of the truck, just beyond the empty red box.

A cold spike of adrenaline hit his nervous system. The light dimmed and he felt dizzy. But he couldn't stop looking at it, even as his knees gave way.

His leather jacket.

20

"LINDY . . ."

She heard it again and this time there was no mistaking it. She stumbled backward, staring at the closet door, hitting her head against the wall behind her. The broom fell to the ground.

She grabbed her chest, trying to breathe. Then reached for the door and yanked it open.

Crumpled inside the closet, arms twisted grotesquely behind her, was Karen.

Dark, furious red blood soaked through her cream blouse. Lindy dropped to her knees, covering her mouth so she wouldn't scream.

"Lindy . . ."

"Don't talk. It's okay. . . . It's okay." Lindy grabbed a cotton hoodie off its hanger and yanked it down. She opened Karen's blouse. A bullet hole. Blood pumped out like a pulsating fountain. She pressed the hoodie against it, but within seconds it turned wet.

She could hear her cell phone ringing. She needed to call 911. Lindy pulled Karen's arm from behind her. "Karen, hold this on the wound. I'm going to go get help."

"I can't . . . I can't feel them anymore."

Lindy started to get up. Her phone was still ringing.

"No . . ." Karen's eyes glowed with fear, with urgency, widening with each breath she took. "I am going to die." Her words sounded like gasps. "I need to tell you something."

Lindy grabbed the doorknob to help lower herself. Her legs were shaking so badly she wasn't even sure she could make it to the phone.

"Mom?"

Lindy turned. The door of the open closet was blocking Conner's view of Karen. She jumped to her feet. "Conner, don't ask questions. I want you to go to your room and close the door. Do you understand me? Now. Go. Don't come out until I tell you!"

Conner backed up, his eyes searching what was sure to be his mother's terrified expression. For once, he didn't question. He just did. She heard the door shut as she dropped to her knees again.

Karen's lips trembled as she tried to speak. "I'm so sorry."

"What happened? Who did this to you?"

"I did something . . ." Her dulling eyes spilled tears onto her pale cheeks. She tried to turn her head a little, but she didn't seem to have much control. "I thought he loved me."

"Who? Is that who shot you?"

"But you told me about you and Vance. And I knew I didn't have that." She gasped again for air. "I thought if we just had some money, we might be happy." She swallowed, her eyes fading, gazing downward. "But you had nothing, and you were making it. . . ."

"Karen, who did this to you?"

"He told me he loved me, but he never . . . I'm sorry, Lindy. You turned out to be . . ." Another gasp for air, this time with less strength. ". . . and I didn't mean to hurt you."

Lindy stared at her, watching the life slip right out of her.

She struggled for two more breaths. "Joe told me it would all be okay . . ."

"Joe?"

"He . . . It went wrong. I came here to warn . . ."

"You're working for Joe?"

"He said he lov . . ." She choked and blood sputtered out of her mouth, sprinkling her lips and chin. Her body hardly moved, but her eyes lit with terror as she tried for another breath that wouldn't come.

Karen's eyes moved up, looked like they were trying to focus. And she said one final word.

"Run."

"Karen? Karen!"

She was gone. The reflected light in her eyes vanished instantaneously.

A sob escaped, even as Lindy held her hand over her mouth. She couldn't believe it. The only friend she had in Redwood City was never a friend.

Run.

She flew to her feet. She had to get to her phone, call the police. Or Vance? She wasn't sure who to call first, but she didn't feel safe. She'd thought Joe was just a thug after money, but she had underestimated what he was capable of.

She stared at Karen's lifeless body shoved into the tiny closet.

A cold piece of metal jammed into her temple, hitting the bone and causing her to wince in pain.

"Don't move."

* * *

Vance tried Lindy's phone again. It rang and went to voice mail. "Pick up!" he yelled as he raced through the streets, weaving in and out of traffic without the benefit of his siren. "Get out of the way!"

He tried to dial 911, missing the numbers. He didn't even know his own address yet. Was it 6850 or 5860? And what was he supposed to tell them? They would take their time getting there if he only offered a simple "Please go check on my wife."

He threw the cell phone down on the seat and grabbed

the wheel with both hands. He blew through an intersection, slipping between two cars. Sweat dripped down his forehead and burned his eyes.

Erin. *Erin?* What did it mean? How could she be involved in this?

A blinding headache electrified his nerves. His vision blurred. Another migraine. They came more frequently now. He clenched his jaw and left the pain to deal with itself. But as he drove frantically down the two-lane road that led to his condo, his concentration was blasted with more images from the past. Picture after picture. The dead. The clues. It was like fear had a substantiated form, touchable, breathing, living. Blood. Death. A ghostly sniper haunting the shadows.

Concentrate. But he couldn't. His mind wandered back to those days, like a helpless child stumbling through a dark forest looking for something familiar. He slowed the car, fearing he couldn't control it.

He grabbed the phone again and dialed Lindy's number. He heard the sound of its ringing. The road in front of him looked misty, and on top of it was a scene that he had lived. He saw himself walking through the trees, looking for clues after they'd shot a middle schooler.

Doug Cantella was by his side, talking him through what to look for.

Then he was in a lower-level parking lot, staring at a woman sprawled on its dark pavement. Then at the gas station, a man's head blown up.

Vance blinked, wiping the sweat off his face with his shirt.

He had to get there. He had to get to Lindy. Something was wrong. Very wrong.

But what did it all mean?

His mind focused on the leather jacket in the truck. Maybe Erin had found Joe first. Shot him. Was going to let Vance know where his stuff was.

Maybe.

He ducked at the sound of a distant shot, of cracking glass. But as he looked around, he couldn't see anything amiss. The windows were fine.

God, help me.

He'd battled these demons. They came and went. But they hadn't forced themselves into his mind like this in years. Not the sound of the bullet. The shattering of glass.

He should talk to Doug. Doug would know what to do.

Lindy.

He screeched around the corner and right into the driveway. Lindy's car was there. But the front door was open. He jumped out and ran toward the condo. Everything was quiet. He broke the silence by shouting Lindy's name.

"Lindy!" He flew up to the porch and into the condo. "Lindy?"

Nothing. Silence. The first thing he noticed was her cell phone. On the counter. He grabbed it and looked at the missed calls. He ran to both rooms. Empty, except for a cluster of books spread out on Conner's floor. He returned to the hallway and stopped midstep.

Blood smeared across the wood floor.

"No . . ."

Bloody handprints. And a shoe print. Was Lindy hurt? A crushing pain sliced through his head and he shut his eyes, holding his hands against his skull.

A few seconds passed and the pain let up a little. He opened his eyes, and the light made him feel like he'd put his face into a fire pit. But he managed to notice blood on the closet door too. He knelt, trying to put together the pieces of what was going on. His wife was gone. His son was gone.

He grabbed the doorknob of the closet and opened it.

God, please . . . no . . . no . . .

Karen Kaye lay crumpled in the closet, her eyes vacant, staring at nothing. Her torso was soaked with blood.

"Lindy!" Vance screamed.

His cell phone buzzed to life. He snatched it out of his pocket. "Lindy?"

"It's Erin."

Vance held his breath.

"And I have her. And Conner."

"Why?" Vance slid down the wall and sat against the hardwood floor, inches from the bloody mess and Karen's dead body. "What are you doing?"

"I only meant to disrupt your life."

"What are you talking about? I want to talk to Lindy. Let me talk to her."

"Shut up and listen to me. I saved your life once and you did nothing to repay me—except abandon me and shove everything wrong in my life in my face."

"That's not true."

"I wanted you to see what it was like to lose everything. Because that's what happened to me. I had to leave what mattered to me most because of your self-righteousness."

"I only wanted you to get help."

"You blackmailed me. So I decided to blackmail you."

"You're behind all this?" Vance lost his breath.

"Yeah. I'm behind all this, Vance. I wanted to take everything away from you because that's what you took away from me."

"You did it to yourself."

"No. See, I saved your life. But you didn't want to save mine."

"I helped you. . . ." Vance felt his throat swell. "It was complicated, Erin. You know that. I needed . . . I needed to be with my wife, and we couldn't—"

"Yeah. I know the story."

"Why are you doing this?"

"I thought I wanted to show you what my life was like. But now I see."

"See what?"

"I want your life."

"What are you talking about?" Vance pulled at his shirt, which stuck to his chest. Sweat dribbled down his skin.

"People think they can blackmail me. You. Joe."

"Erin, don't do this. Whatever it is you think you're going to do. We can talk through this. Just bring Lindy and Conner back to me."

"Lindy and I are going to talk."

"Are you going to hurt her? Did you kill Joe and Karen?"

"I don't have much to lose anymore, Vance. You took everything from me."

"Stop blaming me. I didn't tell you to start drinking. I should have never gone along with the cover-up."

"I realized something," she said. Her voice sounded so smooth, like they were back in the squad car passing the time with conversation. "I realized I tried to take everything, but I didn't take the only thing that means something to you. You were going to walk away from everything in that truck. Even a disc that could land you in front of a DA."

"I couldn't let it keep its grip on me, Erin. And you have to do the same thing. You have to let this go."

"No. I don't. Now your kid's crying, so I have to shut him up. Don't call the police, or you have no chance of getting them back alive."

"What do you want from me? I'll give you anything."

"See. That's the problem. I want . . . wanted . . . you."

"Then take me. Bring them back and take me."

Silence.

"Erin?"

The phone went dead.

21

Vance dropped the phone. Sob after sob escaped him. He couldn't stop it, so he let it pour out of him. Frustration. Anger. Fear. Regret.

He hated the power that Erin had lorded over him for so long. Guilt had caused him distance from his wife. He'd held on to too many secrets. For too long. And now Lindy's life, and Conner's, was in the hands of a woman who was capable of murder.

"Lindy . . ." His eyes swelled with tears again and he could hardly see anything in front of him. He managed to crawl away from Karen and her blank stare, into the living room, which consisted of only carpet and two lawn chairs. He lay on the floor, captive to long chains of memories.

He was at the mercy of all his mistakes rolled into one, in the form of a very dangerous woman. He had wondered about Erin after she decided to leave the department. She always seemed on edge before. Once she left, she grew dark and reclusive. Even before she left, when Vance made the choice to cut ties with her, she was different. Her eyes had turned cold. Intense. Loaded-gun intense. Vance noticed, on the occasions when he ran into her at a crime scene or the officers' club, she blinked slowly. Unfastened to what was around her.

Another piercing pain boomeranged through his head. When would these stop? He had to think. *Think*. But the pain was nearly unbearable. It felt like his skull was cracking.

Call Sammy. He was the tech guru and data analyst with the department. Vance pulled out his phone, looked through his numbers. He had Sammy's cell, he thought, but the numbers and letters were blurry. He held the phone as close to his face as possible, blinking, trying to get the numbers in focus. He decided just to hit Send.

Suddenly he stood over another body. Inside a bus. Sprawled on the steps. *No. Keep focused.*

"Sammy Gunther."

"Sammy, it's Graegan."

"Vance, my man. How are you?"

"I need some help."

"Sandwiches not popular on the West Coast? You should go into the sushi business, man."

"I need you to look up phone records for me."

"You in some trouble, Vance?"

"Sammy, can you just trust me on this one? I need Erin's phone records."

"Erin 'Crazy Eyes' Lester?"

"That's the one."

"Give me a second." The clicking of the keyboard filled the phone, and Vance felt a sense of relief. He was starting the process of tracking her down. And he *would* track her down.

"Got it."

"I need the last ten numbers she dialed." Vance scrambled to his feet and made his way to the kitchen. He searched for a pen and grabbed a paper plate to write on.

"That's easy. They're all 411."

"All of them?"

"Yeah. The whole page is filled with 411 calls."

Vance knew the trick. Clever criminals used it because there was no way to trace the call. The 411 service automatically dialed the number, leaving no record of who was being called. Erin had planned this.

"Thanks, Sammy."

"Is everything okay?"

Vance closed his eyes. Tried to lighten his voice. "Yeah, man. It's cool. I'll call you back. I may need some more info."

"Only for you, because your wife makes outstanding chicken salad sandwiches, which I miss, by the way."

"Thanks." Vance choked out a good-bye and hung up.

Think. Like a detective. He could figure this out. He could find a way back to them.

He dialed information and got the phone number to the Chicago precinct where she worked.

A woman with a deep voice answered the phone.

"I'm calling about one of your officers, Erin Lester." He didn't know where else to start. Perhaps talk to her lieutenant, find out what he could. Obviously they knew *something*. She wasn't at work.

The woman's voice sounded irritated. "You'll have to talk to our media relations spokeswoman."

"But—"

Elevator music. Lengthy, with a single violin stabbing his mind with every high note. Then, "Ellie Fitzgerald."

"I am calling about Erin Lester."

"Sir, I can't tell you anything more than what was in the statement."

"Remind me again what was in the statement."

"Sergeant Erin Lester is on unpaid administrative leave pending an investigation into the accident."

"Accident?"

"Sir, who are you with?"

"An Internet news outlet."

"Well, I'm not going to be your source. Sounds like you need to do more investigative journalism and rely less on people just telling you information. Good-bye."

The call ended, and Vance quickly got on the Internet with his phone. He googled Erin's name and an article came up from an online Chicago newspaper. He read quickly. There had been an accident involving an officer. Four months ago.

She'd struck a car with a family inside, injuring the father and killing a three-year-old girl.

Vance dropped to his knees as he continued to read. There was speculation that she'd been drunk at the time. She was on patrol and had been chasing a speeding motorcycle when she crashed. She was uninjured. An investigation was pending.

Erin had returned to drinking. She was probably going to lose her job. Especially if they found out what he knew. What he'd kept secret for years.

He stayed on his knees for a long time, staring out the back window, which showed only a partial tree from his view. Desperation bled over him, through him, like it had been dumped from a bucket.

What was he going to do? How was he going to find her? *Think. Think.*

But he couldn't. A shotgun blast shattered a window nearby. He ducked. He always knew the snipers were watching him. When they stood over the bodies, he knew they were nearby, with the detectives in their sights.

Think.

He saw Doug walking beside him, pointing to this and that. He'd taught how to look, what to look for, how to search for things unseen.

That's how they'd found the tarot card and the note from the snipers.

Vance got up and turned to the front door. He walked to the porch, his legs shaky and unstable beneath him.

Karen. She was here. But where was her red car?

Erin had been driving a rental. She knew he could trace that, find some information. So she'd switched and took Karen's car, probably abandoning the rental.

Now she was in a red car. That was his first clue.

He turned and paced. Pacing kept away the memories. Sometimes. Where could he look for them? Where would Erin go?

He circled the living room and finally sank into one of the lawn chairs, training his mind to the facts he knew.

But just like the sniper case, it was like Erin was a ghostly mist vanishing into thin air. She could be anywhere. They could be anywhere.

It almost couldn't get worse.

Except it did.

Because suddenly standing in the doorway was one of his worst nightmares. And he couldn't even pull a gun on her.

Joan.

22

"VANCE," JOAN SAID, her voice soaked with displeasure. "You're looking terribly unkempt." She stepped in, her high heel piercing the carpet. "What is the matter with you? Stand up. Get yourself together."

Vance rose to his feet. How was he going to tell Joan? Should he even tell her? He couldn't. She would overreact. And she was never his biggest fan.

"Where is my daughter?"

"She's not here."

"Where is she?"

Vance didn't answer. He only blinked, trying to find a way to get Joan out of the house. He suddenly noticed a small stain of blood on the sleeve of his shirt.

"I'll have her call you, okay?"

"You don't look as if you're feeling well." A black eyebrow, drawn in with what looked like charcoal, rose slowly. "Are you feeling well?"

"Joan, now is not a good time. I'll have her call you."

In her daggerlike heels, Joan stood an inch taller than Vance. But even when she wasn't taller, she still seemed to be able to look down her long nose at him. "She's worried about you, you know."

Vance didn't respond. He looked away, out the front door, praying this woman would leave.

"Which means I'm worried about her. Which is why I came over. To see what I could do to help."

"Or to stick your nose in our business." Vance cut his eyes sideways to her.

"I'm not interfering. But she is my daughter. And I wish to help how I can. Are you broke? Is that it? I can loan you some money, to be paid back with low interest, of course." She walked to his side, looked over her shoulder at him. "You were planning on getting a job once you got out here, right? It's important for a man to have a job, Vance. Even if perhaps he doesn't need the income."

Vance clenched his teeth. "We were going to run the deli together."

"Were?"

"Joan. Please. Just leave, okay? I just want—" Vance stopped midsentence because the color drained right out of Joan's face. And then she screamed.

Vance realized she was staring at Karen.

"Joan, calm down. Please, calm down!" Vance hurried to the front door and shut it. Joan's screams continued, but not as loudly because he reached from behind her and covered her mouth. When he let go, she backed up, her ankles twisting unsteadily in her shoes. She stumbled over one of the lawn chairs.

"Who . . . who is that . . . ?" Her eyes widened with every word.

"I will tell you what's going on, but I need you to calm down."

"Where is Linda?"

"Please, just calm down."

Suddenly Joan was digging through her purse, backing clear up to the front door. She grabbed behind her for the doorknob while her other hand stayed in her purse, fishing frantically. All the while, she spun through expletives her composed self would never dare to utter.

"Joan!"

"You stay back! Stay back!" Black streams of tears fell down each cheek.

"Joan, I didn't do this! I didn't kill this woman!"

Joan finally found her cell phone and held it out in front of her like it was a can of Mace. "I'm calling the police!"

"Please," Vance begged, stepping toward her. "Please don't do that. You're going to put Lindy's life in jeopardy. And Conner's too."

"What do you mean?"

"Just put the phone down."

She didn't, but she seemed to be listening.

"Look, it's very complicated. And I don't have all the pieces put together. But my ex-partner, Erin Lester, has kidnapped Conner and Lindy. She's the one who killed Karen."

Joan's eyes darted to Karen. Her body froze except for her chest heaving up and down.

"I came home and found Karen dead. Lindy and Conner are gone. And I have evidence that Erin's involved. She called me and told me not to call the police."

"You need help, Vance. Lindy came and talked to me yesterday about you. She was worried. She felt something was wrong."

Lindy went and talked to her mother about him? She wasn't even close to her mom.

Another sound of the shotgun. The bullet whizzed by his ear. Wind brushed against his cheek. Glass shattered nearby. They were too exposed. Out in the open.

Distantly Joan's voice whispered in a long tunnel. He fell to the ground, pain searing through his skull.

"Vance . . ." His name was called again and again.

Come out of this. His own words sounded hollow. *For Lindy. Conner. Get out.*

Even as he heard another sound of the sniper's bullet cutting through the air, he opened his eyes.

He was in his living room. His body was soaked in sweat, but he was back. Glass shattered again, and this time he ignored it. Sunlight glared through the house windows. He strained just to focus.

He heard noises, loud, shouting. Frantic.

Tune it out. Think.

But the noises grew louder. He gazed to his right and saw Joan again. She towered over him, her face frozen in panic, the phone held tightly to her chest. The front door suddenly crashed open.

Men scrambled in. They blurred, so he saw only streaks of gray, like strokes of paint on a canvas.

"Get down! Get down!"

He was knocked flat by a strong arm against his back. More yelling.

Glass shattered.

And he let himself slip away. Finally the cracking, splintering pain in his head melted into the darkness.

* * *

Lindy squeezed Conner's hand, kept it in hers. The black mask that had been pulled over her head made it hard to breathe, but she could make out light and dark. And she could hear sound, that they were in a car, driving fairly fast. She had pinpointed where the sun was and knew they were traveling west.

Beside her, Conner would cry in waves, quietly. His little body shuddered in spasms of fear as he tried to hold his sobs in.

"It's going to be okay," she kept telling him.

But she was unsure.

Karen's bloody body kept flashing through her mind. And the cold metal of the gun against her head.

She knew who had her. But she didn't know why.

"Where are you taking us?" Her voice was muffled.

"What did I tell you about talking?"

After that, there was no sound but the zipping wind sheering off the car windows.

Sweat bubbled across her face. The salt slid over her lips. A strong odor from the fabric that was against her face filled her nostrils.

She'd almost hyperventilated earlier. She couldn't get enough air, but Conner's cries caused her to stop and breathe slowly. Use less air. She had to get them out of this.

But first she needed to figure out why they were in this. Why would Erin do this to them? What was her motivation?

She never saw Erin's face. She'd pulled the mask over her before Lindy could get a glimpse. But she would recognize the voice anywhere. She'd heard it many times. At parties. Over the phone. And it always had a bitter aftertaste, like a store-brand diet soda. Every once in a while, it even made her skin crawl.

Vance had never understood it, and she wasn't sure she always explained it well back when the two were patrol partners. Somehow it always came out like she was blaming Vance, and she wasn't. She had just always felt that Erin had ulterior motives and that she couldn't be trusted as far as Lindy could spit.

Conner put his head against his mother, and Lindy moved her shoulder lower to try to get him comfortable. She heard him whisper, "She was nice when I met her."

Erin's warning not to talk still rang in her ears—and she'd already yelled at Conner twice when he started crying. Lindy could now barely hear him, and she sensed that it was by design. But she wondered what he meant. He'd met Erin when he was small, maybe two, but hadn't seen her since then, that she knew of. Not in recent history, for sure. Except last night. Did she talk to him then?

"She came to the house," he whispered again. Lindy tried to make out each word, tried to understand exactly what he was saying. She couldn't ask any questions. That would give them away.

He'd snuggled up against her chest, and she could feel his breath on her neck. It usually smelled like peanut butter. She thought she could feel his heartbeat.

"She isn't scary," he continued, his voice barely audible above the car sounds. "Bad guys are usually scary."

Her hands were cuffed, but she wanted to stroke his cheek. Except she didn't want to make any sudden movements, to attract attention to the backseat.

"She said I was a good boy. A nice boy."

Then it hit her. He was talking about the day he'd been playing outside by himself.

The muscles in her throat cramped as she tried to hold in the sob that wanted to escape. She had to hold it together. She couldn't afford a breakdown right now, but then again, that had been the story of her life since motherhood.

She listened for more, but he remained quiet, so she sat quietly too, imagining what she would do if Erin dragged them out of the car. She tried to pay attention to the sounds. She was fairly certain they were in a populated area.

Erin had been in Redwood City the whole time.

She had plotted this. She had a plan.

Which meant Lindy had to come up with a better one.

* * *

The voices sounded like they were being shouted into the wind, dissolving into light whispers and then silence. They came in waves, until Vance was shaken awake with harsh shouts. A man stood over him, his face blistery red, his eyes bulging and angry.

"Get on your knees!" His voice was staccato, emphasizing every word like a drill sergeant. A clawlike hand dug into Vance's shoulder, yanking him to his knees. His head jerked back and his muscles seized across his shoulder blades.

"For heaven's sake!" Joan's voice, piercing through the chaos. "He's half-unconscious. I don't think he's going to make a run for it."

"Out of the way, ma'am," came another voice.

A scorching pain ripped through his shoulders as his arms were pulled back. Metal. Handcuffs.

He was pulled to his feet. Dizziness swept through him. Nausea lurched against his stomach.

A lot of men milled about. In uniforms. But through the sea of people, a solitary figure stood out. Joan.

Poised once again, she watched him carefully, her scrutinizing eyes undeterred by his harsh stare.

"You're making a mistake," Vance said, but there was a ringing in his ears and he was unable to tell how loudly he was speaking. Nobody seemed to acknowledge that he spoke. He was read his Miranda rights.

Joan pulled a cigarette from the pocket of her pencil skirt and a lighter from her purse. She didn't light up but dangled the cigarette from her thin fingers and snapped the lighter with her thumb.

Two cops argued about who was going to take him to the jail. Vance kept his eyes locked on Joan's. Behind him he could hear them talking about Karen. He heard the click of a digital camera, and its flash bounced off the glass of the windows.

"I didn't kill her. It was someone else. Please believe me." Vance knew his voice was desperate. But that's all he felt at the moment. Utter desperation. "Joan, listen to me. Erin Lester has her. She's the one who killed Karen. You're putting Lindy in even greater danger. You've got to believe me."

He was forced forward by unseen hands and marched outside, where the sun caused him to tear up and blink. Bright flashing lights from the patrol cars strobed out of unison. He made out the shadowy figures of crowds who'd gathered to gawk.

He did what he'd seen a thousand bad guys do in his lifetime as a cop—ducked his head. Why? He wasn't guilty.

But it sure felt like it.

A large hand grabbed the top of his head, pushed him toward the open door of the patrol car, guiding him in. A smaller man reached over and buckled him in. The handcuffs cut into the skin of his wrists.

A flash went off. From the crowd. He looked away. The car smelled like urine.

He looked out once toward the condo as the patrol car pulled from the curb. Joan stood in the window, her unlit cigarette stroking her cheek like a small wand. Joan Webster had no idea what she'd done.

Vance couldn't stop the tears. He watched out the window, stared at the looming redwood trees he'd come to adore. Just a few days ago he was worried about his couch and his microwave and awards that had been tucked away in boxes.

He'd give it all up in a heartbeat just to see Lindy and Conner one more time.

He rode silently to the police station, sorrow stripping away hope.

23

Vance sat with his back to the cold concrete wall. Cheap blue carpet, stained and smelling of mildew, stared him down. The chair was uncomfortable, with a break that kept threatening to pinch his leg again. He tried to maneuver, but there wasn't a comfortable angle on plastic.

The table was small, metal, sticky on the corner, and one end butted up against the concrete walls. The ceiling was stained with water marks, and a camera hung visibly near the door.

Erin had told him not to call the police. But now here he was. Should he try to explain the truth? Or make something up? Was he putting Lindy in more jeopardy by exposing

Erin? Or would the entire thing sound so absurd that they'd start firing up an electric chair somewhere?

What would Lindy do? Lindy would tell the truth.

And Conner would be praying his little heart out, with his hands clasped together so hard, they'd turn white at the knuckles.

Red marks were still visible on his wrists. He stared at his hands. Somehow, though bigger and stronger, they seemed unable to match Conner's childlike faith. He pictured his little boy's hands clasped together, but his own just stayed in his lap.

His whole life he'd been riddled with doubt.

And guilt joined in for the last decade.

What kind of prayer could he utter that would have any power in it?

He needed a sign. He needed to know God was real because he couldn't afford to put his hope in nothing.

But what did he have to lose?

The metal door to the room swung open. Two detectives walked in. The taller one had crew-cut sandy blond hair, streaked with gray, and a neatly trimmed mustache. His sideburns were long, rectangular, out of the wrong decade. He wore his tie loose, but his eyes had a stubborn stare to them. He introduced himself as Chuck Randall.

The other said his name was Bob Grist. He looked more scholarly, like he might be happy to stare at a folder of clues and never leave his desk. He pushed too-small glasses up his face. Clenched his broad jaw. Smiled vaguely.

They sat on the other side of the table but scooted their chairs away, both stretching out their legs.

Vance automatically read the body signals. It's what he did. What he became good at when he was a detective. And he knew they were reading his. So he sat still, didn't make a move, only watched both of their faces and waited for them to begin.

After a moment of awkward silence, Bob jumped in. "The woman in the closet. You know her?"

"She was an attorney that my wife met when we first moved here from Maryland. She was helping us with a situation. . . . Our possessions were stolen by the moving company. Held for ransom, basically."

"Uh-huh," said Chuck, who looked to be taking notes, though he probably wasn't. Everything was being recorded, Vance was certain, by the camera's big eye. "Well, Mr. Graegan, already we've caught you in a lie."

Fear prickled his skin. He hadn't lied. Had he? His head started hurting.

"What are you talking about?"

"The woman in the closet. The dead woman in the closet."

"What about her?"

"She's not an attorney," Bob said, his voice smooth and calm. "Her name is Karen Bedshaw, and she's well-known around here."

"For what?"

"Mostly prostitution. More recently writing hot checks."

Vance's eyelids drooped with exhaustion. He didn't know what to make of it. Lindy had trusted this woman. Counted her as her first friend since moving to Redwood City.

He could try to lie his way out of this, but if these two were worth anything, they'd know it.

"You were a detective, correct? Back in Maryland?"

Vance nodded.

"So why'd you quit and move all the way across the country?"

"We just wanted a fresh start," Vance said. He definitely shouldn't mention a fresh start to their marriage. He was pretty sure right now he was their prime suspect—not only in Karen's murder, but in the disappearance of his wife and son. He leaned forward, put his elbows on his knees, tried to gather his thoughts. The truth, he knew, was the only way to go, even though the truth sounded crazy. "Look," he began, "this is a complicated mess."

"Then try to straighten it out for us."

"You know the old warehouse district off Duncan Street?"

Bob nodded.

"You'll find a body there. The person who took my wife also killed this man and took all of our belongings. There's an old mechanic's shop with a chain-link fence around it. Behind there is a truck. It has all of our possessions in it. And a man named Joe."

Bob nodded at Chuck, who left the room, presumably to go check the details.

"I found him when I was trying to locate my belongings."

"This person who took your wife and child. Who is he?"

"Her name is Erin Lester."

"A female?" Bob might've actually written that down.

"She's my former partner back in Maryland."

"You two have an affair or something?"

"No. But it was a complicated relationship." Vance looked down. How to explain it? He sounded guiltier with each word. "She saved my life while we were on duty. And I guess I've never been able to pay her back enough."

"So she takes your wife and kid?"

No. It was more complicated than that. But he wasn't sure he wanted to go there.

"I just found out she's been suspended from the Chicago Police Department. She was in a wreck while on duty. They think she was drinking at the time."

"So she comes and kidnaps your family?"

Vance sighed inwardly. This guy was no pushover. But could he tell him more? Would he believe him? This was sounding more ridiculous by the minute. His only hope was that once they found Joe's body, they could link the forensics with Karen and show that it wasn't his gun that killed either of them. Then they could get somewhere. They'd call to make sure his story about Erin matched what was going on in Chicago. It was probably being done even as they spoke.

But could he tell this detective what had happened all those years ago? He'd been willing to expose his darkest secret to Lindy. He wanted to. He wanted the weight off his shoulders. But now, would it help him get Lindy back or hinder him?

And what a tangled mess to try to explain to a guy who thought he was looking a murderer in the face.

Bob leaned back in his chair, quickly stretched, and then tapped his pencil lightly on the top of his pad. He looked Vance directly in the eyes and seemed to be thinking something over.

"Vance," he said, taking a lighter tone, "I understand you worked the D.C. sniper case."

"That's right."

"That was some kind of crazy, wasn't it?"

Vance nodded, trying to figure out where he was going with this.

"I can't imagine working that case, to tell you the truth. That was a brutal month."

"It was."

"Is that why you left the force?"

"No."

"But it was stressful on you."

"It was stressful on a lot of people."

"Do you think that maybe it put more stress on you than you think?"

"What are you saying?"

Bob paused, pressing the pencil against his thin lips. "I'm saying that maybe you've underestimated what that ordeal did to you."

Vance looked away. "It was difficult. But I'm fine."

"Are you sure about that? We found you unconscious on the floor of your home. Your mother-in-law says your wife has been worried about you. I'm just wondering if we should be looking at post-traumatic stress disorder."

Vance tried to hold a steady expression, but he felt the muscles in his jaw twitch. "That's not what's going on here."

"You didn't snap? Maybe you didn't mean to, but you felt out of control?" Bob leaned forward. "It's understandable, Vance. You've been through a lot. I'm a detective, and I can tell you that had I worked that case, there would've been fallout."

Vance slumped in his chair, sliding the thumb of his left hand up and down the cold metal leg of the chair. "You're not believing me, are you? That it's my ex-partner." He glanced up. "Please, Detective, you have to believe me. My wife and child are in an incredible amount of danger. This woman is capable of murder. She's already killed two people. Please listen to me. I think she's driving a red Cadillac. It's the car that this Karen lady was driving. And I have no idea where she would be taking them." Tears welled up in his eyes as he thought about how scared they must be. He prayed they were together, wherever they were.

Vance took a deep breath, trying to pull it together. "Erin called me. She told me that she had Lindy and Conner. Check my phone records. The call came in around noon."

Bob took some more notes. "Sure. We can check all this out. We will. But look . . . I know this is hard to hear, okay?

I had a buddy who served in Iraq, right? And he thought he was okay. But he wasn't. Had nightmares. Thought he heard bombs going off. Maybe that's happening to you. Are you hearing things that aren't there, Vance?"

Vance blinked away the rest of the tears and stared at the carpet. His head was starting to hurt again, and he was having trouble concentrating. Bob's words rang in his ear. But the images were taking over. First it was Karen. Then he was at a gas station, watching blood drain out of a young woman.

"Vance?"

Vance looked up, pulling himself out of the dark places.

The door to the room swung open. Chuck stood in the doorway, his expression nothing but sober, unemotional lines. "Bob, can I talk to you for a second?"

Bob stood, taking his notepad with him.

The door closed, and Vance sat still, listening to his heart pound violently in his chest. Were they dead already? Had Erin taken their lives? Wouldn't he know in his heart if they were gone?

And where was this detective getting PTSD? That seemed to come from nowhere. Still, Vance couldn't deny that on occasion—especially when he was stressed—reality seemed to fade into the fabric of fear, and he would hear glass shattering. He was sure he heard bullets punching through the air.

But it wasn't anything that affected him. It wasn't clouding his judgment.

Except the mud flaps. He still couldn't explain seeing them on the truck. And then finding the truck without them.

But that was the least of his concerns.

The door opened again. Bob returned, with Chuck trailing. Both wore grim expressions, and Vance felt any hope he had for Lindy and Conner drown right there in the room.

"What's wrong?" he asked as they both slowly took their chairs.

Chuck looked at Bob and Bob looked at Vance.

"We have some bad news," Bob said, his hand stroking his tie so slowly that it hadn't made it to the bottom before he continued. "We found the mechanic's shop you were referring to."

"And?"

Chuck spoke, his thin voice contrasting with his thick features. "There was no truck. And there was no body."

24

It seemed like they'd been driving for hours. Maybe they had. Conner complained of being hungry and was told to shut up. Then he wet his pants. Lindy could feel the warm liquid against her leg, sliding down the leather seats.

"I'm sorry, Mom," he whispered.

She squeezed his little hand. And hate grew in her heart. Erin had no regard for them. Either of them.

She thought they must be miles from home. It was dark out now. Conner had fallen asleep against her arm and she'd nodded off too. She felt dizzy from the lack of oxygen. Nauseated. The mask suffocating her was soaked with sweat and more uncomfortable than it had been.

She tried to rest. She was going to need to be sharp-minded for whatever Erin had planned for them.

She awoke, startled, as the car stopped. Turned off.

Erin spoke calmly. "We are going to get out of the car. I am going to take your mask off. If you scream, I will hurt you and your kid. And frankly, Lindy, I don't have much to lose here. So behave."

The front car door opened and she heard Erin get out. A few seconds later, her door opened. The mask was pulled from her head. Lindy opened her eyes, breathed deeply, her nostrils flaring with fresh air.

Erin grabbed her hair. "Now, I want you looking down. At your feet. Don't look around. Don't look up. You got it?"

Lindy obeyed and kept her gaze at the ground as Erin yanked her out of the car.

It was dark. Pitch-black like it was the middle of the night. She grabbed Conner's hand and pulled him out with her, then kept him close by.

"Kid, just walk and obey and I won't hurt your mommy, okay?"

"My name's Conner."

"Honey, shh," Lindy said. She looked him in the eyes and was never more thankful to do so. She tried a soft smile.

She quickly discovered they were at a motel. She could see the bottoms of doors and then their numbers as they climbed metal stairs to the second floor. Erin already had a key.

The fact that they weren't out in a field being executed

meant that she needed them alive for something. What, though?

The room glowed with amber lights from three different lamps. There were two beds, a table and chairs, and a TV.

Erin shut the door. "Go sit down."

Lindy sat with Conner on the end of a bed and studied Erin as she threw the keys on the table. The night before, she could barely even look at the woman.

The last time she'd seen Erin, she was a striking blonde with long, wavy hair that never seemed out of place. She never wore much makeup. She didn't have to. Lindy always thought her best feature was her sparkling blue eyes, like a glimmering ocean. But in those eyes, Lindy also saw a threat. They never looked kind. Or safe.

Now her hair was cropped short and was dishwater blonde. Her eyes were still the same blue but looked stained with life, like old carpet trying its best to hold up. Her mouth was drawn down, sad without intention.

Nearby a train rumbled past, shaking the lamp on the table, its whistle blowing through the shoddy Sheetrock.

"What do you want from us, Erin?"

"You shut up and I'll do the talking."

"Then talk."

"I've got the gun and the power here. You need to remember that if you want to get out of this alive."

Lindy held her tongue. This wasn't just a threat. She'd killed Karen, so she was capable of anything.

"Get over here."

Erin took out a pair of handcuffs and cuffed Conner's right hand to the bed rail. She next uncuffed one of Lindy's hands and cuffed her left hand to the other bed rail.

Then Erin grabbed a chair from the small table by the window and moved it over by the bed. But instead of sitting, she lifted a sleek black laptop out of a bag already in the room and set it on the chair. Silently she took out a disc and inserted it into the computer, then opened the screen. She turned it so they both could see.

"I'm going out to get some food," she said, those severe blue eyes staring hard at Lindy. "I want you to watch this. You'll want to see it. And we'll have a lot to talk about when I get back."

* * *

The jumpsuit was bright orange like a roadside hazard cone. It draped over Vance as if meant for a man twice his size. He wore socks with rubber slides. Lindy hated socks with any kind of sandal. He'd tried it at the pool one time because he had a blister on one toe, and she told him it was as atrocious as an elderly man wearing a thong at the beach. He didn't make that mistake twice.

He sat in a cell by himself, though there were two beds. He'd been thoroughly booked and had the ink stains to prove it. White orbs still hovered in his line of sight from the flash.

How had a move across the country to try to keep his family intact resulted in his landing in jail, unable to help his kidnapped wife and son? His body was numb with the grief of it, and his mind ran circles around his emotions. He could do nothing but stare at the bare concrete walls.

The numbness turned to cold. The blanket on the bed looked old and smelled of strong detergent.

It was a strange sensation to be unable to get up and go, to not even know what time it was. He was at the mercy of the legal system, which almost always went with statistics, and statistics said that he was the one who did it.

Karen's bloody body.

Bob's voice, asking him if he was going crazy.

He was certain he wasn't.

Except there was no truck. And no body in a truck.

What was real and what wasn't? Had he done something to harm Karen? Or his family? Could he do that and not remember it?

His hands trembled in his lap. He couldn't imagine it.

But he'd never gone to get help after the sniper case. He'd told Lindy he had, but he never showed up for his first appointment and never told her otherwise.

Instead, he struggled through the images, pressing them into the back corners of his mind, where his childhood memories mingled with the bloody details of bullet-punctured bodies. Each day it seemed easier.

But sometimes the memories were like a sea monster, like the kraken lifting out of dark waters, thrashing around, and grabbing anything it could with long, strong tentacles.

It used to remain mostly quiet. But not these days.

He heard metal clanging against metal and stood to look out the small window of his solid steel door.

"Back up to the far wall," an officer ordered. He obeyed, and then the officer asked him for his wrists. "You have a visitor."

Vance followed the two officers down concrete stairs into a large room, glowing white from fluorescent lights. Outside it was still pitch-black.

The room was empty, though it had a dozen tables and yellow plastic chairs, except for a very small man. He couldn't have been over five feet two, and with fluffy white hair and a thick mustache, he looked a little like Albert Einstein, had Einstein been black. He appeared tired, with one side of his hair sticking up like he'd just risen out of bed. He stood as he saw Vance.

Vance shuffled over to him and sat down. The officers locked his hands to the table and left.

"I'm Conrad Biggs, your attorney."

Funny. Had she not been dead—and a prostitute in real life—he would've called Karen to avoid a court-appointed attorney.

"You've been charged with second-degree murder. You'll be arraigned tomorrow. Well, today, actually." Biggs checked his watch, moving it closer and then farther away from his face like the numbers were blurry. "At 1 p.m." He peered over his reading glasses. "I don't normally take clients charged with murder. I prefer the hard white-collar crime cases." He smiled slightly.

Vance blinked. He had no recollection of anyone asking him if he had an attorney, but he was tired and hadn't slept.

The lawyer took out a yellow legal pad and a Bic. "Tell me about this PTSD."

Vance didn't say anything.

"They mentioned it when they filed, which is probably why they didn't charge you with first-degree murder. According to the charges, you had the woman's blood on you?"

"I guess."

"And who was this woman?"

"My wife's attorney. A prostitute."

Biggs smirked. "Not fond of attorneys?" Then he offered a full-toothed grin that put Vance at ease.

Vance managed a small smile. "I'm a big fan right now."

"Good, son. Good," Mr. Biggs said. "Because I'm afraid I'm the only friend you've got at the moment." He flipped a page on his notepad. "Why don't we start from the beginning?"

"No offense, Mr. Biggs," Vance said, "but nobody asked whether or not I wanted my own attorney. This is a big case, and I know court-appointed attorneys are every bit as savvy as their hired counterparts, but I'm just wondering if I should hire an experienced criminal defense attorney."

Biggs's gentle eyes left his notepad and settled onto Vance. "I'm not court-appointed," he said. "I was hired to take care of you. And that's what I'm going to do."

25

LINDY AWOKE, startled by a sound she didn't recognize. She yanked her arm and a searing pain shot through her shoulder. She realized she was still cuffed, still in the motel room. Conner was asleep next to her.

The noise came from the motel door. It sounded like a key. Soon it opened and Erin walked in. The heavy drapes had been pulled shut. She glanced at the computer, where the screen saver had come on.

"I brought you something to eat. And your kid a change of pants and a package of underwear." She plopped a Walmart sack on the table, then pulled out a container of chicken strips. "Here."

Conner woke up, and Erin walked over to him. Lindy scrambled to a sitting position. "Don't you dare touch him!"

"Chill out," Erin growled, ignoring her and unlocking his handcuff. "I'm sending him to the bathroom so he doesn't pee himself again. Should've bought the kid some Pull-Ups." She looked at Conner. "Hurry up. Go get your business done. Look in that sack. There are some sweatpants and underwear. Change into them." She gave him a menacing wink. "And if you're real good, kid, I'll make sure and not tell your whole class that you peed all over yourself, okay?"

Conner's wide-eyed stare turned to Lindy, who tried to give him a reassuring nod. "It's okay—go change and then we'll eat."

"I heard the train last night. It made the walls shake. It must be big." Conner pulled out a pair of sweatpants from the sack. And then the package of underwear.

"Just go do what I said," Erin snapped.

He walked to the bathroom slowly, like he was keeping his options open.

Erin took a chicken strip and then pulled another chair over from the table, sitting next to the one with the laptop on it. "You watch it?"

Lindy looked away. "What happened to you? You look horrible. You used to be pretty."

Erin laughed. "In a threatening sort of way?"

"Apparently I'm the threat."

Erin's laugh cut short. She nodded toward the computer. Casually crossed her legs. "Did you see it?"

"Yeah. About a billion times before the screen saver started."

"What'd you see?"

"A woman crashing her car. Then stumbling around on the dark street like she was drunk." The car had slammed into a light pole, doing quite a number to the vehicle but not demolishing it.

"That woman is me."

"I know." She listened for Conner. The toilet flushed.

"It was captured on a security camera."

"I still don't understand what this has to do with me."

"I traveled a very long way to get this disc." She laughed a little. "And the kicker is—it doesn't matter much anymore."

Lindy didn't know where Erin was going with it. She'd noticed that the time/date stamp was October tenth of 2002. Four fifteen in the morning. The image was pretty grainy, but she had made out that it was a woman and deduced it was Erin. She wanted to get as much information from Erin as she could before Conner came back.

"Your husband had this disc."

"Why?"

"Because he thought he was helping me, I suppose. There was a time when Vance cared deeply for me, as you know."

"Maybe you should just spell this all out for me," Lindy said.

Conner came out of the bathroom, standing by its door, clinging to the frame.

"Get back over here," Erin said.

Conner obeyed. "Can I have some chicken, Mom?"

"Sure. Go ahead."

Lindy looked back at Erin, trying to decide if this woman had enough tact to not discuss all this in front of Conner.

"Conner," Erin said, "get over on this other bed. I'll turn on some cartoons. You like cartoons, don't you?"

Conner slid onto the bed, a chicken strip in his fist. Erin turned the TV on. It was already on a cartoon channel, which Lindy guessed was by design. He'd been without a TV for so long, Lindy wondered if that was a vulnerability for him. He didn't even look over to see if it was okay.

But soon he was engrossed in SpongeBob, and Lindy was thankful. She turned her attention to Erin, who'd moved back to the chair.

"This," she said, "is what Vance held over my head for many, many years. In one sense, he saved me. I could've been fired over this. But then he got all self-righteous about it."

"I still don't understand."

"He discovered this one night when he was monitoring security footage during the sniper attacks. He was put in charge of watching the camera footage in a four-block radius. It was about four in the morning when he came across this and knew it was me." Erin stood and took another chicken strip. She went to the Walmart bag and grabbed a water bottle, opened it, and took a swig. The lines on her face were so hard. Every crease seemed to deepen by the hour. "So he did me a favor. He erased that portion of the security footage. He was protecting me."

She sat back down and bent forward, trying to get Lindy

to look her in the eye. "That's what partners do. They protect each other. I protected him. And he protected me." She leaned back in her chair and took two bites, slowly chewing, seeming to contemplate something. "But he took something and he shouldn't have. Before he erased the disc, he burned a copy for himself. And he threatened me with it."

"What do you mean threatened?"

"Let's just say it wasn't a free gift. He told me if he ever caught me drinking again, he'd turn the footage over to the captain. So I had a lot of pressure, as you can imagine."

"Is that why you moved to Chicago?"

"I moved to Chicago for a fresh start, much like you were doing. Everyone needs a fresh start, don't they? My father lives there, in a suburb. Besides, Vance had grown cold toward me. Maybe it was the superiority complex he got from moving inside, getting that detective title. Or maybe it was because you kept harping on him to keep his distance from me. I'm still not sure. Whatever the case, he forgot what he owed me."

"Yeah. You never did quite get over that savior complex, did you?"

Erin's eyes narrowed. "You know, I lost everything that mattered to me when I left Maryland. And he never got that. He said it was a good thing, that I could make a good life for myself." She took another long drink of water. "I needed him to understand how it felt to have one's life completely disrupted. Like mine was."

Lindy's heart continued to quiver, but she tried not to

show it. "Erin, you had a drinking problem. I don't know what that disc's about. As I'm sure you know, I had no idea it existed. But I can only imagine that Vance was trying to help you."

"Hmm." Erin rose and stood next to Lindy. She bent down to whisper in her ear. "I saved that man's life, and he discarded me like a cigarette. He stomped on me to put me out." She walked to the computer and started the footage again. "Watch carefully."

Lindy watched, but she'd seen it over and over. She wasn't sure why she was being told to watch it again.

"Don't you see it?"

"I don't know what I'm looking for. All I see is you, the wreck."

"Watch again."

She played it again and Lindy tried to look for details.

Then Erin paused the video and pointed to the top of the screen. "See that?" Her finger was on the corner of a dark sedan, speeding out of view of the camera. It had just passed by the accident.

"I see a dark car."

"You want to know what I see? I see something that is going to cost him dearly. He's tried to hide it for years, and he is going to pay for it. If not criminally, then with his reputation. And you know how much he loves his reputation."

A cold shiver raced over Lindy's skin. She looked at Conner. He stared mindlessly at the TV, and she guessed he hadn't been paying attention.

But then she looked at his hands. They were clasped together, white at the knuckles. He'd heard every single word. And he was fighting the best way he knew how.

* * *

Vance managed to rest, though fitfully. He lay on top of his bunk, expecting to be joined by another prisoner, but no one ever came. His lawyer said he was being arraigned at 1 p.m. He'd been served breakfast, but nothing else.

He dreamed of Lindy and Conner playing at the ocean. They'd not yet made it there as a family. They'd been too busy dealing with the mess that had become their life.

The clanging of metal startled him to his feet. An officer entered, and before he knew it, he was being led to the visitor's center again. Which was strange, since Biggs had told him he would see him again that day in court.

His lawyer had listened to everything he'd said, taken fastidious notes, and seemed completely drawn in by Vance's account of what happened.

But then he ordered a psych consult. Said they probably wouldn't get it in before the arraignment. Instructed him to enter a not-guilty plea. Then said he was headed to IHOP.

This time the visitor's room was more crowded. Vance looked around, trying to find Conrad Biggs. Didn't spot him. He was guided to a table near the center.

Then he saw her.

Vance shot her a cold look as they secured him to the table. "Where is my family?"

Erin gave him a coy shrug, but her eyes were as cold as a deep freeze. She waited for the officers to leave before leaning forward and smiling.

"We're having a grand old time. That kid of yours. Cute as can be. Except how he pees himself."

"Why are you here? What do you want?"

"Does your life feel disrupted, Vance? Because that's what I really want. I want you to feel how I felt when I had my life pulled out from underneath me."

"You're the one with the drinking problem."

"And you appointed yourself judge, didn't you? Well, now I get to play judge." She traced an imaginary line on the table. "I have to tell you, this was unexpected. I wasn't counting on you being framed for that lady's murder."

"I figured you were in control of it all."

"You know me. I roll with it. I thought you'd be hunting me down, and I had a plan for that. But this . . . well, this makes things a lot easier." She looked casually around the room as she spoke. "I've been one step ahead of you the whole time, but there were some kinks in the hose. I didn't count on Joe double-crossing me."

"He disappeared from your radar, took my things, and was going to keep the ransom for himself."

"He and his little whore of a girlfriend, who gave me a good fight, I'll tell you that, even with a hole in her chest." She sighed and gestured toward him. "But I have to say, this is not nearly as fun. I mean, I thought we'd play some hide-and-seek, you know? I'd outmaneuver you, make you feel like you were chasing ghosts. We'd spar. Have that thing going we always had. That chemistry. But this is lame. Here you sit, shackled to a table, unable to do anything at all. You can't save your wife and kid. You can't do anything."

"I will do what you want. Just don't hurt them."

"Funny how you're worried about people getting hurt. You weren't always like that, were you, Vance? I mean, you weren't worried about me."

Vance steadied his breathing. "That's not true."

This caused an angry, startled expression to pass across Erin's face. "You're trying to tell me that you *cared* about me?"

"You never saw it as caring, but what I did was for your own good. You were ruining your life with alcohol. Yeah, I'll admit it—I made a mistake with the disc. A grave mistake. I was scared. Scared of where your life was going. Scared of the mistake I'd made by missing the sniper's car. I've lived with guilt for years because of it."

"So you just stop talking to me or returning my phone calls?"

"Erin, you know as well as I do how complicated that was. I needed to restore my marriage. I needed to show Lindy I was committed. I had to let go of some things, and you were one of them." Vance clenched his jaw as he tried to deliver the lie. "And I regretted it." It made him sick to even say it, because the truth was, it was the best thing he ever did.

Erin sneered. "Yeah. I bet you regret it now, don't you? Just like Joe regrets ever double-crossing me."

"What'd you do with the truck and the body?"

Erin locked her gaze on him, her blue eyes more intense than he'd ever seen them. "I am going to get everything from you, Vance. I am going to take everything you have. Your things. Your wife. Your kid. And lastly, your money."

"I know something happened in Chicago."

Surprise lit up her eyes. "Wow. Good detective work, Graegan. So yeah, I'm going to need a new start. I'm going to have to leave the country for a very long time. I've murdered two people, and by the time I'm done, it's going to be . . . more."

Vance's eyes stung with tears. Anger flushed his cheeks. "You're going to kill Lindy and Conner. That's what you're telling me?" He couldn't believe it had come to this. He couldn't believe what she had turned into.

"You always told me everything works out in the end. You were right." She shrugged. "I mean, it's not perfect. I was never a fan of Mexico. But it's all going to work out for me. Not so much for you, but for me, yeah."

She stood.

"Erin, don't do this."

She spoke softly. "I like to see the desperation in your eyes. I'm sorry you were never able to see it in mine." She walked out the door and disappeared.

Vance looked at his hands. They were squeezed together, knuckles white. He prayed. He had no other recourse. He screamed a prayer out in his soul and begged a God he'd rarely talked to, to have mercy on him.

The officers returned and led him from the room.

As he walked back to his cell, he realized Erin had made her first mistake.

By coming to see him, she revealed that she was nearby. And if that was true, he'd be able to find her. But first he had to get out of this place. So he prayed for that, too.

26

THEY'D BEEN LEFT alone again. Erin had unplugged the
clocks, but it seemed like afternoon. They watched cartoons
and that put Conner at ease. Lindy tried for a while to get
the handcuffs loose or find a way around the bed railing, but
to no avail.

She prayed. It was uncomfortable, but it was a release. She
kind of wanted to ask Conner if she was doing it right, but
then she figured there was really no wrong way. She'd watched
her little boy pray all kinds of different ways, in all kinds of
different places. She'd been embarrassed by it, wondered if
he was suffering from some disorder, had been discouraged
when the doctor told her not to worry about it.

Yet she was amazed at how often his little prayers were

answered. His bike would suddenly start working again. The rain would clear up when he wanted to go to the park. And once, he'd accidentally left his Etch A Sketch on a mall bench. He prayed for its return. And when they went back, it was sitting just where he'd left it. But there was a maturity when he didn't get his way, too. He'd ask and, most of the time, accept the answer, whatever that was.

Maybe it wasn't his faith that made her uncomfortable. Maybe it was the lack of her own.

She drew a great deal of comfort from knowing for certain that Vance was looking for them. And he was good at looking for things. She wondered if he knew it was Erin. Maybe it wouldn't take him long to figure that out.

Strangely, she also longed for her mother. As tumultuous as the relationship was, as cold and distant as her mother was, she still longed for her. That longing always gave her peace in her own mothering journey. It made her sure that Conner would always love her, even if he couldn't show it.

Conner suddenly giggled a little at the cartoon, forgetting he was cuffed to a bed. Kids were amazing.

Her mind wandered to the video that was now forged in her mind. She could see it clearly when she closed her eyes. Vance had covered up something very big, for the sake of Erin, and that caused doubt to rattle the cage of her heart. She thought she knew everything about him, but she hadn't known this, and it felt like a betrayal.

Yet there was something that her heart kept returning to, and it was the knowledge that this man loved her. And maybe she knew why he hadn't told her. Erin had always been a tough topic for them to tackle. They could never get past the anger and resentment. Lindy hated that she felt like she had to compete against another woman. Vance hated that she ever thought she was in competition.

And things got more complicated from there.

But looking back, the resentment now seemed trivial. Handcuffed to a bed, being threatened by a murdering lunatic, she wished their time had been spent more wisely.

Her gaze traced the line of her arm up to her hand, which was flat against the wooden post of the bed. It reminded her of one of Conner's drawings, after he'd watched the Sunday morning preacher. He'd drawn Jesus on the cross. It was out of proportion, as any six-year-old draws, with the arms too long. But it seemed to perfectly depict the strain of a man trying to hold his body weight up by nails through his hands. She remembered carefully studying the crayon drawing of Jesus with red droplets of blood pouring out of each hand. Big, tear-like, out of proportion again, but strangely accurate.

He drew Jesus smiling, but with blood gushing out of every part of his body. She'd asked him why Jesus was smiling if he was dying so miserably. And Conner said, "He was thinking of me."

She stared across the grimy motel room at her little boy, so innocent, so full of faith. Why couldn't she just believe? Why was it so hard for her to ask God for help? To consider Him a friend like Conner did? To consider herself likable enough to be loved so much that Someone would die for her?

She supposed it was because she didn't like herself very much. She was a critical person, and she'd been far too critical of Vance. He'd gone through a horrible tragedy, and she never tried hard enough to understand where he was coming from. She only criticized. Questioned. Berated. All because she felt her needs weren't being met the way she thought they should be.

If only she'd taken the time to let him work things out.

He was sick. She knew he was sick. He was visiting dead detectives. But she still loved him, with everything in her, and if she got a second chance, she would do anything to help him. Anything.

Her second chance was looking less likely. Tears spilled onto her cheeks as helplessness engulfed her. There was nothing she could do for her husband. There was nothing she could do for her child. It was simply hopeless.

Except.

On the other side of that crayon drawing had been another Jesus, this time standing in a bright blue robe, with yellow sunbursts popping out from all sides of him. Conner had written *RIZEN* in orange. He'd boasted with a big grin, "He's a powerful dude, Mom. He's like all superheroish and stuff, except better, because He can come back from the dead, and superheroes can't. They can crush metal and stop bullets, but once they're dead, they're dead."

Dead was pretty hopeless. The way things looked, she was halfway there.

But maybe there was hope, drawn clearly in crayon.

* * *

In another small concrete room, Vance waited in handcuffs. Conrad Biggs stood next to him quietly. Vance smelled aftershave, the kind his grandfather used to wear. And syrup. A large, securitylike camera hung from the ceiling. Eye-level to Vance was another camera, which he would speak into when he talked to the judge.

"The judge will ask you how you plead, and you say, 'Not guilty,'" Biggs said as if needing to fill in the silence. "Respectfully."

Vance sighed. "I know the drill. Not this particular drill, but I've been in court a time or two." The monitor to his right was gray, indicating the judge hadn't arrived yet. "I used to testify against people like me. I'd raise my right hand, take the oath, do everything I could to put them away."

Biggs stared forward. "Did you ever wonder if you put an innocent man away?"

"No. I figured that was for the court to decide. I just presented the evidence."

"The evidence against you looks pretty bad."

Vance acknowledged this with a nod.

"You and Lindy had a rocky relationship. That's never a good sign when a wife and child disappear."

Vance kept his eyes on the monitor.

"One of the victims' blood was all over you. The other victim, who you claimed would link the murders together and show evidence that you didn't kill either, is apparently nonexistent."

Vance glanced at him. "You're starting to sound like a prosecutor."

Biggs grinned. "You gotta think like a prosecutor to beat one."

"Do you believe me? That I didn't kill Karen and that my family was kidnapped?"

"Too early to say."

"Why would you take me on as your client, then?"

"The money's good. Real good."

"By law, I am pretty sure you have to tell me who hired you."

"Doubtful," he said. "But your next option is a chain-smoking, drunk, burned-out, court-appointed attorney who will most likely lose the case."

"How do I know that you're not going to deliberately lose my case?"

He smiled. "Because there's not enough money in the world for a lawyer to purposefully allow himself to look stupid in front of his colleagues and a judge."

Whatever. Vance knew everyone could be bought. The question was, who wanted to purchase him, and why?

The gray TV screen flickered to life.

* * *

Lindy took the downtime she had in the hotel room to sleep. It was fitful, and she wasn't even sure that she'd really fallen asleep because it seemed she heard the running slapstick jokes of the cartoons. But when she opened her eyes, she felt slightly more rested and her body ached less. Her hand was numb, though. The cuffs were too tight.

Conner had fallen asleep on the other bed, and she was thankful. The thought of his captivity was almost too much to bear, so she tried instead to figure out how to get out of this mess. How to contact Vance, at the very least, to tell him they were okay.

But she wasn't sure for how much longer. She still wasn't even sure what Erin's plan was or why she wanted to hold them captive. It was fairly evident she wanted to get back at Vance, but what was her long-term goal? What did she plan to do? Why did she need them?

She heard footsteps and saw a shadow under the door. It stayed there for a long time. Erin listening, she assumed.

Soon the door opened and she walked in. She was backlit. Her hair looked windblown and wispy. Lindy couldn't see her face to gauge her expression.

Erin threw her keys down on the table and finally closed the door. The drapes were still closed, but she stepped into the lamp's light. Conner continued to sleep. Erin stood for a long time and observed him. Lindy's hands balled up. She didn't even like her looking at him. There was a detached iciness to her gaze.

"How long are you going to keep us here?" Lindy asked.

Erin blinked slowly and turned her face toward Lindy.

"He's a little boy, Erin. You can't just keep chaining us up everywhere."

"Really."

"People are looking for us. You're not going to be able to keep this up much longer. What is it that you want? Let me help you get it."

Erin flopped into the nearby chair, her hands dangling over the sides. She then crossed her legs and smoothed her hair. She rested her head against one hand as she observed Lindy for a moment. "You think Vance is searching for you? at this moment?"

"Of course he is," Lindy said. "He will do anything to get us back. You know that. Do you really think you're going to get away with this?"

"I do." She smiled, her expression warming except for the eyes, shimmering like shards of broken glass against pavement. "I will. I am owed this."

Lindy sighed, staring at the ceiling. "You know, what you never understood was how much Vance cared for you." She glanced sideways. The remark startled Erin; she could tell. The catty smile was replaced by a straight line on her lips. "He really did. That was the source of many of our arguments."

Erin recovered her smooth expression. "He sure had an awesome way of showing it."

"He cared about what happened to you. After you started drinking, he worried endlessly about you. I told him to write you off, but he never would. He kept saying that you were a good cop and that you were just going through some tough times."

"He blackmailed me, Lindy. That's the bottom line. He blackmailed me with that footage."

"He could've turned you in, Erin. He should've. But he didn't because he believed in you." Lindy searched her expression, trying to find some kind of humanity there. "Why are you so desperate now?"

"You'll never understand. No. Never. You can't possibly understand."

"Understand what?"

"Understand what it's like to carry the entire family name. I was an only child, and all the expectations were set on top of me." She stood, went to the window, cracked the drapes open a bit as she peered out. "My father thinks that I moved to Chicago for more of a challenge and that I planned to make it all the way to chief. That's what he wanted for me. That was his dream for himself, and then it became his dream for me."

"Does he know about your drinking?"

"One drunk knows another. But it's not discussed." She let the drapes close and turned to stare at Lindy. "Early on, I didn't really think this plan would work. A lot had to fall into place."

"What if it hadn't?"

"You don't want to know." She went to the door, checked the lock. "I'm capable of killing people. I killed someone else in Chicago." She paced the small length of the floor, staring at the carpet as she walked. "A child."

Lindy gasped, then covered her mouth.

"Shocking, right?" Erin asked, pausing a moment to glance at Lindy. Then she continued to pace. "I was pursuing a motorcycle, and I slammed into the back of a car. Killed a three-year-old girl. Annie." Her voice cracked. "Curly hair. Ringlet curls like baby dolls used to have. I laid her on the concrete and tried to revive her but couldn't get her heart started." The small bit of light that was seeping through the crack in the curtains shone against Erin's teary eyes. "She died right there in my arms, with her mother screaming behind me."

"I'm sorry," Lindy whispered.

"So I don't have much to lose, as you can see." Erin sat back down. "I'm below the lowest scum of the earth."

"But haven't you inflicted enough harm?" Lindy chose her words carefully and poured them out with as much compassion as she could feel for this woman. "Let Vance and me help you. What kind of life will you have running from all your mistakes?"

"I am going to be kicked off the police force and probably put in jail. Whatever life I have on the run, it will be worth never having to see that look on my father's face again. And he won't have to have a constant reminder of the enormous disappointment I am to him."

A long pause stretched between them. Then Lindy said, "I get that, you know."

"Get what?"

"I'm a constant disappointment to my mother. She didn't want me to marry a cop. She'd divorced my dad years ago and blamed his career as a cop for all their troubles. When I married Vance, it was like a slap in the face."

Erin raised an eyebrow. "You? Seems like you'd be any-body's perfect child."

"Far from it."

"Vance thought you hung the moon."

"Right."

"You were all he'd talk about some nights when we were on patrol. Lindy this and Lindy that. I was a little disap-pointed when I met you and you weren't wearing a tiara and glass slippers. I think you were wearing a ponytail and no makeup."

Lindy didn't know what to say. She figured all Vance did was gripe to Erin about her. Conner stirred in the bed but went back to sleep. Her instinct was to wake him up, know-ing he wouldn't sleep tonight. But he looked peaceful. She thought it was funny how motherly instincts never waned.

"Vance never recovered, you know. From the sniper case."

Erin shrugged. "I wouldn't know. That's about the time he decided I wasn't worth his time."

"Look, Erin, he was dealing with a lot of pressure at home, and I didn't help matters. I didn't understand how stressful the case had been on him."

"Like he couldn't stand in open spaces anymore."

Lindy nodded, but she hated that Erin knew that. And those were the kinds of things that had kept them arguing well into the night. What Erin knew. What she didn't. On and on it went, until all Lindy could focus on was Erin. It had consumed her.

But her instincts were right. This proved it. Erin was never the innocent woman. She'd had an agenda. Lindy just wished she could've believed more in her husband.

"Well," Erin said, "it's been nice chitchatting with you, but we've got business to take care of."

Lindy's frustration surged. "Vance is going to find us, Erin. He will do whatever it takes."

Erin fingered the small key ring she'd pulled from her pocket. "Vance is in jail, charged with murder. So I wouldn't count on being saved."

27

Biggs said he'd be in touch. Vance was returned to his cell. He'd missed lunch and his stomach rumbled with nerves and hunger.

All he could think about was Lindy and Conner. He wanted so badly to plead with someone, try to convince someone, anyone, that he was innocent and that his wife and child were missing and in danger.

But there was no one. Not even a cell mate. Just him.

"Daddy, I found out that you don't have to kneel. The preacher said you can pray anytime you want. And in your head too. God is a mind reader."

Tears dribbled down his cheeks as he thought of all the

times he'd brushed Conner off, telling him to stop the embarrassing rituals.

"It's not a religion, Daddy. That's what I keep trying to tell you. It's like how you and me talk."

He noticed his hands. His forearms were braced against his knees and his hands were clasped together, his fingers laced between each other, just like Conner prayed. His little boy uttered many prayers with those hands clasped together. White-knuckled, no less, like he was squeezing the prayer out of every pore in his body. His eyes squinted shut like he might be peering through a bright light to see heaven itself.

Vance's stomach rumbled again, and he thought of Lindy and her sandwiches. The Italian beef was his favorite, but she'd never gone wrong on one. He'd never cared for the chicken salad, but he wasn't a fan of grapes, almonds, and mayo together, so that was probably why.

What he wouldn't give for a simple Saturday, outside on a lawn chair, eating a double-decker and watching over his family.

He was supposed to watch over them. Keep them safe.

He stared at his hands for a long time, thinking about the wise counsel his son had given him over the past couple of years. One phrase in particular blew through his mind like a gust of wind. He couldn't remember exactly how it went, but it had something to do with fear and how perfect love casts it away.

It was all he felt in the pit of his stomach. Absolute fear. Total hopelessness.

Vance closed his eyes, though he was not accustomed to it. Normally he liked to keep tabs on everything and everyone around him. He'd gone to church once, sat in the back row because even in church he trusted nobody.

But who was likely to sneak up on him in this jail cell?

At first, he just focused on the black nothingness that stared back at him in his mind. Disbelief. Numbness. Fatigue. But then something stirred inside him. It was deeper than his heart. Wordless but not meaningless. He wanted to reach for it, wanted it to pass through his soul again, but it left as quickly as it came. It was like a whisper that vanished against any sound.

He kept his eyes closed, squeezed his hands, hoped for its return. The blackness was filled with utterances. *Help. Believe. Need. Save.*

And then another whisper, like a thin veil fluttering against the wind. It caused him to breathe deeply. It felt clean and pure, like a cold-water creek left undiscovered in the middle of the woods.

Graegan, stand up.

The words rattled him, yet even as clear as they were, he still could hardly believe he heard them.

Then a clanging metal sound opened his eyes, and he saw an officer standing at his door. Vance stood, offering his wrists.

"No need for that," the officer said, looking sideways at him as he opened the door farther and gestured for him to walk out. Vance obeyed, unsure why protocol wasn't being followed. The officer pointed him to the left, then followed closely behind him. The clanking sounds of the prison faded against the small words in his soul: *I guess prayer does work.*

Vance kept walking, his eyes forward as he'd been instructed. The officer opened a door with a slide of his key card, and another officer escorted him through a second key-guarded door until he was in a hallway that he'd not been in before. He wondered if he was going to the warden. But why wasn't he in shackles?

The officer said, "Sit here. They'll call your name in a second."

"What's going on?" Vance asked, noticing one young man sitting on the bench.

"You don't know?"

"What are you talking about?"

"You posted bail."

"That's impossible. It's a hundred-thousand-dollar bail."

"Graegan. Vance Graegan."

The officer shrugged and nodded toward the woman who sat behind a wall with a square box for a window. "I guess you know some pretty powerful people, then."

The officer turned, and Vance walked to the window.

The woman didn't acknowledge him but seemed to know he was there. Her bored-looking eyes drifted over some paperwork that she was reading line by line. "You Vance Graegan?" she finally asked, still not glancing up.

"Yes."

"All right. Your bail has been posted. You must appear on

your appointed court date, or the city has the right to return you to jail. Do you understand?"

Vance wanted to ask if there might be a mistake, but he figured he should just take this opportunity and run. Literally. He knew mistakes could happen. Twice he'd helped track down fugitives who'd been mistakenly released from jail. He signed the papers she slid through the window.

She smacked her lips together and shook her head. "You don't look rich."

"I'm not," Vance said. He shoved the papers back to her.

She left her desk momentarily and returned with a paper sack. "Here's your stuff. We've included a complimentary white T-shirt since your shirt was confiscated by the police."

The paper sack rattled loudly as she handed it to him.

"There's a changing room down the hall, right before the exit. Please put your prison-issued uniform and shoes in the large basket in the corner of that room. Have a nice day."

Vance took uncertain steps as his rubber-soled flip-flops slapped against the concrete floor. He found the room easily and quickly changed. His jeans were like comfort food, but the white T-shirt was thin and about a size too small.

Minor things to worry about. Right now he just needed to hightail it out of there. He fingered through his wallet. He had about forty dollars cash and his credit cards were still there.

An officer opened the door for him, like he was leaving the Marriott or something. The bright sunlight assaulted him, and he raised his arm for shade.

As his eyes adjusted, he noticed a slick, dark luxury car idling nearby, its windows black as night and reflecting the sun's rays. Its headlights seemed to stare him down.

He stood at the curb, figuring out what he should do. How to get home. He needed his car to try to find Lindy. And his phone was dead. He was going to have to recharge that. He thought he'd call Mr. Biggs, see about having his private investigator help him out.

Thought after thought raced through his head, so many that they seemed to spill right out of his ears.

The door to the black car opened, and an older gentleman with a white goatee, white dress shirt, and silver tie beckoned him. "Vance Graegan." It wasn't a question. This man knew who he was.

"Yes?"

"Get in the car."

"Why?"

The man didn't answer. He slipped back into the car, under the cover of the black-tinted windows.

Vance clenched his teeth and made a smooth walk toward the car. Whoever was in there had to know who they were messing with.

He took a private breath and opened the car door.

28

"You've looked better."

Vance stooped, peering into a car that was nearly foggy with odor spray. The seats were leather. The floor mats spotless.

"Joan?" Vance wasn't sure whom he expected to be in the car, but it certainly wasn't his mother-in-law.

"Get in, get in. You're letting all the air freshener out."

Vance climbed in and was suddenly very aware of how tight his shirt was. He pulled it over his belly a little.

Joan lifted a critical eyebrow. "I see jail time hasn't improved you."

"What is going on? You posted bail for me?"

"Indeed."

"Why? You're the one that called the police on me."

"That's true as well."

"I'm not following."

"No reason you should. You were never as bright as Linda. I told her that, you know, the day before your wedding. I told her you'd always be trying to keep up with her."

Vance looked out the window, biting his tongue. He really just wanted to bite her head off. "Look, I realize I've never been your favorite person. But right now I've got to find Lindy and Conner. They're in a lot of danger."

"Oh yes. We will. You will." She leaned forward. The emotion she always tried to hide glistened mildly in her eyes. "Arnold, to the hotel, please."

"A hotel? Joan, listen to me. They are in danger. Erin is very dangerous. She's lost her mind. I need to go home, get my car, try to track them down."

"You can't go home. It's a crime scene. I mean, technically you can, but you shouldn't."

Vance clutched his jeans at the knees. Frustration was building as it always did when he was around Joan, but it was doubled this time. He tried to calm himself. It wasn't going to help to get mad at Joan. It never did. She was a cool, emotionless woman who was unfazed by harsh words. Mostly her own.

She cracked the window of the car and poked a couple of fingers out. "They didn't let you bathe, dear?"

"Erin visited me at the jail," Vance finally said.

This caught Joan's attention. She looked at him.

"She has Lindy and Conner. She's planning on fleeing to Mexico. But I don't know what she's capable of. She's already killed Karen. And Joe. Joe double-crossed her. But Karen just got in her way."

Joan's default expression of unending disgust changed. She looked worried. "Arnold, please hurry."

"Two minutes out," he replied.

"Why did you post bail for me?" Vance asked.

"I did more than that," she said smoothly. "I hired Conrad Biggs too, or didn't you notice?"

"I noticed. Thank you."

"It wasn't a gift," she said, her words purring against the car noise. "I wanted to know."

"Wanted to know what?"

"If you did it. Killed that woman. Hurt my daughter." A hint of fear warbled in her voice. "And as much as I dislike you, Vance, I decided to take Conrad's advice. That you didn't."

Vance let out a sigh of relief and didn't try to hide it. "I would never hurt Lindy or Conner."

The car turned in to the large half-circle drive of a luxury hotel, at least twenty stories high. A bellhop opened the door and was about to announce a formal greeting when Joan shooed him away and closed the door. "I've read the entire police report—it helps to have friends in high places. I also read the entirety of the notes Conrad wrote up."

"That's confidential information."

"Nothing is confidential when the price is right." She smiled, the jagged wrinkles over her top lip smoothing against the stretching skin. "I've concluded a few things. First, I believe that you were not involved in Lindy and Conner's disappearance."

"You already said that."

"But I do believe you're suffering from post-traumatic stress disorder."

Vance swallowed, looked away.

"I've been a therapist for thirty years, Vance. I know when someone is sick. And by the way, I am not the only one who knew. Lindy suspected it herself."

"Lindy?"

"I am her mother. Daughters confide in their mothers."

Vance looked sideways at her. "You two don't have that kind of relationship."

"Maybe it's unconventional, but she's still my daughter. . . ." Her voice trailed off, and she grabbed a tissue from her purse, poking it to the outside of each eye. "I couldn't live if something happened to her." She sniffled. "And that is why I have given you the full resources you need to find her."

"What are you talking about?"

"Follow me." Joan exited the car gracefully, and Vance followed her through the swooshing gold-plated doors into the lobby. Her long strides carried her across the marble floor and to the elevator, which opened as if it sensed her coming.

They rode to the top floor, twenty-two, and exited straight

into a luxurious suite with two walls of solid windows. It was bigger than his condo.

Vance was startled to find a man sitting on the couch, facing away from him. He instinctively grabbed for his missing gun, just as the man stood and greeted Joan with a handshake.

"Harmon, thank you for meeting us here on such short notice."

"My pleasure."

"This is my son-in-law, Vance Graegan."

Harmon nodded but didn't offer a hand.

"I don't understand what's going on," Vance said. He noticed the dining table. It was covered with all kinds of papers, whereas the rest of the suite looked perfectly tidy.

Joan walked to the table and looked at Vance. "I took the liberty of pulling all the phone records, all the documents, all the paper trails you might need to locate them."

Vance exhaled. He looked at Joan. He couldn't stop the tears that rushed to his eyes. "And Harmon?"

"He's your own private investigator. He cost me a pretty penny, but I hear he's worth every cent. He'll do whatever you need him to do."

Harmon nodded and Vance saw the twinkle in his eyes of a man who loved justice.

"I am going to need a—"

"Gun?" Joan smiled and motioned to Harmon, who reached for a small bag and pulled out a Glock 17. "Done. What else?"

Vance looked at the table. "Time. But I'm afraid we don't

have much." He walked to the glass wall that overlooked Redwood City. "I know one thing. She's still here. And that is her first mistake. It's going to cost her."

"We'll get to that in a minute." She looked at Harmon, who somehow read in her expression a signal that he should move to the other room. "Sit down," she told Vance.

Vance sat at the dining table, eyeing the paperwork, wondering where he should begin, wondering what this delay was for.

Joan slid into a chair, crossing her thin legs at the ankle. "First, you and I have some business to discuss."

"What is this about? I need to get to my wife and son." The words hurt as they came out of his throat.

She picked up a tablet and pen that sat next to her. "Do you have headaches?"

"Pardon me?"

"Headaches, Vance. Surely you don't need a definition."

"What do you need to know that for?"

"Do you or don't you?"

"Yes," Vance said, the word barely escaping his gritted teeth. "Often. Migraines, I think."

"What about anger? Do you feel it constantly?"

"I feel it right now," he said. He ignored her writing notes and grabbed Lindy's phone records. Almost all the calls were to him or to a local number that he assumed was Karen's. Something stood out to him, though. She'd called the Montgomery County Police Department. His police department. There was also another Maryland number that he didn't recognize.

"What about nightmares?"

Vance glanced at her. "Yeah, Joan. Those too. Not every night, but yeah, I relive it sometimes."

"What about when you're awake? Do you see the scenes of those days when you're awake?"

Vance didn't answer. Did he win for having the most intrusive mother-in-law on the planet?

"Vance," she said, and there was actually a twinge of kindness in her voice. Maybe she could muster that up when she was playing therapist. "I need you to look at me. Concentrate on me."

"Why? What is the point of this?"

Her stern eyes narrowed. "Because you're getting ready to go save your wife and son, and PTSD is triggered by stress. I am assuming you're under a great deal of it right now." She put her bony arms on the table and leaned in slightly. "You've got to understand what is happening to you. You're going to have to reason your way out of this illness to stay in reality and find Lindy and Conner. And the only way you'll be able to do that is to grasp what is happening in your mind."

Ironically, a mild headache was shifting around his skull. He looked away. He hated those scrutinizing eyes. "I hear bullets whizzing past my head. It even feels like my hair moves as they go by." He glanced at her. She didn't look startled, which, strangely, brought him some comfort. He moved his gaze to the window, a beautiful scene of redwoods surrounding a bustling city. "I get skull-crushing headaches. I used to feel numb. I couldn't get any emotions to kick in."

"Go on," she said. She'd slid reading glasses on and was peering through them, down her long nose, as she wrote notes.

He didn't want to go on. But he did. The last thing he needed was for her to hound him, and she would if he didn't answer sufficiently. "I still can't stand in open spaces."

"Uh-huh," she said, writing quickly.

He didn't say anything else, and she finally looked up. She waited but he remained quiet. Then she said, "All right. I want to go back to this feeling of a bullet going past you. Tell me more about it."

Vance sighed and wore his disgust heavy on his shoulders as he talked. "Sometimes I hear glass shattering, like the bullet has gone through a window and broken it. Maybe a car window."

"Do you hear anything else?"

"No."

"What about other diversions from reality."

"Like what?"

"Do you hear people? See people?"

"No." But his conscience whispered otherwise.

She wrote some final notes, then took the glasses off her face. "When did all this start?"

Vance stared at the table. "It started about three or four months after we wrapped up the investigation, I guess."

"Did you ever seek professional medical help?"

Vance hesitated. He'd told Lindy he had. It was one of many lies he'd told her that led to the unraveling of their relationship. But he never could understand how talking about what happened was going to relieve him of his pain. The other detectives and officers had seemed to recover fine. He always suspected that this lingered because of the lie he buried, the cover-up he tangled himself in trying to save Erin's career and get her off the bottle.

For a while, the problems seemed to dissipate on their own. His headaches never left, but they happened less frequently. He thought he was getting over it.

"Vance?"

"What?"

"Did you ever seek professional medical help?"

The word felt impossible to speak. "No. I told Lindy that I did, but I didn't. I didn't think I needed it."

Joan's expression morphed from concern to fear. Vance wasn't sure what the trigger was until she said, "I already knew that."

"Then why did you ask me?"

"A woman called me when you first moved here to tell me that very fact."

Vance eyed her, trying to figure out her angle. "What are you talking about?"

"Just what I said. A woman called anonymously, and all she said was that you never went to therapy like you told your wife."

Vance stared through the stark reality that was facing him. "Erin called you."

"I can only assume it is the same woman who took Lindy

and Conner." Joan sighed harshly, the first sign she might be as flustered as he felt. "I played right into her hands. She knew I'd tell Lindy."

"She told me she wanted to disrupt my life. She wanted me to see, feel everything that she's going through."

"How dangerous is she?"

"I never would've believed she was capable of this. But she's killed two people. I think she was sent over the edge by a drunk-driving accident. A child died."

Joan leaned across the table, her posture as straight as if it'd been starched, and her eyes locked on him like he was prey. "You find them, do you understand me? You do whatever you have to do, but you find them."

"I will. Now can I get to it? without interruption?"

"I will see to it you have whatever you need. But, Vance, be aware of your circumstances. Your condition. It is triggered by stress." She then put her purse on the table and pulled out an unmarked pill bottle. She handed it to him.

"What's this?"

"I want you to take these. Morning, noon, night. It will help. It's what we can do in the short term."

"Are these antipsychotic meds?"

"Just take them." She rose, didn't wait for a rebuttal. "Now, I am going to go get you a proper meal." Joan whisked her purse onto her shoulder and walked out the door.

The private detective, Harmon, came back into the room. "Where do you want me to start?"

Vance took a nearby notepad and scribbled some information onto it. "This is the car we're looking for. It's cherry red, and I wrote down the make and model. I don't know the tags. It was Karen's, and Erin took it when she grabbed Lindy and Conner. For all I'm learning about Karen, it may have been stolen to begin with."

"Got it. I'll see what I can find out."

"I'm fairly certain Erin rented a car when she flew here. Find out what you can about that, though I'm certain she's dumped it by now. Also," Vance said, trying to keep his emotions in check, "I need to find out whether Erin bought a round-trip ticket or a one-way."

"Does that matter at this point?" Harmon asked.

"Yeah," Vance sighed. "It will tell me how much she planned on this and what her intentions were. If she bought a one-way, then there's literally no going back for her."

Harmon handed him a cell phone. "Use this. I'll call you as soon as I have any information."

Vance watched him leave and tried to find a place deep within himself where he could push out the fear and focus, be a detective, search for the clues. It was possible, but waves of fear crashed over him every few minutes, when the gravity of the situation weighed on him and he understood the consequences of failure, consequences he knew he could not live with.

He picked up the paper with Lindy's cell phone history. Why would she call his former police station? Maybe she was just getting records. Something simple like that.

Except there was something nagging at him about it.

So he called. He knew who would answer the phone, and he knew she knew everything that went on at the police station. If Lindy talked to her, she would remember and probably know why she had called.

"Montgomery County Police Department."

"Adelle?"

"Vance Graegan, is that you?"

"How'd you know?"

"Honey, I'd recognize that sweet voice of yours anywhere."

Vance smiled, mostly to try to keep his voice light. "Adelle, it's good to hear your voice too. I really miss all of you."

"Of course you do! There ain't nobody like us around, now is there. And I sure enjoyed talking with your beautiful wife the other day too."

Vance tried not to sigh with relief, but this was going better than he expected. "Oh yeah? What was Lindy calling about?"

"Strange, actually."

"Oh?"

"Well, she was wanting to see about how to get ahold of Doug Cantella."

The sounds around Vance disappeared like they'd been sucked into a vacuum, and he felt the pulsing of his blood against his eardrums. "Doug?"

"I know," Adelle said in her singsongy voice. "I guess she hadn't heard that Doug had passed away."

"No . . . I guess not . . ."

"Anyway, how is California? You guys taking over the West Coast one Reuben at a time?"

"Something like that," Vance said, but he was breathless. "Good talking to you, Adelle."

"You too, sweetheart. Where can I direct your call?"

"Andy Drakkard."

"You got it."

But he hung up as soon as Adelle made the transfer. He stood and went to the large window that faced west. His forehead pressed against it, he stared not at the brilliant and beautiful scenery, but at the lie that must've slapped Lindy in the face.

Of course Doug was dead.

Vance swallowed as he thought of Lindy hearing that news. Because Vance had said that he was very much alive.

And lately he was.

He knew of course he wasn't.

But he was.

Vance never wanted Lindy to see him like that. He was her protector, and more than anything he wanted her to feel safe, most especially around him.

He'd fought through a lot of emotional detachment and even rage, which had perhaps been the biggest monster he had to slay.

Mostly, he was okay.

And when he wasn't, he was always able to come back. Sometimes he just needed to slip away to a darker place. The light always looked brighter when he returned. And he'd always been able to return.

Vance walked back to the table. Another Maryland number appeared on her cell phone records. He dialed it, unsure of who might answer the phone.

"Dr. Nancy Sullivan's office."

"Sorry, wrong number." Vance threw down his phone. She knew. She knew! These phone calls pointed to one thing, and that was that his wife really was beginning to discover things about Vance he'd never wanted her to know.

He regretted the lies. So much. And then when he came to the conclusion that he couldn't lie to her anymore, it was too late. She might never know how much he regretted keeping these things from her. And she might die believing that he didn't trust her enough.

It wasn't her that he didn't trust. It was never her. It was always himself. At all costs, he had to get her back. She deserved to live much more than he.

The orange pill bottle stared him down. He opened it. A handful of tiny white pills were crowded at the bottom.

He poured a few into his hand. He needed his mind sharp. And these were certain to have side effects.

But his mind was where he was most likely to be betrayed.

Vance closed his hand around the pills.

His focus spread wide over all the papers. Joan was right. Stress triggered a lot of dysfunction in his mind. Could he stay calm? Could he keep his grasp on reality?

The tarot card glided through his thoughts. Had he imagined the mud flaps?

He tried to focus. That wasn't important now. He had to get his family back. That's all he needed to focus on.

The papers blurred in front of him. His head throbbed with a sudden pain that cracked through his skull like an invisible whip. He squeezed his eyes shut, trying to set aside the pain. He took deep breaths. He had to stay calm. His wife's and child's lives depended on it.

Detach, he told himself. *Try to think like a detective, not like a husband.* He opened his hand and wondered at the tiny white pills. Antipsychotic? Antianxiety?

One pill could relieve him of this. But he was certain his mind would not be as sharp. He'd be lethargic. Sleepy. Still, could he work and fight off his demons, all at the same time?

A nearby trash can caught his eye. He opened his hand again. They were so small.

29

"How much money do you have in your bank account?" Erin sat at the small table in their motel room, stacks of cash piled upon it.

Lindy's anxiety level had risen. Erin had uncuffed Conner, and he was standing next to her, gawking at the cash. It was like he'd forgotten she was the bad guy.

"How much money is this?" he asked. He stuck out a finger, touched one of the piles. Erin smiled at him and that smile made Lindy's stomach roll. It was the smile of manipulation. She was up to something.

"Thousands," Erin said, grinning at him. She took one of the bills from a rubber-banded stack and handed it to him.

"A twenty? Is this mine?"

"Sure. And if you continue to be a good boy, there's more to come."

Conner turned and held out the money to Lindy. "Mom! Look at this. I could buy at least . . . Well, how many, Mom?"

Lindy tried to catch his attention with her eyes. "How many what?"

"Action figures could I buy with this?"

She didn't want to alarm him, but maybe she should. Everything she'd always taught him about taking things from strangers seemed to be flying out the window.

Erin grinned at Lindy, then turned her attention to Conner. "Check out the fridge. There's a Coke in there."

"I'm not allowed to have caffeine."

"Well, I'm making the rules now, and I say you can have all the caffeine you want."

Conner turned and started toward the refrigerator. But Lindy's intense stare seemed to grab him by the chin and turn his face toward hers. When he saw her expression, he stopped dead in his tracks.

"Um . . . I better not." His voice was soft, regretful, but he eyed the refrigerator like he'd just turned down pure gold.

Erin stayed at the table, still counting her cash. "That's too bad. Life's no fun following all the rules."

Conner walked back to the table. "Yeah, I know what you mean. But life's no fun with your mom mad at you, either."

"Good point," Erin said.

Lindy yanked at her handcuff. What was Erin doing now? Trying to bond with her son?

"Tell me how much is in your bank account," Erin said.

"Close to fifteen thousand."

"That's what you were planning to start this big business with? A measly fifteen thousand?"

"I make a heck of a sandwich. Figured word would spread fast. Wasn't planning on a lot of advertising. And we were going to try to get a loan."

"Good for you," she growled. "Luckily Joe and what's her name provided some side cash." She sighed, scraped her fingers through her hair, seemingly thinking hard. "To withdraw your money, you're going to need your ID."

"It's at the house."

"Figured as much."

"The place is swarming with police."

Erin smirked. "Lindy, you still don't get it, do you? The police have their guy. He's in jail. And I'm just here to tell you, when they think the husband did it, they're looking for bodies. They may not say it, but they're thinking it. So yeah, there are cops out looking for you, but they're in the woods and off the highway. And if they ever do put all the pieces together, I'll be long gone. So. We're going to the house tonight after dark. We're going to get your ID. And then we're going to finish up my plan."

"Then are you going to let us go?"

Erin started putting the stacks of money into a black

duffel bag. She never looked up. "I never planned on killing you, Lindy."

Except her words had a haunting echo to them, and the whisper reeked of lies.

Darkness set down, but not before stretching long shadows across the motel room, through the wispy white curtains that hazed any view but let some light in. The sun, like a blood orange, melted into the horizon, and now only a single lamp lit the room.

Conner was still watching cartoons but was fidgety. He rolled on and off the bed, did handstands against the wall, tried to do the splits, all the while focusing on the TV. And that was without caffeine.

Erin was in the shower. The walls were thin and Lindy heard her pull the curtain shut. She hoped she'd be in there a long while.

She could send Conner out of the room for help. She eyed the chain on the door. He probably couldn't reach it, but he could pull over a chair. The dead bolt, though . . . sometimes those were hard to unlock.

"Mom, I'm bored."

"I'm sorry, honey. I'm sorry for all of this." She choked out the words, tried to make it sound like they were just on a long errand. "But we're going to get out of this, okay?"

"We could call the police," he said, pointing to the phone.

"She cut the line."

"Oh." He sighed and threw himself on the bed, grabbing

the remote. "I'm tired of cartoons. I want to watch something else."

Erin hadn't mentioned anything about his turning the channel. And he didn't ask. He just started turning. Lindy sighed and tried to occupy her mind with how they were going to get out of this.

Conner was whizzing through the channels, but something caught her attention. She thought she heard her name. "Conner, wait. Go back."

"To what?"

"Just a few channels. Slowly."

Conner obliged, channel by channel, until they hit the news.

"Stop. Here." She leaned forward. "Turn the volume up, just a little."

The scene was their condo. Police cars parked along the street, lights flashing. Detectives going in and out.

"That's our house," Conner observed, sliding onto his belly.

"Yeah," Lindy said, but she was more tuned in to what they were saying.

"Police have arrested Vance Graegan in connection with the murder of the woman found in the closet and are saying that he is responsible for the disappearance of his wife and son," the report said. "Sergeant Craig Champion said that they are unsure whether Linda Graegan and their eight-year-old son, Conner, are still alive. A source tells us that if they were harmed, it does not appear to have been inside the home." They cut to a shot of both their cars being towed away. Yellow police tape fluttered against the wind.

Lindy gasped as a picture of her and Conner came to view. It was older, maybe two years ago. She had sent it to her mother for Easter.

The shower stopped. The news story didn't. "Vance Graegan is a former police detective from Maryland and is currently out on bail."

Lindy gasped, then covered her mouth. Hope rushed through her. "Conner, we have to pray."

Conner looked away from the news, which had moved on to another story. "You mean it?"

"Yes, yes, sweetheart, I mean it. I'm sorry I didn't listen to you before about prayer. Sometimes adults don't know very much."

Conner grinned. "Well, first you put your hands together."

Lindy laughed as she looked at her hand cuffed to the bedpost.

"Oh," Conner said. "Well, that's okay. You don't have to always do that. But it helps you to concentrate. Do you think you can concentrate?"

Lindy nodded.

"Okay. Then bow your head."

Lindy didn't know what she was expecting when she announced they should pray, but she wasn't sure it was for her little guy to lead the whole thing. Of course, he was way more versed in it than she.

"Dear Lord, we want to thank You for this day . . ."

Lindy peeked, wondering if he could hurry it along. She listened and could hear Erin still in the bathroom.

". . . and thank You for my family. Lord, we ask that You forgive us of our sins . . ."

The toilet flushed. Lindy's eyes flew open. Should she tell Conner to skip to the part where they ask to get rescued?

"And thank You, Lord, that my mom now understands how important prayer is . . ."

"Conner," Lindy whispered, "we need to hurry up, honey, and pray that Daddy can come save us."

Conner opened one eye. It blinked at her. "Mom," he said, exasperated, "you have to always thank God first. That's important. If you don't be thankful, then you miss out on what God's doing. You don't see it."

"But let's pretend we're getting ready to be in a car wreck, and we need God's help fast. Then what kind of prayer do you pray?"

"You don't pray then, Mom," he said. "You just trust that He's there."

Lindy's heart melted with conviction as she saw deep wisdom in that one peering eye. She'd never trusted God. Not one day in her life. She'd never really trusted anybody but herself. She was the only one who could make sure her life didn't fall apart. Except now. And before . . . well, she obviously hadn't been doing that great of a job either.

Lindy nodded. "Okay, we're going to trust God," she said, smiling through proud tears.

The bathroom door opened and Erin walked out, eyeing

both of them as she toweled her hair. "We're leaving in fifteen minutes." She looked at the TV, noticed the cartoons
weren't on.

"Can we rent a movie or something?" Conner blurted.

"Chill out, kid," Erin said. "Things are just about to get
real exciting."

30

"Vance . . ."

The voice was quiet but many, like a thousand people were calling his name all at once, exactly the same way. But then, like a horse at a race, one voice emerged, just a nose ahead of the rest.

"Doug."

"You have to listen to me."

"You can't be here."

"If you don't listen to me, you will never find them."

"That's not true."

"It is true. I've been the voice guiding you, Vance. You know this. You listen to me."

"No."

"We understand each other in a way few others do. We've been through a lot together. We can trust one another."

"I can't trust you."

"You can."

"But you're dead."

"What does that have to do with the price of tea in China?"

"You're dead. You're dead."

"Then why am I standing here?"

A gasp shook Vance's body and he bolted up, blinking into the dimly lit room. His hand covered his chest, which held in a wildly beating heart. He took in air and the comfort of knowing it was just a dream. Doug could show up in his dreams. That was okay. Dead people showed up in a lot of people's dreams.

He must've fallen asleep at the table.

Nearby, Joan moaned and mumbled but stayed asleep, curled up in a corner of the couch, her legs tucked beneath her, her spiked heels having fallen off her feet and to the floor. He checked his watch. A little after 2 a.m. Harmon was out tracking down a lead. He'd heard someone had tried to sell a red Cadillac at a nearby car dealership.

Vance looked at the table before him. With all the white laid down over it, it looked like Christmas snow had fallen. Except it felt more like Halloween. Everything haunted him. Each piece of paper seemed to laugh wickedly, giving small clues leading only to dead ends.

He stood and paced the room, trying to get the blood stirring in his brain. It seemed a horrible irony that the detective couldn't find his own family. He knew Erin was smart and that she'd covered her tracks well, but one thing he knew about criminals—especially desperate ones— was that eventually they made a mistake. It usually came from impatience. Or desperation. And it usually involved money.

He rubbed his eyes. His mind was still aching for sleep. He'd slept little in the past seventy-two hours and it was starting to affect him. Objects in the room came in and out of focus. But he couldn't sleep. Time was wasting.

He tried to ponder Erin's motivation. So she wanted to disrupt his life. That was done. What else did she want? She'd not planned on Joe's double-crossing her, and from there, Vance suspected, things got out of control quickly.

But how desperate was she? How far was she willing to go?

Vance went to the bathroom and splashed his face with cold water. As he rose and grabbed a towel, he heard a voice say, *Go to the house.*

He turned, eyeing the room for any sign of Doug. But nobody was there. Water dripped off his face as he clutched the sink. What *was* that?

Then, right outside the bathroom, he heard movement. He yanked open the door.

Joan yelped and fanned her face, her eyes blinking rapidly. "Good grief, Vance. Trying to scare a barely aging woman to death?"

"Sorry . . ."

"In a polite world, one normally just opens the door at a minimal speed. Why is there a need for yanking?"

"Did you say something?"

"Obviously you don't live in a polite world."

"No, I mean . . . sorry, obviously you said something. But before. Before I opened the door. Did you say something?"

Joan peered at him with those narrow eyes, like a door barely cracking open. "No, Vance, I did not say anything. I don't shout out things in the middle of the night. That might startle someone and that would be impolite."

Vance moved past her, out of the space where she seemed to suck all the air from the room. The drowsiness was lifting. Nothing like the threat of a mother-in-law to slap some life back into you.

She followed him to the living area. "What have you found?"

"Harmon is checking on a lead right now, word of a Cadillac being sold."

"That's good, correct? It will give us something to go on?"

Even through her piercing features and scrutinizing words, Vance could see a mother's worry.

"Yes, yes. That's a very good lead." He emphasized each word and could see her brighten right before him. "I'm going to need your car."

"My driver can take you wherever you need to go."

"Not everywhere." He made a bold move and put a hand on her shoulder. He felt her shudder. "Joan, if you want your daughter and grandson back, you're going to have to trust me. I've got to go back to the house."

* * *

"Hurry up," Erin hissed. The house would've been pitch-black had it not been for the full moon spilling its light through the curtainless windows.

"I'm trying," Lindy said. She'd hidden her wallet in the house somewhere, just in case Joe tried to break in and take it. But now she couldn't remember exactly where she'd put it.

"Hey, kid. No. Stand right here."

Conner began to wail and Lindy jerked upright to see what was going on.

"Kid, shut up, for crying out loud."

"I just want my toys!"

Lindy hurried over. "Erin, let him have some of his toys. They're in his bedroom."

"Shut up. Go look for the wallet."

"Listen to me. Kids are kids, and he could throw a big fit right here and not care the least bit that you have a gun, so if I were you, I'd let him go grab some of his toys."

Erin eyed Conner, whose big eyes puppy-dogged their way through the darkness.

"Fine. Go, kid. What are you, five? Get a couple of things."

Conner started to race to his room, but Lindy grabbed his elbow and walked him down the hallway and around the blood.

"Now," Erin said, "hurry it up. And I swear if you are messing with me—"

"I'm not," Lindy said, scraping hair out of her face. "I just don't remember where I put it."

Lindy went back to the kitchen and searched through the drawers. She watched Erin pace the length of the hallway, glancing into Conner's bedroom and monitoring him for a moment before coming back to the kitchen.

"The police are looking for you," Erin suddenly said.

Lindy looked up. But it didn't appear Erin was talking to her.

"They're watching this house." That was true. They'd spent an hour waiting to see how often a patrol car drove by. Once in an hour.

So instead of coming through the front, Erin had them come in from the back, through the woods behind their house.

"They'll be monitoring your credit cards, your ATM card . . ." Erin shook her head, pacing again. She went to check on Conner, then returned. "This wasn't the plan. I wanted money. I just wanted money." She glanced at Lindy, who was frozen as she listened to her. She gestured with the gun. "Get to looking."

Lindy suddenly remembered. She'd hidden it behind the paper plates in the pantry. She hurried over, reached to the back, and found it. "Got it."

Erin turned, her expression relaxing at the news for just a moment. She walked over and snatched it from Lindy's hands. She fingered through the cards, pulled out the cash, which was only fifty or so dollars, and pocketed it.

"This is never going to work." She clawed at her cheek, her eyes darting to one thing after another in the house. Lindy hadn't seen her this nervous. So far she'd played it very cool. "I'd planned on you getting the money out, but that was before they thought you were kidnapped and possibly killed by your husband. They're watching him, but they'll find me if I don't handle this right." She cursed, shoving the wallet into her bag. "We need to get out of here. I need to think."

Lindy stood next to her, watching her coolness unravel right before her eyes. She wasn't sure if an unstable Erin was better or not. Which one could be better played?

"It's under the company name," Lindy said.

"What?"

"The money. The fifteen thousand." She glanced at Erin, whose eyes were frantically oversize. "You have to have two signatures to withdraw money. Mine and Vance's."

Erin cursed again.

"We do have about eight hundred dollars in our regular checking, though." Lindy almost smiled at the statement. She knew that was far less than Erin was expecting. If she couldn't get what she wanted from them, maybe she'd just go.

"Go get your kid," Erin growled, pushing her with the side of the gun.

Lindy stumbled forward, taking soft steps down the hallway. The blood on the floor was now dark, nearly black, but the moonlight caused it to look a little wet. She stepped around it and found Conner in his room on the floor. He was playing with his Etch A Sketch by the blue light of the moon. Lindy smiled at the scene, took it in. For just a moment, all things in their world were right again.

"Okay, buddy, we have to go."

"I don't want to."

"Me neither."

"I hate that room we're in. Are we going back to that room?"

"I think so." She wanted to take a step in but knew Erin was watching her, and if she disappeared, Erin would freak out. "Why don't you grab three or four toys, okay?"

"Okay, Mom."

She studied him, proud of this sudden maturity that had fallen upon him. She watched him grab two books, a puzzle, and one action figure.

"Sweetie, why don't you bring your Etch A Sketch?"

"Don't want to."

"But it's your favorite toy."

"I want to leave it here."

Lindy sighed. Sometimes he was a mystery. If anything could pass the time well, it would be an Etch A Sketch.

"It needs to be here so when I come home, I'll have it." He whispered, "I don't want Meanie in there to steal it, if you know what I mean."

Lindy chuckled. She loved this kid. "I know what you mean. Let's go." She steered him once again down the hallway.

Erin was waiting, but she still looked panicked. "Maybe the ATM. We could withdraw quite a bit before they figured it out." She was mumbling as if nobody else were in the room. She looked up like she'd forgotten about them.

"I don't have an ATM card to the company. Only to the personal."

Suddenly Erin cackled, throwing her head back. It shot out of her mouth so fast, Conner actually jumped right to his mother's side. "This is just *great.*"

"Erin, listen to me. You've got money. Leave us here. Just take my credit cards, take the ATM. Get as much as you can and get out of here. Run to wherever you're going."

"*We're* going." Her tone was cool again.

"Where?"

"I'm going to take you wherever I need to take you to make sure I get what I want." She lowered her voice, stepped close to Lindy. "And let me assure you, I will get everything I want."

* * *

Vance drove Joan's sleek black Escalade out of the hotel parking garage, scanning his mirrors to see if he was being tailed. He wasn't even sure if the police knew where he was. He was ordered not to leave the county. But he was never told not to go home.

It took him twenty minutes by highway to get to the condo. Traffic was sparse in the middle of the night. He opened the sunroof and let the cool night air drift into the car. The wind canceled out a lot of the other noise in his head.

But no matter what, he couldn't clear his mind of images of Lindy and Conner. Squeezing around all the good memories, drifting like a snake through water, was the idea that those might be all he had left. He tried not to think about it. And then, when he could think of nothing else, he tried to reason that Erin was not a vicious killer. She'd slaughtered Karen and had executed Joe, but somehow he managed to convince himself that she wouldn't do that to his family.

They had history. Some bad. A lot good. He had good memories of the fun times they shared on patrol, the pranks they played, the endless stories of how they Turner and Hooched their way through calls. If a cop didn't have a billion funny stories, he should practically hang up his badge.

They had good stories. But frankly, they were all marred the day Erin couldn't set down the bottle.

He wondered how she was faring with that. Was she passing out drunk? Was she driving around with them, drinking her way through stoplights?

He tried to breathe slowly. He needed to keep the stress down, but the dull ache that climbed up his skull reminded him he was not doing a good job.

When he arrived at the house, he drove by slowly, looking for anybody staking it out. Nothing seemed out of the ordinary except the yellow crime scene tape wrapped around anything that stood upright.

Bet the neighbors love that.

It was a stark reminder of how his life had fallen off a cliff.

He circled back around the block and pulled into the driveway, turning off his lights so he wouldn't alert the neighbors that someone was there. He knew, by law, he had every right to be at his house, but he didn't want to draw attention to it.

All the lights inside the condo were off. He took out his keys and unlocked the front door. The air conditioner was set cold, and the temperature change gave him pause. He quietly shut the front door behind him and wondered if he should turn on the lights.

Maybe not. The moon cast an eerie, cold light across the floor of the living room. As his eyes adjusted, he noticed a large cross spanning the carpet. He couldn't take his eyes off it. He blinked, wondering if he was imagining it. It seemed like a sign. His gaze wandered upward, and he saw the window, its panes the source of the mysterious image.

A supernatural sign it was not. But still, he stepped delicately around the cross as he wandered toward the kitchen. He stood there for a long moment, wondering if he was truly going mad. Why was he here? Because he thought he heard a voice telling him to go? What was he, Moses now?

He was glad the ridiculousness was his own private misery. He already had a mother-in-law who thought he was half-crazy. He didn't need people thinking he was hearing things.

But it had been so clear. Like someone had been standing right behind him.

Sometimes the bullet whizzing past his ear sounded real.

Too real. And then glass shattering. So how could he know what was real and what wasn't?

He leaned against the counter, held his head in his hands, rubbed his temples, tried to think. Where would Erin take them? What was her purpose for holding them?

Then he heard a noise.

31

Vance pulled his gun.

Bang. Like the sound of a door or a cabinet closing. It wasn't loud, but in the silence of the dead house, it was enough to get his attention.

It sounded again. He turned, following it, stepping lightly, his gun guiding the way. He had a clear view of the living room and kitchen thanks to the moonlight. The hallway, though, was darker.

He listened. Again. It was coming from the back of the house. He wondered if he should check the bedrooms first, but the sound beckoned him. He turned the corner and aimed his gun toward the back door.

Everything seemed calm and quiet. He lowered his gun cautiously and focused on the noise, which led him directly to the door. It was slightly open, and the wind was catching the screen and then funneling through it to pull and push the wooden door against the frame.

Why would the back door be open?

A crime scene was typically locked down well. No police force wanted to be blamed for a burglary because they forgot to lock the doors when they left, assuming the doors were still on the hinges.

He slowly opened the door and pushed the screen outward, raising his gun again. The backyard was small and normally dark, thanks to a streetlight that had been out since they arrived. The moonlight glowed against the grass, though, and he could see fairly well. Everything looked in its place.

But the door hadn't been closed, and that bothered him. The detective in him told him to pay attention to it. So he did. He walked out into the grass, eyed everything he could, tried to find another thing out of place.

He tried to use all his senses like Doug had taught him. He listened. He heard normal street traffic and the creaking, brushing sounds of the high-away limbs of the redwoods. He smelled only pine and freshly cut grass and the hint of salt from the ocean.

With a deep heaviness, he turned and walked back to the condo, thinking about the cross that was laid out before him. It had even seemed to point to the back door. But here he was again, with nothing to help him.

He trudged up the first of two steps that led to the small porch. His foot slipped slightly, as if he'd hit a lone piece of gravel. He stepped back and looked down. But it wasn't gravel.

Stooping, he set his gun near a flowerpot and scooped the ring into his hand. He turned so he had the light of the moon beaming down onto it.

It was Lindy's wedding ring.

Vance laughed out relief. This was it. The clue he needed. The back door. Her ring on the porch. She was trying to tell him she was still alive, that they'd been to the house. The crime scene folks would've found this had it been left earlier.

But when? How long ago?

Vance clasped it in his hand. The metal soothed him. He squeezed it and thanked God. It felt weird to thank God. He'd never done so, though he watched his son do it every time he ate a meal. Or even a snack. Vance would close his eyes, or at least pretend to out of respect, but mostly he was annoyed that he had to wait while his son performed the ritual.

But right now, he was sure he'd never been so thankful for something in his life. It was like a little seed of hope planted right in his heart.

And he realized something. The ring wasn't cold as metal would become if it were sitting out through the night. It was still warm.

She'd been here recently.

If Lindy had left this clue, maybe she'd left others. He started to hurry up the steps, then looked back at the woods. Maybe he should try the woods. Maybe they went that way.

His indecision was interrupted.

"Freeze."

* * *

Erin had rehandcuffed Lindy. She wasn't sure why, but she hated that she couldn't hold Conner's hand as they plodded through some thick brush. She hadn't been back here. The sign against the fence in their yard indicated it was private property and to keep out. From what she could tell, it was dense but not long, a patch of land preserved among all the development.

But walking through it at night, it seemed to go on forever.

Maybe it was because Erin appeared to be unraveling right before her eyes. She was talking to herself, spilling out her plan to the trees and bushes and dirt. She marched ahead, glancing back often to make sure they were behind her.

Lindy had already tripped twice and couldn't brace herself for the fall very well. Her elbow was bleeding.

Conner was concerned about it, but Lindy played it off. "It makes me look tough, right?"

"You need a Band-Aid," he said sternly.

"We'll get one, sweetie. No worries. It doesn't even hurt," she lied.

For much of the walk, Conner was engrossed by the forest, staring straight up through the trees to get glimpses of the bright, starry night. Patches of moonlight guided their way. Lindy couldn't imagine doing this without the moonlight. It was haunting and comforting all at once.

She played with her ring finger. She couldn't remember the last time she'd taken her ring off. She slept with it. Showered with it. Gardened with it. She knew it was a long shot when she casually, quietly dropped it on the porch as they left. She also hadn't pulled the door completely shut, and Erin had been so distracted by her money situation that she didn't even notice.

Then she prayed that the ring would be found. If anyone could find it, it would be Vance. Once, before Conner was born, he'd found her contact on a stark white floor, and an earring back at a restaurant when she wasn't even sure where she'd dropped it. He had an eye for detail and for things out of place. That's what she loved about him and what sometimes drove her absolutely crazy.

Erin suddenly stopped talking. Midsentence. And it was just as alarming as all her babbling. Conner noticed and glanced at Lindy, who tried to convey to him through her expression to stay calm.

Then Erin stopped walking and they stopped too.

"What's wrong?" Lindy asked.

She didn't answer. She was looking up, just like Conner had been. Lindy did too, wondering what she was staring at. It was a beautiful sight as the wind danced through the tree limbs, tickling the leaves. The three of them stood there for a long moment, in the silence of Mother Nature.

Then Erin looked at Lindy. "I have my plan."

Lindy tried to lock eyes with her. "Does it include letting us go?"

"You're going to rob a bank."

"What?"

"You heard me."

"You're crazy."

"Not really. It's the only plan that's going to get me enough money to get out of here."

"I won't do it."

"Really." Her dark gaze set on Conner.

Lindy tried not to let it rattle her. Even through the darkness, she could see the desperation in Erin's eyes. She was running out of time. She couldn't take them very many places without their being recognized. But having Lindy rob the bank would certainly put a new twist on the investigation. It would distract the police long enough for Erin to get wherever she wanted to go.

Erin's hard stare was back on Lindy. "You know what I'm going to say."

"If you hurt him . . ."

"I know, I know. You'll hunt me down and kill me. But will that be before or after his funeral?"

Lindy's glare was cut short by her worry over what Conner was hearing. She looked at her son and it was obvious that he understood. The toys he'd brought from home were clutched tightly to his chest. He stared at Erin as if he finally realized how dangerous she really was. Before, she was just a woman who handcuffed his mom and brought them chicken tenders and let him watch cartoons.

Erin pulled Lindy closer to her. "I will do anything to keep from going to jail. Do you understand me? I'll say it again. I have nothing to lose."

Conner suddenly spoke. "God loves you, miss."

"Conner, honey, shhh."

"She needs to know this." His eyes gleamed against the moonlight and shifted back to Erin. "And He forgives all sorts of things. You can't do anything that He can't forgive."

"Conner, sweetie—"

"Let the kid talk," Erin said, hands on her hips, looking down on Conner.

"I've been praying for you, you know," Conner said, not backing down from her hard stare. "You're a bad lady."

With the speed of a snake strike, Erin slapped Conner across the cheek. The pop against his skin shot through the night's darkness. Conner fell to the ground, his toys flying through the air and landing nearby.

Just as fast, Lindy pounced on Erin, knocking her down. With the full force of a mother's rage, Lindy threw down a blow against her cheek with the sharpest part of her knuckles, but it was hampered by the cuffs. A burning pain shot through her hand as their bones clashed. A long line of blood trickled down Erin's face, and her eyes widened with a madness that caught Lindy's breath in her throat. With what seemed like one continuous move, Erin threw Lindy off her body, onto the ground, and drilled her knee into Lindy's shoulder.

Erin yanked her head back by the hair. Her fist pushed hard into Lindy's spine.

Lindy yelped. "Stop it . . ."

"Stop it? You want me to stop it? I should just kill you right now."

"Stop!" Conner's tiny voice was thin with fear. "Don't hurt my mom."

"Shut up, kid."

"No! Don't hurt her!"

Lindy tried to turn her head so she could get a glimpse of Erin. "Listen to me. He is getting ready to get hysterical. And he's going to start screaming."

"Not if I can help it," she growled, pinning Lindy's shoulder down even more.

Her eyes welled up from the fiery pain shooting through her back. "Erin, don't do this. Please. He's just a kid. He didn't know what he was saying."

"He knew exactly what he was saying." Erin lifted her knee off Lindy's back and gave a slight release to her shoulder. "And he's right."

Lindy lowered her head, her cheek set against sharp twigs and small rocks in the ground. Adrenaline caused her entire body to quiver as she waited to see what Erin would do. She was ready to tear her own limb out of the socket to keep Conner safe. And a mother could throw a gorilla off her back if she had to.

She couldn't see Conner, but she could hear him crying

nearby. She wanted to scream, *Run!* She was pretty sure a fast kid like Conner could beat Erin through the woods.

But not quite sure enough.

"I'll do it," Lindy said, clenching her teeth through the pain. "I'll get you the money."

Erin climbed off her. Her fingers clawed into Lindy's arm as she grabbed her and hauled her to her feet.

Conner raced over to her. "Mom, I am so sorry." He buried his face in her side. "I said a mean thing and then you got hurt."

Lindy ran her fingers through his hair, stroking his little face. "No, it's not your fault. It's not your fault at all." She eyed Erin, who was pressing the back of her hand against the cut on her cheek, then looked down to make sure Conner was all right. His left cheek looked like it was swelling a little bit. "Are you okay?"

"I'm fine, Mom," he said, but he was clutching her shirt so tightly, Lindy thought it might rip.

Erin gestured with her gun, which she'd pulled from her waistband. "Let's go. And, little man, no more trouble from you. You don't want your mom to get hurt, now do you?"

Conner quietly, submissively, gathered his toys. It broke Lindy's heart.

They continued forward, and Lindy could only think about that ring and pray that Vance found it. Her finger felt naked without it, and she realized the power it symbolized. They were together, even though separated. And they'd stuck together even when everything fell apart.

He rescued her when she didn't realize it. Everything they'd been through together had changed her. She saw clearly now. She understood his struggles, understood her own.

What she wouldn't give for one more chance to say, "I love you."

So she whispered it to Conner instead.

* * *

Vance slid the ring onto his pinkie and raised his hands slightly. The voice was male. And sounded somewhat young. His radio crackled. A cop.

"Officer, this is my house."

"I'm going to need to see some identification."

Vance turned slowly, lowered his hands as he watched the officer lower his gun. He glanced down, toward the flowerpot, to see if his firearm was visible as he handed over his wallet. He definitely didn't have the papers to be carrying a gun. "I need to get a few things. Check on my property." Vance looked hard at him, keeping the kid's attention on him. "Which is my right."

"Let's step inside," the officer said. He couldn't have been more than twenty-five years old.

They walked through the back door and into the kitchen. Vance switched on a light. He wanted to see as much as possible, see if another clue had been left.

The officer took out his cell phone. "I'm going to call my supervisor. Just stay right here."

Vance eyed everything, looking for anything that would point to them.

"Yeah, this is Carter. I've got a guy here, says he's Vance Graegan. . . . Yeah, at the house. . . ."

Vance tuned the conversation out and focused. The closet door where Karen was found was still open. There was blood on the floor. The front door had been locked . . . Maybe Lindy had her keys, but it seemed more likely that they'd come and gone through the back. He hadn't installed the new lock on the back door yet, and the old one would've been easy enough to pick.

The woods. They'd fled through the woods. Probably parked half a mile away.

There was a convenience store, two of them, near where the woods ended and more commercial property started. Maybe someone would remember seeing them come out and get into a car or would have noticed a car parked at the curb.

". . . yeah, to get a few things, he said."

"Clothes, some food," Vance said. He knew he had the right to be there. He was only charged. Not convicted. He figured the supervisor was probably telling the kid to go get the tag numbers off his vehicle.

"All right, sir. . . . Yes . . . Thanks." He hung up the phone and turned to Vance. "Sorry for the inconvenience," he said, handing the wallet back. He eyed him, the nearby living room, then walked out the front door.

Vance wanted to shout at this kid, tell him that he knew

his wife was still alive and had probably gone through the back woods just recently. But he knew it was useless. He was their suspect. They weren't going to look for anyone else.

He watched through the window as the officer took out his pad and wrote down the tag numbers before climbing back into his squad car. So much for being inconspicuous.

He then hurried through the house. Yeah, he needed clothes, but that wasn't his concern. He wanted more clues. He went to their closet, grabbed a duffel bag, and stuffed a couple of pairs of jeans and some shirts in. Lindy's clothes did not look like they'd been touched. So why had they been here? What would be the reason for returning?

Something from the crime scene, maybe. Something Erin had left that would link her to it?

What else? Money. Maybe she thought they had money stashed. They didn't.

Guns. Maybe Erin needed more weapons.

He dug through the back of their walk-in closet to his gun safe. It was open, and the guns were gone, but there was a better chance that the police took them for their investigation to see if any of the guns matched the one used to kill Karen.

His mind trailed back to the money again. He wondered if Lindy had her wallet with her when she was kidnapped. If not, maybe that's why Erin had returned. She wanted credit cards. ATM cards. It would be a stupid move to use them. The police would be tracking those very things to search for Lindy and Conner.

But if she was desperate enough for money . . .

Lindy had become paranoid of a break-in at the house, so she'd been hiding her wallet various places. The last time she'd hidden it, he was pretty sure it was in the pantry. He hurried there and looked but found nothing. He wasn't sure what that meant, but maybe it was something.

He looked through everything in the bathroom to see if there was anything misplaced. Lindy's toothbrush was there. Her hairbrush. Makeup.

Vance sighed. There didn't seem to be anything else to find. He walked out of the bathroom and stopped at Conner's room. His books and toys were spilled across the empty room on the carpet. The tent was still erected.

His heart ached to smell Conner's little boy smell, a mix of sweat and warmth and sugar cereal. He missed his smile. His giggle. He gazed down at the small pile of books and toys and noticed Conner's Etch A Sketch. How was he surviving without it? He was probably asking for it constantly, wherever he was.

He knelt and picked up the Etch A Sketch. Tears trickled down his face, knowing how much his son was missing this toy. He studied the drawing, which filled up the entire gray window.

There was writing at the top, sloppy but pretty good cursive for his age.

Dad help.

Vance peered harder at it. Was that what it said? *Dad, help?*

He traced the lines of the drawing. He wasn't sure what it was. There seemed to be a train or something and then a building.

At the bottom right-hand corner were more words. *Yucky hotel.*

Conner was trying to tell him they were at a hotel! A run-down one. But the train . . . ? Maybe it was a hotel by train tracks. A motel more likely. Vance studied the drawing. Yes, the doors were on the outside of the building that Conner drew.

Vance took the Etch A Sketch, careful not to shake it, and grabbed his duffel bag. Back in his car, he reversed out of the driveway.

He turned north. There were railroad tracks by the warehouse where he'd found Joe. He could follow those.

He squeezed his hands together over the steering wheel, and he knew God had heard his desperate plea for help. He'd answered with an Etch A Sketch.

32

In his patrol days, Vance used to get a kind of high off the adrenaline surge while en route to a call. The siren wail against the city noise. The engine's roar. Yet he glided effortlessly around cars, like wind around skyscrapers.

But this was different. There was no high. The headache had returned with a vengeance. He could hardly see straight. He leaned forward on the steering wheel just so the white lines of the road would come into focus.

The railroad spread for miles, but he had an extra clue. *Yucky.* That was probably the most important piece of the puzzle. He would be looking for a motel in a lower-income part of town.

The sun was rising. Brilliant orange. And giving enough light to help him figure out where to start. He'd passed by a business district, a shopping district, and a lot of housing, but nowhere that seemed to be a place a motel might be located.

A train passed him, its long trail of cars rumbling loudly in the quiet morning air. Normally it might be mesmerizing. He always liked trains. But not this morning. Its whistle sounded like a shrieking seagull.

If he could just shake the headache.

The bullet. Then the shattering glass.

No . . .

Stay here. Don't . . . just don't . . .

He listened and the phantom sounds stopped. He diverted from the railroad. Nearby were slum houses, and he thought he might find motels nearer to the city. But his head hurt.

He pulled over. The entire road was blurry. His phone rang as he parked against a curb and closed his eyes. "Yeah?"

"It's Joan. Where are you?"

Vance paused. He was unsure how much to tell Joan. She was known to overreact, like calling the police at the wrong time. "Following a lead."

"Please tell me you've found something substantial."

"I have."

"What's wrong? You sound different."

"My head . . . it's killing me."

"Migraine. Possibly a cluster headache. Did you take those pills I gave you?"

"Yes." He was tired of lies. But he could live with it if he didn't have to hear his mother-in-law gripe at him.

"Vance? Vance!"

"What?"

"Vance, what happened?"

"What do you mean?"

"I've been saying your name over and over. You weren't responding to me."

Vance blinked. She had? He thought they'd just been in a conversation. Had he blacked out?

"I'm here. I think the phone is getting bad reception." But he was shaken. He'd lost a small chunk of time.

"I'm going to see about getting you some migraine medication."

"Okay. That would be good." Even talking was excruciating. But he couldn't stop looking for them. He knew he wouldn't stop, not to go all the way back and get some meds.

The migraine would lift. It always did. But usually he had to sleep for a while. "Have you heard from Harmon?"

"Yes. He got word of a woman and child up north. They'd stopped at a convenience store off the highway. They fit the description of Lindy and Conner, though the cashier was pretty vague about the details of what they were wearing. Harmon thought it was worth checking out."

"All right," Vance said, though he wished he had Harmon nearby. They could cover more ground that way. "Have him call me as soon as he can, okay?"

"Certainly. And please call me when you have more information."

Vance hung up and gripped the steering wheel, resting his forehead against it. He closed his eyes and it offered temporary relief. But not enough. The pain was nearly unbearable.

He sat up a little and tried to open his eyes, focus on the road. Finally everything stopped spinning, though nothing came into focus easily. But he had to press forward.

He pulled away from the curb and prayed for relief.

*　*　*

Lindy tried again for sleep, but she was often yanked away by fear like a kite that couldn't be reeled in. Conner was sleeping soundly when Erin rose from the chair she'd fallen asleep in.

Sometime before dawn, she'd finally stopped her babbling. The entire kidnapping incident had been terrifying, but what Lindy saw out in the woods scared her the most. Erin was losing control. She wasn't thinking clearly, and the underlying rage that Lindy thought was there all along finally reared its ugly head. Lindy still couldn't believe she'd slapped Conner. Her little boy's cheek burned pink from it. Her own shoulder ached from being pulled off the ground.

Lindy pretended to be asleep but carefully watched Erin move around the room. She was busy, but Lindy couldn't really figure out with what. She was on her computer, then would write something down, then would get something out of her duffel bag.

She walked over to Lindy's bed and stood above her. Even with her eyes closed, Lindy could feel her shadow crossing the bed as she blocked the dawning light.

"Get up."

Lindy opened her eyes. Erin unlocked her hand and threw the cuffs on the bed. Her demeanor was different, like the subtle change of the air right before a storm arrives. But her expression remained neutral. "Sit up. We've got to get prepared."

Lindy obeyed, though her body ached from fatigue and from being pummeled. Erin took her laptop off the table and brought it over to the bed. She pulled up a chair, then glanced around Lindy at Conner. It was all Lindy could do not to shove her.

"I'd like to only have to say this once," Erin said, her voice quiet. "And I'm saying it now so I don't have to say it with him awake. I think you will appreciate that gesture."

Lindy nodded, trying to be as compliant as possible.

"If you don't do exactly as I say, you're never going to see your little boy again."

Those words caused tears to gather in Lindy's eyes. She pressed the back of her hand against her cheek, trying to stop them. She gazed at Erin, trying to find an ounce of humanity in her. "Erin," she whispered, "I know you're desperate. I get that. But I can't see you deliberately killing a child. I know there was the accident, but that wasn't your fault . . ." Lindy tried not to look away, though that lie stung all the way up her throat. Of course it was her fault. But if she could just get Erin to see this in a different way. "Look at that little boy over there," she continued, still wiping the tears. "You're telling me that you're going to kill him? You are actually going to do that?"

Erin stared at Conner for a long time, then with one shift of the eyes was staring at Lindy. "Who said anything about killing him?"

"What do you mean?"

"I'm not going to kill him," she said, her mouth curving into an unsettling smile. "I'm going to take him."

Lindy lost her breath. "What?"

"With me. To Mexico or South America or wherever it is I decide to go. You'll never be able to find me, Lindy. Or him." She fingered the sleeve of her shirt. "It would be horribly ironic, me raising Vance's child, acquiring his greatest possession."

Conner stirred.

"What do you want me to do?"

"There is a bank about eight blocks from here. It's been robbed twice in the last twenty-four months." Erin pulled the laptop closer, brought up a picture of it. "It's in a poor neighborhood, so it probably can't afford a security guard. And if it does have one, they'll bring him in during high-traffic times, like in the afternoon or on the first or fifteenth, when many people get paid. It's also close to the highway and far from the police station. This is our target." She tapped her finger against the screen of the laptop.

Lindy studied the picture. It was a simple, free-standing

building that looked newer than some of what she'd been able to observe nearby.

"We're going to wait until some of the morning traffic has subsided. Once people are at work, around nine thirty, we'll strike."

"I don't know what I'm doing, Erin."

"You're going to learn. Fast. Basically," she said, "the people behind that counter have to believe that you're willing to shoot them for what they have in their trays."

"I can't shoot anybody . . ."

Erin glanced at Conner, then back at Lindy. "I'm certain you'll do what you have to do to get your boy back." She rose and went to her duffel bag, pulling out a gun and a ski mask. "This is a Glock." She lifted it.

Lindy nodded, wide-eyed, but she already knew that.

"I'm going to teach you how to use this, so pay attention."

Lindy watched, but she already knew that too.

* * *

His stomach grumbled with hunger, then swirled with nausea. Any need his body felt was canceled out by utter desperation. If he had to run faster, he would. If he had to lift the heaviest object, he could. But this . . . chasing after a ghost . . . was unbearable. He was grasping at thin air. There seemed to be nothing he could do to speed things along.

Vance ignored two calls from Joan. He had nothing to report. As he drove up and down streets, gazing at every building, he felt sorrow for the fact that even the police wouldn't help him. If he had their resources, he knew he could find them. Probably within fifteen minutes.

But it was just him.

Yucky hotel.

He pictured Conner in the room, turning the Etch A Sketch knobs, not giving up hope that his daddy would find him.

Tears streamed down his face, causing an already-blurry road to fade like a watercolor. And his skull felt like it was being crushed by a vise.

But he drove. And he drove.

And then . . .

A motel.

It sat close to the road with a circular, covered drive. Tattered vinyl, green and scalloped, hung over it, probably fancy in better times.

The front doors were glass, dirty as if they'd not been cleaned for years. There were a few rooms facing the road, but it looked like most were on the side and back.

Vance turned in and parked in one of the spaces. He tucked his gun into his waistband and slowly got out, taking in everything. Only two other cars were parked in the front. He studied them. Nothing stood out to him.

There were two breezeways, one on each side of the motel. He took the one on the right. The sidewalks were cracked and weed infested. The breezeway led to the center court-yard, which featured an empty pool with chairs and tables still around it. Dusty umbrellas. Overgrown grass snaked through a small white fence.

He searched the doors of the rooms, looking for movement. All was quiet, as if hardly anyone was here.

He walked through another breezeway that led to the back of the hotel. As he rounded the corner, he lurched to a stop.

The red car. Karen's red car.

The police most likely didn't even have a record for her driving that car if it had been stolen and retagged. He slowly walked toward the parking lot so he could get a good view of the rooms. There was nothing to hide behind. He had to hope that he would be graced with the element of surprise. But first he had to figure out which room they were in.

Hope drifted around him like the faint scent of wildflowers. But then a stench.

"Draw your gun, Graegan."

Vance squeezed his eyes shut, willing Doug to go.

"Your gun, Graegan. This isn't a shopping trip. She's dangerous."

"I know. . . ." Vance put his hand on his gun, trying to ignore Doug and the vicious, stabbing pain through his head.

"Hello, sir."

Vance turned at the sound of a woman's voice. Hispanic. Pushing a cart filled with towels and cleaning supplies. He withdrew his hand.

She gave him a pleasant smile. "Can I help you with something?" Her accent was thick but easy to understand.

"Ignore her," Doug's voice said. "She's not real."

Vance glanced around but didn't see Doug nearby. He swallowed. She looked real. If he could just reach out and touch her.

"I'm looking for my sister," Vance said—barely audible, he knew.

"Excuse me, sir? Speak up, please."

"My sister. I am looking for her."

"What does she look like?"

"Short blonde hair. Thin and kind of tall."

"I have seen a woman like that. I believe she is in room 288. On the second floor." She nodded as she pulled out a rag. "Yes, I believe that is correct. She has not wanted maid service for the entire time."

"Thank you," Vance said.

"She is strange, your sister. Sad eyes. Very sad eyes."

Vance nodded, and then the woman disappeared into a nearby room to clean.

"You don't believe me. Is that it?"

Vance turned. There he was, with his hands in his pockets and his shirtsleeves rolled up. That's how he always used to stand at a crime scene. It could be the bloodiest, most horrific scene imaginable, and Doug would stand casually over it like he was observing Bermuda grass.

"You have to leave," Vance whispered.

"I'm here to help you. You shouldn't have talked to that woman."

"I found out where they are. Right up there."

"You have a plan?"

Maybe if Vance ignored him, he would go away. He drew his gun, looked to see if anyone else was nearby, and then climbed the metal stairs.

Behind him, he heard Doug's footsteps.

He didn't have a clue what he was going to do. But surprise was going to be to his advantage.

Suddenly a door opened. Vance pointed his gun but quickly hid it as a businessman in a cheap suit walked out. Luckily he didn't notice Vance until he'd shut his door. Vance leaned against the railing, pretended to be interested in the drab view.

"Mornin'," the man said and walked past uneventfully. He got in a pickup and left.

Vance squeezed his eyes shut. The pain reached all the way to the fillings in his teeth.

"Vance, you've got to get it together, man."

"Shut up," Vance whispered.

Then the bullet, gliding through the air, parting it. Glass shattering.

He was losing it. Quickly.

Harmon. Call Harmon.

He reached in his pocket for his phone but grabbed nothing but material. It was in his car. He couldn't leave now and risk their coming out and getting away.

"Why are you just standing around?" Doug's voice was harsh, accusatory.

He wouldn't listen to it. It was just a figment of his broken imagination. Everything in him was broken.

"Just kick the door down, Graegan," Doug barked.

Sweat poured down his face, and in periodic spurts, everything would go black; then light would creep back in. His mind felt like one giant echo.

"Go in there and get your family back. What are you waiting for?"

What was he waiting for?

There was another voice.

Quiet. Simple. Wordless.

It seemed to be carried by the wind, through his soul, and it calmed him.

But he wasn't quite sure he could hear it. Wasn't sure if he should hear it.

What was real proved distant.

He clutched the railing, afraid the dizziness might topple him over.

Vance heard more voices. He turned. He was pretty sure these came from room 288. They were muffled.

The voices danced around one another, Doug barking orders, the wind whispering another plan, and his gut, for the first time, completely indecisive.

He stared at the window. The curtains were drawn. If only he could peek inside.

He knew he had to do something. The question was, which voice was real?

*   *   *

Lindy pretended to be interested in Erin's instructions on how to use the gun, but instead she was trying to figure out how to use it to get Conner back. She wondered if she could shoot someone for the sake of saving her son. Shoot an innocent person?

Let Conner go, forever?

The only answer was to never go in the bank. She imagined Erin handing over the gun, probably in the bank parking lot. That would be the moment she would need to make her move. Shoot Erin point-blank. Right in front of Conner, if he came with them.

She wondered, would Erin leave him here, chained to the bed?

Erin slid the safety back on and set the gun in the duffel bag. "You got any questions?"

"Yeah. Where is Conner going to be during all this?" She kept her voice low. She wanted Conner to keep sleeping.

Erin turned, her eyes narrow. "He'll be in the trunk."

"In the trunk?" Lindy gasped.

"Tied up, with tape on his mouth."

"Erin, please. Don't do this. He's just a little boy."

"Exactly. Unpredictable. With his prayers. And his God talk. Plus," she said, zipping the bag, "I figure there will probably come a point where you'll need some extra incentive, and I think that'll be a good picture for you to keep in the forefront of your mind if you get to thinking about doing something heroic. Or stupid."

Knock.

Knock.

Erin turned, grabbing a small gun out of her waistband.

She cursed and mumbled something about putting up the sign that they didn't want room service. She stepped to the door, bracing her shoulder against it. There was no peephole.

"No room service."

Knock.

Knock.

Erin repeated, in Spanish, what she'd said before. This time her voice was louder. More tense. Conner sat up, rubbing his eyes and looking for Lindy. Lindy got off the bed and went to him, holding his shoulders and stroking his head.

"Don't you move," Erin whispered to Lindy, waving her gun at them. For a third time, she repeated herself through the door.

Silence.

Then two more knocks.

33

HE STOOD THERE face-to-face with her. Her eyes gleaming and wide. He could practically see the thoughts screaming through her mind.

"I'm unarmed," Vance said, raising his hands. Sweat poured down his face, into his eyes. He wiped it away with his arm. His shirt was soaked.

The door was cracked about a foot.

"Kick it in. She'll go flying to the ground."

But Vance stayed motionless against Doug's voice, only blinking to try to keep the sweat out of his eyes. He couldn't see into the room. "Is my family here?"

A gun was now visible, staring him down like a pit bull.

"You've made a horrible mistake coming here." Erin glanced to his left and right, her face coming out of the shadow of the door. "I thought you were in jail."

"We need to talk."

"Don't. I will kill them." She looked him up and down. "You look horrible."

He could barely stand. He held on to the doorframe. "I'm the one you want."

"Yes, well, the one I wanted. But you made it clear that you're not interested."

"I've had time to think."

"You're here for your family," she snarled. And then she yanked him forward. He tripped over her foot as he fell to the ground, hitting his head. Everything went black. But sounds smothered his thoughts.

"Vance!" It was Lindy. He tried to open his eyes and realized they were open, but he could see nothing. The pain canceled nearly everything out. He thought he heard Conner but wasn't certain.

A kick in the stomach caused him to gasp for air. It wouldn't come for what seemed like minutes, and then his lungs filled. Slowly he began to see light. And then objects. He tried to sit up but only got to an elbow.

Erin peered at him. "You came here with no gun?" She laughed. "What? Did you think you were going to talk me down with your charm and good looks?"

"I want to talk to Lindy."

"Get on your belly," Erin ordered.

Vance obliged, and Erin patted him down for a weapon. Then she used her foot to kick him back over. Right in the ribs. She knelt beside him. "You're quite the hero, aren't you?

Stumbling in here. Are you drunk? Look at you. You're a mess. But I already knew that." She stood, towering over him. "Does your wife know you talk to imaginary people? I mean, fun for your son and all that, but a little disturbing when it comes to you, don't you think?" She smirked. "I saw what I saw. At the beach."

Vance rolled to his side. Lindy sat on the bed. He tried to focus on her, but she split into three. Wavy like fun-house mirrors. "Lindy . . ."

"Shut up, you pathetic sicko." There was a tense urgency in Erin's voice. "Now what do I do? You've complicated things, Vance, and when things get complicated, things get messy."

"You were right," Vance said. "We've been through a lot together. You understand me, Erin. You understand what it means to be a cop." The words hurt coming out, but it was his only chance. He looked at Conner, who sat frozen on the other bed, his eyes unsure. Vance tried a smile, but maybe it was a grimace.

He got to his knees, trying to catch his breath. His rib cage felt like it had come unhinged. "Erin, I need to tell Lindy the truth."

Erin looked confused. Vance tried not to pause.

"Conner, go to the bathroom and shut the door. Don't come out until I tell you to. No matter what happens."

"Stay right where you are, kid. I give the orders around here," Erin said.

"What I have to say, he can't hear."

Erin, who was closer and in better focus for him, eyed him before nodding to Conner to go to the bathroom. Vance watched him. His hands were clenched together, his small fingers threaded through one another.

As the bathroom door closed, Vance continued. "Lindy, we had a window of time to try to make it work. But our window is closing. We tried, but that was our window, you know?" He tried to breathe, sound calm, look into her eyes. But the pain in his head still blurred everything. "And now a different window has been opened for me."

"Vance, what are you saying?" Lindy's voice was pained.

"Yeah, Vance, what are you saying?" Doug stood beside him. His shadow crossed over Vance's face, but Vance didn't turn to him.

"I'm saying that we had our last shot. We tried to find our target. And then we thought we had our window, but there's just too much history. Our window has closed."

"You said you wanted Lindy, not me," Erin said.

"I wanted to try to make it work. I owed her that much." Vance closed his eyes for a moment, trying to manage the pain. "But I don't think she'll ever understand me. And that's not her fault. It's mine. Erin saved my life. I owe her a debt I can't repay. But now I want to try. She gave me the gift of life, and I want to live it to its fullest."

Erin suddenly sat down in the chair by the table, flopping herself into it like she didn't have the strength to stand. "After it's all come to this, Vance? Now you decide?" Her voice tensed with anger. "I am going to Mexico. My life is sunk. I have nothing left."

"That's not true," Vance whispered. These words burned his tongue. "Let them go."

Silence.

Erin stroked the metal of her gun, her eyes tired, stressed, contemplative. "You never knew what you had," she said quietly, turning her eyes toward Lindy. "He was there the whole time, and he was never good enough for you, was he?"

Vance looked at Lindy, trying to focus on her. She was still blurry. He couldn't see the details of her face.

Lindy sat silently. "Vance is right," she finally said. "We had our window. We had our one shot."

"You're unbelievable," Erin spat, staring at Lindy. "This is what I've been trying to tell you all these years," she said, now looking at Vance.

Vance nodded. Each movement caused a stab of pain through his head.

Doug's shadow passed over him again, but he couldn't see him.

"Get out of here," Erin said, waving her gun. She sounded tired, her voice thin. Disgruntled.

Nobody moved.

"I said get out of here," Erin repeated through clenched teeth.

Lindy stood. "You're just going to let us walk out?"

"Not *us*," Erin hissed. *"You."*

34

LINDY FROZE. Something in Erin's eyes terrorized her more than usual. She looked at Vance. She'd never seen him like this. He was sweating profusely and seemed to be in terrible pain. He was blinking and unable to focus on her. He grabbed his head again and again and sometimes even looked over his shoulder like there was something there.

When she saw him at the door, hope had swelled in her heart. He was here with them. But he didn't seem to have a plan, and that was unlike him. She was surprised he didn't kick down the door, guns blazing.

She glanced at Erin, who nudged her toward the door with the tip of her gun. Lindy turned toward the bathroom.

"Where do you think you're going?" Erin asked.

"To get my son."

"Your son is staying here. With his father. Where he belongs."

Lindy's hand went over her mouth. She shuddered. "What are you talking about? I am not leaving Conner here."

"He is my ransom," Erin said. "My leverage. You walk out of here and go call the police, right? I mean, that's what any reasonable person would do. And Cripple here might not be trustworthy. Might want to get clever. So no, the kid stays with me." She sighed, wiped her brow. "Now get out of here before I have to break another rib."

Lindy's entire body shook. She couldn't even get her feet to move. Suddenly Vance, stooped over like an old man and holding his ribs with one hand, shuffled toward her. Erin pointed her gun at him, but he didn't stop.

"I need to say good-bye," he mumbled. His eyes were clouded, withdrawn, but his face held an intense expression that Lindy tried to read. He stood a little taller, grabbed each of her shoulders gently. He was breathing hard, his face oily with sweat. Dark circles clung to the skin under his eyes, weighing them down. "The window was our only shot," he whispered to her. He touched her hair. She peered deeply into his eyes. And he looked at her, the mistiness seeming to lift a bit. "All I have left is a bullet whizzing past me and the sound of shattering glass."

That was all he said. Tears welled in his eyes and she expected more, but that was it. Lindy was confused. She wasn't buying his sudden devotion to Erin and figured it was a ploy to get her out of there. But then his words seemed so startling, said with intense conviction. They'd had one shot. One window of time.

Those were the words that seemed to hang in front of her. Once, before she began to understand the whole picture of her husband, she'd believed their window had closed.

But did he?

"You have to keep Conner safe," Lindy said, tears gushing down her face. She sobbed into her hands.

Vance slowly peeled them away. Lindy searched his eyes, his face, his lips, for anything, any answer.

Suddenly a hand grabbed her shirt, ripping it at the shoulder. She was pushed toward the door, a fist shoving her right between the shoulder blades.

"Time to go."

Lindy felt herself growing hysterical. Sobs turned into hyperventilation. She couldn't catch her breath.

"I will take care of him," Vance said to her, but his voice brought her no comfort.

Until she noticed something.

His hands. On his pinkie finger was her wedding ring.

And both hands were clasped together. Like Conner's.

Then a soft, warm tingle spread over the top of her head and down her body. It felt like a warm shower, except inside. In her soul.

She stopped crying. Heaving. Shaking.

Something was happening in the room, something she couldn't explain.

She looked at Vance, who gave her a slight nod. Then she stepped backward, out onto the concrete—the very thing that everything in her told her not to do.

Erin kept the gun close, but visible. "If you call the police, this is going to get very ugly. And very bloody. Stay out of sight for two days. I'll be in touch. And don't worry. Once we reach Mexico, I'll send one of them back to you."

The door shut. Lindy stood staring at its stark gray metal. Its black numbers. *One? Which one?*

Hysteria bubbled up, but something kept her steady. She didn't know how, but she was in complete control.

And then she saw it.

A gun. Sitting on the concrete.

Right below the window.

* * *

Vance's heart felt shredded. He was their only hope? His stupid, idiotic plan. He'd felt compelled. It had made sense at the time. But Lindy looked hopelessly confused. He thought they would have a connection, that she would see what he was trying to say to her.

Now a cold-blooded killer was staring him down.

"Daddy?" Conner called from the bathroom.

"Stay in there, Son."

"But it stinks."

"Just a little longer."

Erin pushed Vance into the chair she'd sat in. She circled him like a vulture, the shiny black gun dangling by her side. "You've completely lost your mind, haven't you?" There was glee in her voice. "I mean, Vance, dude, I was just going to mess with you a little. The call to your mother-in-law was intended to be pretty torturous. I knew how much you hated that woman. I figured she'd stir plenty of chaos into your life."

"The mud flaps."

"You saw those too, huh? Yeah, I thought that was a nice touch. Subtle, though, right?" Her crooked grin contrasted with her cold eyes.

Then her expression melded into sadness. He'd seen the same expression the day he'd told her they had to part ways. "You know we're probably not going to make it out of this alive."

Vance didn't answer. But he noticed something. The pain in his head was fading. His vision was becoming less blurry. It felt like he'd been crushed by a mountain and now something was lifting it away.

Erin stared him down. "You're looking a little better. You've got color in your face. For a while there I thought you were about to drop dead."

"We need to leave for Mexico soon."

She smiled a little. "I like the sound of that. *We.*" She scratched the side of her face with the barrel of her gun. "But I'm not buying it."

The pain was now gone, like it had never been there. He saw clearly. The ringing in his ears subsided. He glanced around. Doug had vanished.

He felt strong, like he'd just woken up from a good night's

sleep. His mind was clear. But he was troubled immediately by the disjointed plan he'd come up with to try to save his family. Lindy was free, but he was certain she did not know what to do with the freedom.

And Erin wasn't buying his story. Which was making the passing minutes more and more desperate.

Erin shook her head. "Except . . . here you are, like the plague's been lifted from you. Was she that great of a burden to carry? Just minutes ago you were sweating like a pig. Now you look perfectly normal."

Vance had no explanation for it either. But he wasn't complaining. He needed his mind back. Fully.

And he put it to work immediately. He wondered if he could take Erin down. She had a gun and also two decades of martial arts training. He'd seen her take down men twice her size. He tried to talk to her while he thought through his options.

"When did you decide to come to California? after we talked? You got here fast."

"Vance," she said with a small laugh, "you don't get it."

"Get what?"

"I've been here the whole time."

The hair stood straight up on his arm.

"Those times we talked on the phone, I was already here, trying to find that thug that thought he could double-cross me. But now," she said, "I guess I'm getting what I really wanted. You. Suffering. That's really all I wanted. Yeah, I am probably not going to make it out alive. You either. But at least I am going to get to see you go through what I've suffered for several years now."

"Daddy!"

Vance rose, stepped toward the bathroom. "Stay put, Conner."

But just as he felt his mind coming together, he felt a hand on his shoulder. It was heavy. He could feel the individual fingers press into his skin.

He whipped his head around. "Get out of here."

It startled Erin. She raised her gun. "Who are you talking to, Vance?"

Nobody was there. But when he turned back to face Erin, the hand grasped his shoulder again.

If this was how he was going to have to live the rest of his life, he wasn't sure it was worth living. He couldn't imagine a constant toggling between reality and distortion.

The hand was increasingly heavy, so heavy that his knees buckled underneath him, and he dropped to the ground.

Erin's eyes lit up with fury. "You're as pathetic as I thought you were," she said, and her arm stiffened, her fingers moving over the trigger of the gun.

Vance saw a shadow pass in front of the window. He looked at Erin. "I guess the question is, who's crazier? You or me?"

Erin glared and aimed her gun.

And then he heard it. The bullet returned, whizzing right over his head. Glass shattered and crashed.

He looked at Erin as he dove to the ground. Her face turned the color of cement. Her mouth gaped open. Her eyes shifted sporadically, and blood soaked her chest. The gun fell with a thud to the ground, and Erin toppled forward, her head crashing against the bed frame. She was out of Vance's sight.

Lindy stood in the frame of the glassless window, both hands on the gun. She lowered it and tears streamed down her face.

Vance stood and ran to her, his feet crunching against the glass on the carpet. At the window, he touched her bruised face. "Are you okay?" He gently took the gun from her.

She nodded. "I thought you'd lost your mind. Our window of time. One shot." She shook her head. "I don't even know how I understood."

"I didn't think I was making sense."

"Somehow we always understand each other." She smiled and leaned into his chest, over the windowsill.

"Dad!" The bathroom door opened.

Vance hurried to Conner and picked him up, pushing his head against his shoulder so he wouldn't see Erin as he carried him out.

Outside the room, a gentle breeze cooled his neck as he wrapped his arms around his family.

Maybe he had lost his mind. But somehow reality had intersected with faith at the crossroads of insanity. And he had a feeling that two little hands squeezing together in a tiny motel bathroom made it happen.

35

"CAN YOU PLEASE state your full name?"

"Lindy Graegan."

"Your real name is Linda. Is that correct?"

"Yes."

"Your middle name?"

"Michaela."

"Mrs. Graegan, do you know why you're here?"

"Yes."

"You've waived your right to an attorney. Is that correct?"

"Yes."

"And for the record, your husband is Vance Mitchell Graegan, correct?"

"Yes."

"For your information, you are being tape-recorded."

"Fine."

"Mrs. Graegan, do you understand that you are being questioned in the death of—"

"I understand. I have nothing to hide. Just ask me the questions, okay? Can we just get on with it? Can I get a drink of water or something? Coffee?"

"We can get you a drink of water."

"Thank you."

"Let's start from the beginning."

"I'm tired."

"I understand. But we need to piece together exactly what happened."

"You can't possibly understand it all. You can't possibly know what this has done to my family."

"If we could just start from the beginning."

"Well, I fell in love with a cop. And that was my first mistake."

The detective brought in a cup of water, set it on the table, then joined his partner.

"No offense, boys," Lindy said with a subtle wink. "Wouldn't trade him for the world."

"Ma'am, I know I'm skipping ahead here, but how did you know where she would be? The drapes were closed."

"Look," Lindy said, leaning forward. "This is going to sound nuts to you, okay? But I have a little boy who prays a lot. And I mean a lot. It's kind of embarrassing, but sort of wildly radical too. When they say you can move mountains, he believes it."

"So what does that have to do with it?"

"I don't know how to explain it, except to say that I knew my son was in the bathroom, and for the first time in my life, I had to completely trust my husband. I picked up that gun and I pointed it toward the window and I closed my eyes. I'm a good shot. As you probably know, every cop's wife knows how to fire a gun—and pretty darn well if we've been forced to go to the range over and over. But nobody knows how to shoot at a blind target." She looked at them. One was taking notes. The other was staring at her as if he needed more. "Is there an explanation for this? Yeah, I'd say there is. But you have to have faith to believe in it."

Note Taker looked at Baffled. "Well, I'm kind of fond of cold, hard facts, but in this case, I'd have to agree. That was some kind of mountain you moved."

"You see," Lindy said with a small, tired smile, "that's just it. It wasn't me."

* * *

Vance and Conner sat in a small holding room with fluorescent bulbs that flickered now and then. Vance couldn't stop looking at his son. He wanted to take everything in, over and over. Despite what he'd just been through, Conner looked remarkably calm and unaffected.

"Conner, here in a little bit, the police are going to take you into a room and ask you some questions."

"That's where Mom is?"

"Yes."

"What do I tell them?"

"The truth. Tell them everything that you saw."

Conner nodded, but he was busy playing with his fingers, seeing how far he could twist them around each other. Vance wondered if he was hearing anything he said. He knew Conner was having a hard time sitting still. His leg was swinging under the chair like a pendulum on steroids.

"By the way, big man, thanks for the Etch A Sketch drawing."

Conner's face brightened up. "You got it?"

"Yeah. That's how I found you."

"I drew that—no kidding, Dad—in under five minutes. I pretended I was playing with my toys, and then I got that idea."

"*Yucky hotel* was perfect."

"Oh, Dad, it was so gross. I saw cockroaches. And did you see the pool?"

Vance nodded. "Disgusting."

A little more silence passed.

"Buddy?"

"Yeah?"

"When we start our *new* new life over, Dad's going to have to get some help."

"What kind of help?"

"Help I should've gotten a long time ago. Sometimes adults get prideful, and we think we can handle things on our own, but we can't. I've got to . . . I've got to get my mind healthy."

"What's wrong with your mind?"

Vance was really hoping he wasn't going to ask that. This was hard to explain, and he probably shouldn't. It was too complicated for an eight-year-old to understand that his dad was seeing things, hearing things, feeling things that weren't there, and that when he got stressed, his head felt like it was going to explode.

Already Joan had put him in touch with a doctor who specialized in PTSD. A former cop, no less. And one who was willing to give him a financial break until they could get their feet under them.

It was a relief he couldn't describe.

"Dad?"

"Yeah?"

"I understand needing help. It's okay. I need help sometimes too. Like in that bathroom."

"What do you mean?"

"I really wanted to come out. But I didn't."

"Why?"

"The hand."

"The hand?"

"Yeah. There was a hand on my shoulder, and when I stood up, it sat me back down. Twice."

Vance pulled his son near him. Emotion caught him off guard and he tried to wipe his tears away quickly.

"So maybe I'm not as crazy as I think I am," he said, smiling at his son.

Conner smiled back. "Just remember, Dad, it's like the

TV preacher says about praying. *Before* all else fails, do this!"

But Vance was starting to understand something profound. *Before everything*, God's hand had already been moving in their lives. Bullets and shattering glass. Etch A Sketch obsessions. He'd been there even before they needed Him.

Or wanted Him.

He clasped his hands together, finger through finger, as tight as he could.

Acknowledgments

I CAN HARDLY BELIEVE this is my seventeenth book. As with each child, this one feels as special and as important to me as my very first one. And at least with my "kids," it's true that it takes a village to raise them! I'm especially grateful to Jan Stob, Stephanie Broene, Karen Watson, and Sarah Mason for their vision and work on this book. Thanks also to the entire Tyndale family for their hard work and professionalism. I'd also like to thank Ron Wheatley, my technical adviser, and Janet Kobobel Grant, my agent, for always being there for me. And as always, thanks to Sean, John, and Cate for their support and love. You three are my most treasured possessions. And to my heavenly Father for allowing me the privilege of being a wife, mother, and storyteller.

About the Author

RENE GUTTERIDGE is the author of seventeen novels, including four suspense novels from Tyndale House Publishers (*The Splitting Storm, Storm Gathering, Storm Surge,* and *Listen*). She is also known for her Christian comedy novels and sketches. She studied screenwriting while earning a mass communications degree, graduating magna cum laude from Oklahoma City University and earning the Excellence in Mass Communication Award. She served as the full-time director of drama for First United Methodist Church for five years. She now writes full-time and enjoys instructing at writers conferences and in college classrooms. She lives with her husband, Sean, a musician, and their children in Oklahoma City.

An Interview with Rene Gutteridge

Many readers are familiar with your comedies, but how many suspense novels have you written, and what made you decide to write another one?

This is my sixth pure suspense. Suspense is actually my favorite genre in which to write. When I was a kid, the very first novel I attempted was a ghost story. Suspense lets me explore good and evil and all the fears that I sometimes don't want to admit are there. It lets me believe that there are still heroes in the world. It helps me gain perspective on my life. And I can relax a bit in the writing process. To be a great comedy writer, you have to have suffered a bit. Many comedy writers are intense and dark, like you'd expect a suspense writer to be. Suspense writers are usually very witty and engaging, like you'd expect a comedy writer to be. Thankfully, my split personality allows me to toggle between both.

How did the idea for *Possession* come to you?

It sort of came from two different places. I'd read a magazine article about people whose possessions were being held for ransom by illegitimate moving companies. And that was about the time we were watching people lose all their belongings when the economy crashed. I read news stories about dads killing themselves and their entire families because they lost their jobs or lost their homes. So I wanted to explore the idea of losing everything and what that means and how to gain perspective on life . . . on what really matters.

The story opens with Lindy at the police station. Why did you start there? Were you worried about giving too much away?

I always like to start stories with a little mystery, a small amount of information that readers can carry with them. I like the opening because it casts a tiny shadow of doubt over every chapter until the end.

A lot of the spiritual content in the story comes through Conner, and the innocence of his faith is so powerful. Where did you come up with the idea of Conner's becoming a Christian by watching a televangelist?

I got the idea from my own son, who'd somehow gotten to a televangelist one morning while surfing for cartoons. For days after that he would talk to me about what he heard in that sermon. I had this funny picture in my head of Conner watching this evangelist, his white hair slicked to his head, his hands shooting in the air, and Conner just totally picking up on that, not a thought about denomination or what's comfortable or uncomfortable for him. Since I wasn't raised charismatic, I thought it'd be fun to explore how a mom would react to her kid acting like a little charismatic televangelist. And how, in the end, she finds her own faith through something that used to embarrass her.

Vance suffers from post-traumatic stress disorder. How did you research this? And what made you decide to give Vance this illness? Are hallucinations like Vance's conversations with Doug Cantella common to PTSD?

I've been interested in PTSD since my experience with the Oklahoma City bombing in 1995. I was there for the whole thing and saw a lot of disturbing things but never had any PTSD symptoms—no flashbacks or anything else—except my eyes water every time I hear sirens, fifteen years later. It's just this weird physiological reaction that happens every time I hear a siren. And that was one of the things that made such an impression on me that day: the sirens never ended. They just kept coming and coming, all through the city. All through the night. I feel fortunate that I was able to come through that without psychological damage. But it gave me a small glimpse into Vance's struggle with PTSD.

In my research on PTSD, I found a lot of interesting symptoms that coincide with the disorder, including the flashbacks that he experiences, the sounds of the bullets and shattering glass. Hallucinations, however, are extremely uncommon, and there you're actually bordering on psychosis. But for the story, I wanted Vance to really struggle with reality and delusion and then find faith in between. It fit well for what he'd been through with the D.C. sniper case, which is a case I'd been fascinated with since it happened. I always wondered what it was like for those cops, trying to hunt down what must've seemed like a ghost.

Lindy's mother, Joan, is an intriguing character. She is the proverbial ice queen, yet we see that she truly loves her daughter. How did you develop this character?

Joan was a lot of fun to write. It's always fun to play with the mother-in-law/son-in-law relationship. I saw Joan clearly from the moment I decided to put her in the story. But what I really enjoyed was ice-picking my way through her coldness, to find her humanity underneath.

Where did you get the motivation for Erin's character?

She's a whole lot of badness wrapped into one! She's misguided, selfish, living for all the wrong things. Rarely does one get this extreme, but I think the thing that makes the bad guy (or gal) so chilling is when we get a little glimpse of ourselves in that character. Erin and Vance both lost their way, but her pride and her own desires kept her from finding the healing that Vance eventually finds.

What do you hope the reader takes away from this story?

The first and most obvious thing is that I want readers to examine what really matters in their lives. It's so easy to get caught up in the extras of life that were intended as blessings but become harmful when we elevate them over what truly matters. But I also love the story between Vance and Lindy, and how through utter material devastation, they find the compassion and truth they need to restore their marriage. There can be so many obstacles that stand in the way of a marriage thriving, but it is sometimes those very things that cause all the layers to be peeled away so that healing can begin. Lastly, always, *always* read the fine print!

Discussion Questions

Use these questions for individual reflection or for discussion within your book club or small group. If your book club reads *Possession* and is interested in talking with me via speakerphone, please feel free to contact me through my Web site at www.renegutteridge.com, and I'll do my best to arrange something with you. Thanks for reading!

1. At some point, Vance and Lindy realize they may never see their possessions again. How do they feel about losing their things? Do you think it changed what they valued?

2. Lindy tries to convince Vance to let their possessions go. What do you think would have happened if he followed her advice?

3. Have you ever been in a situation where you had to choose between getting what is rightfully yours and letting it go? How did you feel?

4. Lindy and Vance decide that Vance should leave his job and they should move across the country. Why do you think they had to make such a drastic move? Have you ever been in a situation where you wanted to pick everything up and move far away? Would it have solved your problem?

5. Early in the story we see Vance sitting at his desk in the police station. His retirement party is over, yet he doesn't head home. Why do you think he was hesitant to leave?

6. Joe is gruff and somewhat rude when he shows up at Vance and Lindy's house with the moving van. Why do you think they trusted him to take their stuff? Are there people in your life whom you trust as experts? Are there times when you should be more careful in checking their credentials?

7. Vance quickly signed the agreement with the moving company without reading the fine print. Have you ever found yourself contractually obligated by something because you didn't read the agreement carefully?

8. Why does Vance go to Chicago to see Erin? Does he have feelings for her?

9. Erin has an unhealthy attraction to Vance. How do you think Vance could have handled it differently? Should Lindy have handled it differently?

10. After Conner came to faith through a televangelist, his parents found his talk about God and his behavior very strange. Has anyone ever thought you were strange because of your faith? Have you found someone else's expression of faith strange?

11. Lindy and Vance try to protect Conner from everything going on, yet in some ways Conner seems better equipped to handle the situation. Why do you think Conner adapts so easily?

12. Erin holds Vance responsible for everything she's lost. Is her anger justified?

13. What is on the disc that Vance hides from the authorities? Why was he trying to protect Erin? Have you ever been in a situation where you had to decide between telling the truth and protecting someone you cared about? Would you have handled this differently?

14. Vance continues to see and have conversations with Doug Cantella, but we later learn that the conversations are in Vance's mind. Why do you think Vance communicates with Doug? What does Doug represent to Vance?

15. When Vance is arrested, Joan believes that he's responsible for her daughter's disappearance but later changes her mind. Why do you think she hired a lawyer for Vance? What made her decide he was innocent? Have you ever suspected someone of something only to discover his or her innocence?

16. While Erin is holding Lindy and Conner hostage, her approach to Conner seems to change. Why does Erin tell Conner to help himself to a soda? Did you find it more disturbing when Erin was mean to Conner or when she was nice?

17. When Joan discovers that Vance is suffering from post-traumatic stress disorder, she gives him medication. Why doesn't Vance take it? Do you think this was the right decision?

18. It's obvious that Joan is against Vance and Lindy's marriage. Why is she so distrustful of Vance? Have you ever been fearful that your children will make the same mistakes that you have? Or have your parents ever shown a similar fear?

19. After Vance arrives at the motel and gives Lindy verbal clues, Lindy walks out of the room, sees the gun on the ground, and shoots through the window. When does she realize that Vance was giving her clues? What does her shooting blindly into the motel room represent?

20. In the end, Conner tells his father that he wanted to
    come out of the bathroom but he felt a hand pushing
    him down. How was this similar to Vance's experience?
    What do you think held them both back? Have you
    ever had a similar experience?

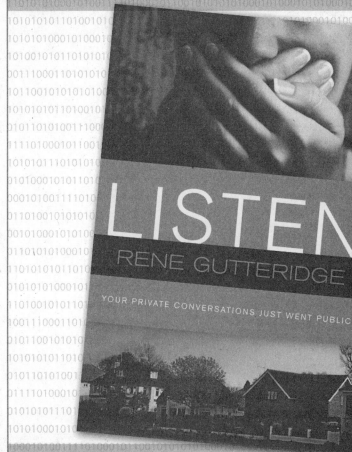